ARTEMIS
FOWL

THE ETERNITY CODE

OTHER BOOKS BY EOIN COLFER

GRAPHIC NOVELS

Artemis Fowl: The Graphic Novel

Artemis Fowl: The Arctic Incident: The Graphic Novel

Artemis Fowl: The Eternity Code: The Graphic Novel

The Supernaturalist: The Graphic Novel

AND FOR YOUNGER READERS

Eoin Colfer's The Legend of Spud Murphy

Eoin Colfer's The Legend of Captain Crow's Teeth

Eoin Colfer's The Legend of the Worst Boy in the World

ARTEMIS FOWL

THE ETERNITY CODE

EOIN COLFER

Disney • HYPERION

Los Angeles   New York

Can You Crack the Code?
The code that runs along the bottom of the book has been specially
created by the author. Decipher it to reveal a secret message.

Gnommish alphabet created by Alicia Grace Martin

Copyright © 2003, 2018 by Eoin Colfer

All rights reserved. Published by Disney • Hyperion, an imprint of Disney Book Group. No part of this book may be reproduced or transmitted in any form or by any means, electronic or mechanical, including photocopying, recording, or by any information storage and retrieval system, without written permission from the publisher. For information address Disney • Hyperion, 125 West End Avenue, New York, New York 10023.

First Hardcover Edition, May 2003
New Paperback Edition, July 2009
10 9 8 7 6 5 4 3 2 1
FAC-025438-18264
Printed in the United States of America

This book is set in American Typewriter ITC Pro, Courier New, DIN Next LT Pro, ITC Novarese Pro, Perpetua MT Pro/Monotype; Neutraface Condensed/House Industries
Designed by Tyler Nevins

Library of Congress Control Number: 2003046431
ISBN 978-1-368-03695-5
www.artemisfowl.com
Visit www.DisneyBooks.com

SUSTAINABLE
FORESTRY
INITIATIVE

Certified Chain of Custody
Promoting Sustainable Forestry

www.sfiprogram.org
SFI-01054

The SFI label applies to the text stock

To the Power family
In-laws and Outlaws

Excerpt from Artemis Fowl's diary, disk 2 (encrypted)

For the past two years my business enterprises have thrived without parental interference. In this time, I have sold the Pyramids to a Western businessman, forged and auctioned the Lost Diaries of Leonardo da Vinci, *and separated the fairy People from a large portion of their precious gold. But my freedom to plot is almost at an end. As I write, my father lies in a hospital bed in Helsinki where he is recovering after a two-year imprisonment by the Russian Mafiya. He is still unconscious following his ordeal, but he will awaken soon and retake control of the Fowl finances.*

With two parents resident in Fowl Manor, it will be impossible for me to conduct my various illegal ventures undetected. Previously this would not have been a problem, as my father was a bigger crook than I, but Mother is determined that the Fowls are going straight.

However, there is time for one last job. Something that my mother would not approve of. I don't think the fairy folk would like it much either. So I shall not tell them.

PART 1
ATTACK

Knightsbridge, London

Artemis Fowl was almost content. His father would be discharged from Helsinki's University Hospital any day now. He himself was looking forward to a delicious lunch at En Fin, a London seafood restaurant, and his business contact was due to arrive at any moment. All according to plan.

His bodyguard, Butler, was not quite so relaxed. But then again, he was never truly at ease. One did not become one of the world's deadliest men by dropping one's guard.

The giant Eurasian man flitted between tables in the Knightsbridge bistro, hiding the usual security items and clearing exit routes.

"Are you wearing the earplugs?" he asked his employer.

Artemis sighed deeply. "Yes, Butler, though I hardly think we are in danger here. It's a perfectly legal business meeting in broad daylight, for heaven's sake."

⚅⚇⚒• ⚅⚇⚒•⚒• ⚐⚑⚒•⚒⚛⚗⚘⚖•⚑⚒⚅

The earplugs were actually sonic filter sponges cannibalized from fairy Lower Elements Police helmets. Butler had obtained the helmets, along with a treasure trove of fairy technology, when one of Artemis's schemes had pitted him against a fairy SWAT team more than a year before. The sponges were grown in LEP labs, and had tiny porous membranes that sealed automatically when decibel levels surpassed safety standards.

"Maybe so, Artemis, but the thing about assassins is that they like to catch you unawares."

"Perhaps," replied Artemis, perusing the menu's entrée section. "But who could possibly have a motive to kill *us*?"

Butler shot one of the half dozen diners a fierce glare, just in case she might be planning something. The woman must have been at least eighty.

"They might not be after us. Remember, Jon Spiro is a powerful man. He put a lot of companies out of business. We could be caught in a crossfire."

Artemis nodded. As usual, Butler was right, which explained why they were both still alive. Jon Spiro, the American he was meeting, was just the kind of man who attracted assassins' bullets—a successful IT billionaire with a shady past and alleged Mob connections. Rumor had it that his company, Fission Chips, had made it to the top on the back of stolen research. Of course, nothing was ever proven. Not that Chicago's district attorney hadn't tried. Several times.

A waitress wandered over, smiling a dazzling smile. "Hello there, young man. Would you like to see the children's menu?"

A vein pulsed in Artemis's temple.

"No, mademoiselle, I would not like to see the *children's* menu. I have no doubt that the *children's* menu itself tastes better than the meals on it. I would like to order à la carte. Or don't you serve fish to minors?"

The waitress's smile shrunk by a couple of molars. Artemis's vocabulary had that effect on most people. Butler rolled his eyes. And Artemis wondered who would want to kill him? Most of the waiters and tailors in Europe, for a start.

"Yes, sir," stammered the unfortunate waitress. "Whatever you like."

"What I would like is a medley of shark and swordfish. Pan seared. On a bed of julienned vegetables and new potatoes."

"And to drink?"

"Spring water. Irish, if you have it. And no ice, please. As your ice is no doubt made from tap water, which rather defeats the purpose of spring water."

The waitress scurried to the kitchen, relieved to escape from the pale youth at table six. She'd seen a vampire movie once. The undead creature had had the very same hypnotic stare. Maybe the kid spoke like a grown-up because he was actually five hundred years old.

Artemis smiled in anticipation of his meal, unaware of the consternation he'd caused.

"You're going to be a big hit at the school dances," Butler commented.

"Pardon?"

"That poor girl was almost in tears. It wouldn't hurt you to be nice occasionally."

Artemis was surprised. Butler rarely offered opinions on personal matters.

"I don't see myself at school dances, Butler."

"Dancing isn't the point. It's all about communication."

"Communication?" scoffed young Master Fowl. "I doubt there is a teenager alive with a vocabulary equal to mine."

Butler was about to point out the difference between talking and communicating when the restaurant door opened. A small, tanned man entered, flanked by a veritable giant. Jon Spiro and his security.

Butler bent low to whisper in his charge's ear. "Be careful, Artemis. I know the big one by reputation."

Spiro wound through the tables arms outstretched. He was a middle-aged American, thin as a javelin, and barely taller than Artemis himself. In the eighties, shipping had been his thing; in the nineties, he had made a killing in the stock market. Now, it was communications. He wore his trademark white linen suit, and there was enough jewelry hanging from his wrists and fingers to gold-leaf the Taj Mahal.

Artemis rose to greet his associate.

� of gnommish symbols⌟

"Mr. Spiro, welcome."

"Hey, little Artemis Fowl. How the hell are you?"

Artemis shook the man's hand. His jewelry jangled like a rattlesnake's tail.

"I am well. Glad you could come."

Spiro took a chair. "Artemis Fowl calls with a proposition, I would walk across broken glass to be here."

The bodyguards appraised each other openly. Apart from their bulk, the two were polar opposites. Butler was the essence of understated efficiency. Black suit, shaven head, as inconspicuous as it was possible to be at almost seven feet tall. The newcomer had bleached-blond hair, a cut-off T-shirt, and silver pirate rings in both ears. This was not a man who wanted to be forgotten, or ignored.

"Arno Blunt," said Butler. "I've heard about you."

Blunt took up his position at Jon Spiro's shoulder.

"Butler. One of *the* Butlers," he said in a New Zealand drawl. "I hear you guys are the best. That's what I hear. Let's hope we don't have to find out."

Spiro laughed. It sounded like a box of crickets. "Arno, please. We are among friends here. This is not a day for threats."

Butler was not so sure. His soldier's sense was buzzing like a nest of hornets at the base of his skull. There was danger here.

"So, my friend. To business," said Spiro, fixing Artemis with his close-set dark eyes. "I've been salivating all the way across the Atlantic. What have you got for me?"

Artemis frowned. He'd hoped business could wait until after lunch.

"Wouldn't you like to see a menu?"

"No. I don't eat much anymore. Pills and liquids mostly. Gut problems."

"Very well," said Artemis, laying an aluminum briefcase on the table. "To business, then."

He flipped open the case's lid, revealing a blue cube the size of a mini-disk player nestled in blue foam.

Spiro cleaned his spectacles with the tail end of his tie.

"What am I seeing here, kid?"

Artemis placed the shining box on the table.

"The future, Mr. Spiro. Ahead of schedule."

Jon Spiro leaned in, taking a good look. "Looks like a paperweight to me."

Arno Blunt snickered, his eyes taunting Butler.

"A demonstration, then," said Artemis, picking up the metal box. He pressed a button and the gadget purred into life. Sections slid back to reveal speakers and a screen.

"Cute," muttered Spiro. "I flew three thousand miles for a micro TV?"

Artemis nodded. "A micro TV. But also a verbally controlled computer, a mobile phone, a diagnostic aid. This little box can read any information on absolutely any platform, electronic or organic. It can play videos, laser disks, DVDs, go online, retrieve e-mail, hack any computer. It can even scan your chest to see how fast your heart's beating. Its battery is good for two years, and of course it's completely wireless."

Artemis paused, to let it sink in.

Spiro's eyes grew huge behind his spectacles.

"You mean, this box . . ."

"Will render all other technology obsolete. Your computer plants will be worthless."

The American took several deep breaths.

"But how . . . how?"

Artemis flipped the box over. An infrared sensor pulsed gently on the back.

"This is the secret. An omni-sensor. It can read anything you ask it to. And if the source is programmed in, it can piggyback on any satellite you choose."

Spiro wagged a finger. "But that's illegal, isn't it?"

"No, no." Artemis smiled. "There are no laws against something like this. And there won't be for at least two years after it comes out. Look how long it took to shut down Napster."

The American rested his face in his hands. It was too much.

"I don't understand. This is years, no *decades,* ahead of anything we have now. You're nothing but a thirteen-year-old kid. How did you do it?"

Artemis thought for a second. What was he going to say? That sixteen months ago Butler had taken on a Lower Elements Police Retrieval Squad and confiscated their fairy technology? Then he had taken the components and built this wonderful box? Hardly.

"Let's just say I'm a very smart boy, Mr. Spiro."

Spiro's eyes narrowed. "Maybe not as smart as you'd like us to think. I want a demonstration."

"Fair enough." Artemis nodded. "Do you have a mobile phone?"

"Naturally." Spiro placed his cell phone on the table. It was the latest Fission Chips model.

"Secure, I take it?"

Spiro nodded arrogantly. "Five-hundred-bit encryption. Best in its class. You're not getting into the Fission 400 without a code."

"We shall see."

Artemis pointed the sensor at the handset. The screen instantly displayed an image of the cell phone's workings.

"Download?" inquired a metallic voice from the speaker.

"Confirm."

In less than a second, the job was done.

"Download complete," said the box, with a hint of smugness.

Spiro was aghast. "I don't believe it. That system cost twenty million dollars."

"Worthless," said Artemis, showing him the screen. "Would you like to call home? Or maybe move some funds around? You really shouldn't keep your bank account numbers on a SIM card."

ᔕ • ᑫᏔ ᕦᒪᔤᕤ • ᕤᏕ • ᕫᏔ ᑌᑌ Ꮤ ᕕᔤ •

The American thought for several moments.

"It's a trick," he pronounced finally. "You must've known about my phone. Somehow, don't ask me how, you got access to it earlier."

"That is logical," admitted Artemis. "It's what I would suspect. Name your test."

Spiro cast his eyes around the restaurant, fingers drumming the tabletop.

"Over there," he said finally, pointing to a video shelf above the bar. "Play one of those tapes."

"That's it?"

"It'll do, for a start."

Arno Blunt made a huge show of flicking through the tapes, eventually selecting one without a label. He slapped it down on the table, bouncing the engraved silver cutlery half an inch into the air.

Artemis resisted the urge to roll his eyes, placing the blue box directly onto the tape's surface.

An image of the cassette's innards appeared on the tiny plasma screen.

"Download?" asked the box.

Artemis nodded. "Download, compensate, and play."

Again the operation was completed in under a second. An old episode of an English soap crackled into life.

"DVD quality," commented Artemis. "Regardless of the input. The C Cube will compensate."

"The what?"

ᚼᚵᛁ • ᚤᚲᚦᛂ • ᛤᚼᛚᛂᚲᚳᚤ • ᛏᚿᛂ • ᚤᚻ • ᚲ

"C Cube," repeated Artemis. "The name I have given my little box. A tad obvious, I admit. But appropriate. The cube that sees everything."

Spiro snatched the videocassette.

"Check it," he ordered, tossing the tape to Arno Blunt.

The bleached-blond bodyguard activated the bar's TV, sliding the video into its slot. *Coronation Street* flickered across the screen. The same show. Nowhere near the same quality.

"Convinced?" asked Artemis.

The American tinkered with one of his many bracelets. "Almost. One last test. I have a feeling that the government is monitoring me. Could you check it out?"

Artemis thought for a moment, then held the omnisensor close to his mouth. "Cube. Do you read any surveillance beams concentrated on this building?"

The machine whirred for a moment.

"The strongest ion beam is eighty kilometers due west. Emanating from U.S. satellite, code number ST1132W. Registered to the Central Intelligence Agency. Estimated time of arrival, eight minutes. There are also several LEP probes connected to . . ."

Artemis hit the mute button before the cube could continue. Obviously the computer's fairy components could pick up Lower Elements technology too. He would have to remedy that. In the wrong hands that information would be devastating to fairy security.

"What's the matter, kid? The box was still talking. Who are the LEP?"

Artemis shrugged. "No pay, no play, as you Americans say. One example is enough. The CIA, no less."

"The CIA," breathed Spiro. "They suspect me of selling military secrets. They've pulled one of their birds out of orbit, just to track me."

"Or perhaps me," noted Artemis.

"Perhaps you," agreed Spiro. "You're looking more dangerous by the second."

Arno Blunt chuckled derisively. Butler ignored it. One of them had to be professional.

Spiro cracked his knuckles, a habit Artemis detested.

"We've got eight minutes, so let's get down to the nitty-gritty, kid. How much for the box?"

Artemis was not paying attention, distracted by the LEP information that the Cube had almost revealed. In a careless moment, he had nearly exposed his subterranean friends to exactly the kind of man who would exploit them.

"I'm sorry, what did you say?"

"I said how much for the box?"

"First, it's a cube," corrected Artemis. "And second, it's not for sale."

Jon Spiro took a deep shuddering breath. "Not for sale? You brought me across the Atlantic to show me something you're not going to sell me? What's going on here?"

Butler wrapped his fingers around the handle of a pistol

in his waistband. Arno Blunt's hand disappeared behind his back. The tension cranked up another notch.

Artemis steepled his fingers. "Mr. Spiro. Jon. I am not a complete idiot. I realize the value of my Cube. There is not enough money in the world to pay for this particular item. Whatever you could give me, the Cube would be worth a thousand percent more in a week."

"So what's the deal, Fowl?" asked Spiro through gritted teeth. "What are you offering?"

"I'm offering you twelve months. For the right price, I'm prepared to keep my Cube off the market for a year."

Jon Spiro toyed with his ID bracelet. A birthday present to himself. "You'll suppress the technology for a year?"

"Correct. That should give you ample time to sell your stocks before they crash, and use the profits to buy into Fowl Industries."

"There is no Fowl Industries."

Artemis smirked. "There will be."

Butler squeezed his employer's shoulder. It was not a good idea to bait a man like Jon Spiro.

But Spiro hadn't even noticed the gibe. He was too busy calculating, twisting his bracelet like a string of worry beads.

"Your price?" he asked eventually.

"Gold. One metric ton," replied the heir to the Fowl estate.

"That's a lot of gold."

Artemis shrugged. "I like gold. It holds its value. And anyway, it's a pittance compared to what this deal will save you."

Spiro thought about it. At his shoulder, Arno Blunt continued staring at Butler. The Fowl bodyguard blinked freely. In the event of confrontation, dry eyeballs would only lessen his advantage. Staring matches were for amateurs.

"Let's say I don't like your terms," said Jon Spiro. "Let's say I decide to take your little gadget with me right now."

Arno Blunt's chest puffed out another inch.

"Even if you *could* take the Cube"—Artemis smiled—"it would be of little use to you. The technology is beyond anything your engineers have ever seen."

Spiro smiled a thin, mirthless smile. "Oh, I'm sure they could figure it out. Even if it took a couple of years, it won't matter to you. Not where you're going."

"If I *go* anywhere, then the C Cube's secrets go with me. Its every function is coded to my voice patterns. It's quite a clever code."

Butler bent his knees slightly, ready to spring.

"I bet we could break that code. I got one helluva team assembled at Fission Chips."

"Pardon me if I am unimpressed by your 'one helluva team,'" said Artemis. "Thus far you have been trailing several years behind Phonetix."

Spiro jumped to his feet. He did not like the P-word.

Phonetix was the only communications company whose stock was higher than Fission Chips.

"Okay, kid, you've had your fun. Now it's my turn. I have to go now, before the satellite beam gets here. But I'm leaving Mr. Blunt behind." He patted his bodyguard on the shoulder. "You know what you have to do."

Blunt nodded. He knew. He was looking forward to it.

For the first time since the meeting began, Artemis forgot about his lunch and concentrated completely on the situation at hand. This was not going according to plan.

"Mr. Spiro. You cannot be serious. We are in a public place, surrounded by civilians. Your man cannot hope to compete with Butler. If you persist with these ludicrous threats, I will be forced to withdraw my offer and release the C Cube immediately."

Spiro placed his palms on the table. "Listen, kid," he whispered. "I like you. In a couple of years, you could have been just like me. But did you ever put a gun to somebody's head and pull the trigger?"

Artemis didn't reply.

"No?" grunted Spiro. "I didn't think so. Sometimes that's all it takes. Guts. And you don't have them."

Artemis was at a loss for words. Something that had only happened twice since his fifth birthday. Butler stepped in to fill the silence. Unveiled threats were more his area.

"Mr. Spiro. Don't try to bluff us. Blunt may be big, but I can snap him like a twig. Then there's nobody between me and you. And take my word for it, you don't want that."

Spiro's smile spread across his nicotine-stained teeth like a smear of treacle. "Oh, I wouldn't say there's nobody between us."

Butler got that sinking feeling. The one you get when there are a dozen laser sights playing across your chest. They had been set up. Somehow Spiro had outmaneuvered Artemis.

"Hey, Fowl?" said the American. "I wonder how come your lunch is taking so long."

It was at that moment that Artemis realized just how much trouble they were in.

It all happened in a heartbeat. Spiro clicked his fingers, and every single customer in En Fin drew a weapon from inside his or her coat. The eighty-year-old lady suddenly looked a lot more threatening with a revolver in her bony fist. Two armed waiters emerged from the kitchen wielding folding-stock machine guns. Butler never even had time to draw breath.

Spiro tipped over the salt cellar. "Check and mate. My game, kid."

Artemis tried to concentrate. There must be a way out. There was always a way out. But it wouldn't come. He had been hoodwinked. Perhaps fatally. No human had ever outsmarted Artemis Fowl. Then again, it only had to happen once.

"I'm going now," continued Spiro, pocketing the C Cube. "Before that satellite beam shows up, and those other ones. The LEP, I've never heard of that particular agency. But as soon as I get this gizmo working, they're going to wish they'd never heard of me. It's been fun doing business with you."

On his way to the door, Spiro winked at his bodyguard. "You got six minutes, Arno. A dream come true, eh? You get to be the guy who took out the great Butler." He turned back to Artemis, unable to resist a final gibe.

"Oh, and by the way. 'Artemis'—isn't that a girl's name?"

And he was gone, into the multicultural throngs of tourists on the high street. The old lady locked the door behind him. The click echoed around the restaurant.

Artemis decided to take the initiative.

"Now, ladies and gentlemen," he said, trying to avoid staring down the black-eyed gun barrels. "I'm sure we can come to an arrangement."

"Quiet, Artemis!"

It took a moment for Artemis's brain to process the fact that Butler had ordered him to be silent. Most impertinently, in fact.

"I beg your pardon . . ."

Butler clamped a hand over his employer's mouth.

"Quiet, Artemis. These people are professionals, not to be bargained with."

Blunt rotated his skull, cracking the tendons in his neck.

"You got that right, Butler. We're here to kill you. As soon as Mr. Spiro got the call, we started sending people in. I can't believe you fell for it, man. You must be getting old."

Butler couldn't believe it either. There was a time he would have staked out any rendezvous site for a week before giving it the thumbs-up. Maybe he *was* getting old, but there was an excellent chance he wouldn't be getting any older.

"Okay, Blunt," said Butler, stretching his empty palms before him. "You and me. One-on-one."

"Very noble," said Blunt. "That's your code of honor, I suppose. Me, I don't have a code. If you think I'm going to risk your somehow getting out of here, you're crazy. This is an uncomplicated deal. I shoot you. You die. No face-off, no duel."

Blunt reached lazily into his waistband. Why hurry? One move from Butler, and a dozen bullets would find their mark.

Artemis's brain seemed to have shut down. The usual stream of ideas had dried up. I'm going to die, he thought. I don't believe it.

Butler was saying something. Artemis decided he should listen.

"Richard of York gave battle in vain," said the bodyguard, enunciating clearly.

Blunt was screwing a silencer onto the muzzle of his ceramic pistol.

"What are you saying? What kind of gibberish is that? Don't say the great Butler is cracking up? Wait till I tell the guys."

But the old woman looked thoughtful.

"Richard of York . . . I know that."

Artemis knew it too. It was most of the verbal detonation code for the fairy sonix grenade magnetized to the under-side of the table. One of Butler's little security devices. All they needed was one more word and the grenade would explode, sending a solid wall of sound charging through the building, blowing out every window and eardrum. There would be no smoke or flame, but anyone within a ten meter radius not wearing earplugs had about five seconds before severe pain set in. One more word.

The old lady scratched her head with the revolver's bar-rel. "Richard of York? I remember now, the nuns taught us that in school. Richard of York gave battle in vain. It's one of those memory tricks. The colors of the rainbow."

Rainbow. The final word. Artemis remembered, just in time, to slacken his jaw. If his teeth were clenched, the sonic waves would shatter them like sugar glass.

The grenade detonated in a blast of compressed sound, instantaneously hurling eleven people to the farthest extremities of the room until they came into contact with various walls. The lucky ones hit partitions and went straight through. The unlucky ones collided with solid cinderblock walls. Things broke. Not the cinderblocks.

⸙⟊⁙⟒⌓ • ⟊⁙⸛⁂⸋ • ⌓⁂⟒⟊⸱ • ⟅⸸⸱ • ⟅

Artemis was safe in Butler's bear hug. The bodyguard had anchored himself against a solid door frame, folding the flying boy into his arms. They had several other advantages over Spiro's assassins: their teeth were intact, they did not suffer from any compound fractures, and the sonic filter sponges had sealed, saving their eardrums from perforation.

Butler surveyed the room. The assassins were all down, clutching their ears. They wouldn't be uncrossing their eyes for several days. The manservant drew his Sig Sauer pistol from a shoulder holster.

"Stay here," he commanded. "I'm going to check the kitchen."

Artemis settled back into his chair, drawing several shaky breaths. All around was a chaos of dust and moans. But once again, Butler had saved them. All was not lost. It was even possible that they could catch Spiro before he left the country. Butler had a contact in Heathrow security, Sid Commons, an ex–Green Beret he'd served with on body-guard duty in Monte Carlo.

A large figure blocked the sunlight. It was Butler, returned from his reconnoitering. Artemis breathed deeply, feelingly uncharacteristically emotional.

"Butler," he began. "We really must talk regarding your salary. . . ."

But it wasn't Butler. It was Arno Blunt. He had some-thing in both hands. On his left palm, two tiny cones of yellow foam.

"Earplugs," he spat through broken teeth. "I always wear 'em before a fire fight. Good thing too, eh?"

In his right hand, Blunt held a silenced pistol.

"You first," he said. "Then the ape."

Arno Blunt cocked the gun, took aim briefly, and fired.

⚶ •)（⧲ ⚶⚶ ⟩⟩ • ⚶ ♋ �️ • ⚶⚶ ⟨ • （⟨ ⚶⚶ ⟟⧲

Haven City, the Lower Elements

Though Artemis did not intend it, the Cube's scan for surveillance beams was to have far-reaching repercussions. The search parameters were so vague that the Cube sent probes into deep space, and of course, deep underground.

Below the surface, the Lower Elements Police were stretched to their limits following the recent goblin uprising. Three months after the attempted goblin takeover, most of the major players were in custody. But there were still isolated pockets of the B'wa Kell triad loping around Haven's tunnels with illegal Softnose lasers.

Every available LEP officer had been drafted to help with Operation Mop-Up before the tourist season got started. The last thing the city council wanted was tourists spending their leisure gold in Atlantis because Haven's pedestrianized central plaza was not safe to wander through. Tourism, after all, accounted for eighteen percent of the capital's revenue.

Captain Holly Short was on loan from the Reconnaissance Squad. Generally, her job was to fly to the surface on the trail of fairies who had ventured aboveground without a visa. If even one renegade fairy got himself captured by the Mud Men, then Haven would cease to be a haven. So until every gang goblin was licking his eyeballs in Howler's Peak correctional facility, Holly's duties were the same as every other LEP officer: rapid response to any B'wa Kell alert.

Today, she was escorting four rowdy goblin hoods to Police Plaza for processing. They had been found asleep in an insect delicatessen, stomachs distended by a night of gluttony. It was lucky for them that Holly had arrived when she did, because the deli's dwarf owner was on the point of lowering the scaly foursome into the deep-fat fryer.

Holly's ride along for Operation Mop-Up was Corporal Grub Kelp, little brother to the famous Captain Trouble Kelp, one of the LEP's most decorated officers. Grub did not share his brother's stoic personality.

"I got a hangnail cuffing that last goblin," said the junior officer, chewing on his thumb.

"Painful," said Holly, trying to sound interested.

They were driving along a magnastrip to Police Plaza, with the perpetrators manacled in the rear of their LEP wagon. It wasn't actually a regulation wagon. The B'wa Kell had managed to burn out so many police vehicles during their short-lived revolution that the LEP had been forced to commandeer anything with an engine and room in the back for a few prisoners. In reality, Holly was piloting a fast-food van with the LEP acorn symbol spray painted on the side. The motor-pool gnomes had simply bolted the serving hatch and removed the ovens. A pity they couldn't remove the grease smell.

Grub studied his wounded finger. "Those cuffs have sharp edges. I should lodge a complaint."

Holly concentrated on the road, though the magnastrip did the steering for her. If Grub did lodge a complaint, it wouldn't be his first or even his twentieth. Trouble's little brother found fault with everything, except himself. In this instance he was completely wrong: there were no sharp edges on Plexiglas vacuum cuffs. If there were, a goblin might think to poke a hole in the other mitt and allow oxygen to reach his hand, and nobody wanted goblins hurling fireballs in the back of their vehicles.

"I know it sounds petty, to lodge a complaint over hang-nails, but no one could accuse *me* of being petty."

"You! Petty! Perish the thought."

Grub puffed up his chest. "After all, I am the only member of LEPretrieval One to have faced down the human Butler."

Holly groaned loudly. This, she fervently hoped, would dissuade Grub from telling his Artemis Fowl war story yet again. It grew longer and more fantastical each time. In reality, Butler had let him go, as a fisherman would a minnow.

But Grub was not about to take a hint.

"I remember it well," he began melodramatically. "It was a dark night."

And, as though his very words carried immeasurable magic, every light in the city went out.

Not only that but the magnastrip's power failed, leaving them stranded in the middle lane of a frozen highway.

"I didn't do that, did I?" whispered Grub.

Holly didn't answer, already halfway out of the wagon door. Overhead, the sun strips that replicated surface light were fading to black. In the last moments of half-light Holly squinted toward the Northern Tunnel, and sure enough, the door was sliding down, emergency lights revolving along its lower edge. Two hundred feet of solid steel separating Haven from the outside world. Similar doors were dropping at strategic arches all over the city. Lockdown. There were only three reasons that the Council would initiate a citywide lockdown. Flood, quarantine, or discovery by the humans.

Holly looked around her. Nobody was drowning, nobody was sick. So the Mud Men were coming. Finally, every fairy's worst nightmare was coming true.

Emergency lights flickered on overhead. The sunstrips' soft white glow was replaced by an eerie orange. Official vehicles received a burst of power from the magnastrip, enough to get them to the nearest depot. Ordinary citizens were not so lucky. They would have to walk. Hundreds stumbled from their automobiles, too scared to protest. That would come later.

"Captain Short! Holly!"

It was Grub. No doubt he would be lodging a complaint with someone.

"Corporal," she said, turning back to the vehicle. "This is no time for panic. We need to show an example. . . ."

The lecture petered out in her throat, because of what was happening to the wagon. All LEP vehicles would have received the regulation ten-minute burst of power from the magnastrip, to get them and their cargo to safety. This power would also keep the Plexiglas cuffs vacuumed. Of course, they weren't using an official LEP vehicle and so it hadn't been cleared for emergency power. Something the goblins had obviously realized, because they were trying to burn their way out of the wagon.

Grub stumbled from the cab, his helmet blackened by soot.

"They melted the cuffs off and started blasting the doors," he panted, retreating to a safe distance.

Goblins. Evolution's little joke. Pick the dumbest creatures on the planet and give them the ability to conjure fire. If the goblins didn't stop blasting the wagon's reinforced interior, they would be encased by molten metal. Not a nice way to go, even if you were fireproof.

Holly activated the amplifier in her LEP helmet. "You there, in the wagon. Cease fire. The vehicle will collapse and you will be trapped."

For several moments smoke billowed from the vents, then the vehicle settled on its axles. A face appeared at the grille, forked tongue slithering through the mesh.

"You think we're stupid, elf? We're gonna burn clean through this pile of junk."

Holly stepped closer, turning up the speakers.

"Listen to me, goblin. You are stupid, let's just accept that and move on. If you continue to fireball that vehicle, the roof will melt and fall on you like shells from a human gun. You may be fireproof, but are you bulletproof?"

The goblin licked his lidless eyes, thinking it over. "You lie, elf! We will blow a hole right through this prison. You will be next."

The wagon's panels began to lurch and buckle as the goblins renewed their attack.

"Not to worry," said Grub, from a safe distance. "The fire extinguishers will get them."

"They would," corrected Holly, "if the fire extinguishers weren't connected to the main power grid, which is shut down."

A mobile food preparation wagon such as this one would have to adhere to the strictest fire regulations before setting one magna wheel on the strip. In this case, several foam-packed extinguishers that could submerge the entire interior in flame retardant foam in a matter of seconds. The nice thing about the flame foam was that it hardened on contact with air, but the not-so-nice thing about flame foam was that the trip switch was connected to the magna-strip. No power, no foam.

Holly drew her Neutrino 2000 from its holster. "I'll just have to trip this switch myself."

Captain Short sealed her helmet and climbed into the wagon's cab. She avoided touching metal wherever possible, because even though microfilaments in her LEP jumpsuit were designed to disperse extra heat, microfilaments didn't always do what they were designed to do. The goblins were on their backs, pumping fireball after fireball into the roof panels.

"Knock it off!" she ordered, pointing her laser's muzzle through the mesh.

Three of the goblins ignored her. One, possibly the leader, turned his scaly face to the grille. Holly saw that he had gotten eyeball tattoos. This act of supreme stupidity probably would have guaranteed him promotion had the B'wa Kell not been effectively disbanded.

"You will not be able to get us all, elf," he said, smoke leaking from his mouth and slitted nostrils. "Then one of us will get you."

The goblin was right, even if he did not realize why. Holly suddenly remembered that she could not fire during a lockdown. Regulations stated that there were to be no

꒫꒫ꗴ • ꕯꙮꔖꔗꕯꙮꕯꕔ • ꕔꕯ • ꙶꕯꔖꙶꕯꔖ

unshielded power surges, in case Haven was being probed.

Her hesitation was all the proof the goblin needed.

"I knew it!" he crowed, tossing a casual fireball at the grille. The mesh glowed red and sparks cascaded against Holly's visor. Over the goblins' heads, the roof sagged dangerously. A few more seconds and it would collapse.

Holly unclipped a piton dart from her belt, screwing it into the launcher above the Neutrino's main barrel. The launcher was spring-loaded, like an old-fashioned speargun, and would not give off a heat flash. Nothing to alarm any sensors.

The goblin was highly amused, as goblins often are just before incarceration, which explains why so many are incarcerated.

"A dart? You going to prod us all to death, little elf?"

Holly aimed at a clip protruding from the fire foam nozzle in the rear of the wagon.

"Would you please be quiet," she said, and launched the dart. It flew over the goblin's head, jamming itself between the rods of the nozzle clip. The piton cord stretched the length of the wagon.

"Missed me," said the goblin, waggling his forked tongue. It was a testament to the goblin's stupidity that he could be trapped in a melting vehicle during a lockdown with an LEP officer firing at him, and still think he had the upper hand.

"I told you to be quiet!" said Holly, pulling sharply on the piton cord and snapping the clip.

Eight hundred kilograms of extinguisher foam blasted from the diffuser nozzle at over two hundred miles per hour. Needless to say, all fireballs went out. The goblins were pinned by the force of the already hardening foam. The goblin leader was pressed so forcibly against the grille that his tattooed eyes were easily legible. One said MOMMY, the other DUDDY. A misspelling, though he probably didn't know it.

"Ow," he said. More from disbelief than pain. He didn't say anything else, because his mouth was full of congealing foam.

"Don't worry," said Holly. "The foam is porous, so you will be able to breathe, but it's also completely fireproof, so good luck trying to burn your way out."

Grub was still examining his hangnail when Holly emerged from the van. She removed her helmet, wiping away the soot with the sleeve of her jumpsuit. The visor was supposed to be nonstick; maybe she should send it in for another coating.

"Everything all right?" asked Grub.

"Yes, Corporal. Everything is all right. No thanks to you."

Grub had the audacity to look offended. "I was securing the perimeter, Captain. We can't all be action heroes."

That was typical Grub, an excuse for every occasion. She could deal with him later. Now it was vital that she get to Police Plaza and find out why the Council had shut down the city.

"I think we should get back to HQ," Grub offered. "The intelligence boys might want to interview me if the humans are invading."

"I think *I* should get back to HQ," said Holly. "You stay here and keep an eye on the suspects until the power comes back on. Do you think you can handle that? Or are you too incapacitated with that hangnail?"

Holly's red hair stood in sweat-slicked spikes, and her round hazel eyes dared Grub to argue.

"No, Holly . . . Captain. You leave it to me. Everything is under control."

I doubt it, thought Holly, setting off at a run toward Police Plaza.

The city was in complete chaos. Every citizen was on the street staring at their dead appliances in disbelief. For some of the younger fairies, the loss of their cell phones was too much to bear. They sank to the streets, sobbing gently.

Police Plaza was mobbed by inquiring minds, like moths drawn to a light. In this case, one of the only lights in town. Hospitals and emergency vehicles would still have juice, but apart from those, the LEP headquarters was the only government building still functioning.

Holly forced her way through the crowd, into the lobby area. The public service lines ran down the steps and out the door. Today, everyone was asking the same question. What's happened to the power?

• (ᚴ♨ᚻ>ᚴ•)(ᒐ5ᘔ • ᚼ♧)( )(♧ ᘔ ᛞ •

The same question was on Holly's lips as she burst into the situation room, but she kept it to herself. The room was already packed with the force's complement of captains, along with the three regional commanders and all seven Council members.

"Aaah," said Chairman Cahartez. "The last captain."

"I didn't get my emergency juice," explained Holly. "Non-regulation vehicle."

Cahartez adjusted his official conical hat. "No time for excuses, Captain. Mr. Foaly has been holding off on his briefing until you got here."

Holly took her seat at the captain's table, beside Trouble Kelp.

"Grub okay?" he whispered.

"He got a hangnail."

Trouble rolled his eyes. "No doubt he'll make a complaint."

Foaly, a centaur, trotted through the doors, clutching armfuls of disks. Foaly was the LEP's technical genius, and his security innovations were the main reason that humans had not yet discovered the subterranean fairy hideaway. Maybe that was about to change. The centaur expertly loaded the disks, opening several windows on a wall-size plasma screen. Several complicated-looking algorithms and wave patterns appeared on the screen.

He cleared his throat noisily. "I advised Chairman Cahartez to initiate lockdown on the basis of these readings."

⚔☻⦿ • ☻⚏⅃ • �(⦶⦶ • ☻⚔⦶ • ⦶⚔

Recon's Commander Root sucked on an unlit fungus cigar. "I think I'm speaking for the whole room here, Foaly, when I say that all I see is lines and squiggles. Doubtless it makes sense to a smart pony like yourself, but the rest of us are going to need some plain Gnommish."

Foaly sighed. "Simply put. Really simply. We got pinged. Is that plain enough?"

It was. The room resonated with stunned silence. *Pinged* was an old naval term from back in the days when sonar had been the preferred method of detection. *Getting pinged* was slang for being detected. Someone knew the fairy folk were down here.

Root was the first to recover his voice. "Pinged. Who pinged us?"

Foaly shrugged. "Don't know. It only lasted a few seconds. There was no recognizable signature, and it was untraceable."

"What did they get?"

"Quite a bit. Everything North European. Scopes, Sentinel. All our cam-cams. Downloaded information on every one of them."

This was catastrophic news. Someone or something knew all about fairy surveillance in Northern Europe, after only a few seconds.

"Was it human?" asked Holly. "Or alien?"

Foaly pointed to a digital representation of the beam. "I can't say for certain. If it is human, it's something brand-new. This came out of nowhere. No one has been developing technology like this as far as I know. Whatever it is, it read us like an open book. My security encryptions folded like they weren't even there."

Cahartez took off his official hat, no longer concerned with protocol. "What does this mean for the People?"

"It's difficult to say. There are best- and worst-case scenarios. Our mysterious guest could learn all about us whenever he wishes and do with our civilization what he will."

"And the best-case scenario?" asked Trouble.

Foaly took a breath. "That was the best-case scenario."

Commander Root called Holly into his office. The room stank of cigar smoke in spite of the purifier built into the desk. Foaly was already there, his fingers a blur over the Commander's keyboard.

"The signal originated in London somewhere," said the centaur. "We only know that because I happened to be looking at the monitor at the time." He leaned back from the keyboard, shaking his head. "This is incredible. It's some kind of hybrid technology. Almost like our ion systems, but not quite, just a hair's breadth away."

"The *how* is not important now," said Root. "It's the *who* I'm worried about."

"What can I do, sir?" asked Holly.

Root stood, walking to a map of London on the wall plasma screen.

"I need you to sign out a surveillance pack, go topside and wait. If we get pinged again, I want someone on site ready to go. We can't record this thing, but we can certainly get a visual on the signal. As soon as it shows up on the screen, we'll feed you the coordinates and you can investigate."

Holly nodded. "When is the next hotshot?"

Hotshot was LEP-speak for the magma flares that Recon officers rode to the surface in titanium eggs. Pod pilots referred to this seat-of-the-pants procedure as "riding the hotshots."

"No such luck," replied Foaly. "Nothing in the pipes for the next two days. You'll have to take a shuttle."

"What about the lockdown?"

"I've restored power to Stonehenge and our satellite arrays. We'll have to risk it, you need to get aboveground and we need to stay in contact. The future of our civilization could depend on it."

Holly felt the weight of responsibility settle on her shoulders. This "future of our civilization" thing was happening more and more, lately.

Knightsbridge

The sonic blast from Butler's grenade had crashed through the kitchen door, sweeping stainless-steel implements aside like grass stalks. The aquarium shattered, leaving the flagstones slick with water, Plexiglas, and surprised lobsters. They skittered through the debris, claws raised.

The restaurant staff were on the floor, bound and soaking, but alive. Butler did not untie them. He did not need hysteria right now. Time enough to deal with them once all threats had been neutralized.

An assassin stirred, suspended halfway through a dividing wall. The manservant checked her eyes. They were crossed and unfocused. No threat there. Butler pocketed the old lady's weapon just the same. You couldn't be too careful. Something he was learning all over again. If Madam

Ko could have seen this afternoon's display, she would have had his graduation tattoo lasered off for sure.

The room was clear, but still something was bothering the bodyguard. His soldier's sense grated like two broken bones. Once again Butler flashed on Madam Ko, his sensei from the Academy. *The bodyguard's primary function is to protect his Principal. The Principal cannot be shot if you are standing in front of him.* Madam Ko always referred to employers as Principals. One did not become involved with Principals.

Butler wondered why this particular maxim had occurred to him. Out of the hundreds Madam Ko had drummed into his skull, why this one? It was obvious, really. He had broken the first rule of personal protection by leaving his Principal unguarded. The second rule, *Do not develop an emotional attachment to the Principal,* was pretty much in smithereens too. Butler had become so attached to Artemis that it was obviously beginning to affect his judgment.

He could see Madam Ko before him, nondescript in her khaki suit, for all the world like an ordinary Japanese housewife. But how many housewives of any nationality could strike so quickly that the air hissed? *You are a disgrace, Butler. A disgrace to your name. It would better suit your talents to get a job mending shoes. Your Principal has already been neutralized.*

Butler moved as though in a dream. The very air seemed to hold him back as he raced for the kitchen doors. He knew what would have happened. Arno Blunt was a professional. Vain, perhaps, a cardinal sin among bodyguards, but a professional, nevertheless. Professionals always inserted earplugs if there was any danger of gunfire.

The tiles were slick beneath his feet, but Butler compensated by leaning forward and digging his rubber-soled toes into the surface. His intact eardrums picked up irregular vibrations from the restaurant. Conversation. Artemis was speaking with someone. Arno Blunt, no doubt. It was already too late.

Butler came through the service door at a speed that would have shamed an Olympian. His brain began calculating odds the moment pictures arrived from his retinas. Blunt was in the act of firing. Nothing could be done about that now. There was only one option. Without hesitation, Butler took it.

In his right hand, Blunt held a silenced pistol.

"You first," he said. "Then the ape." Arno Blunt cocked the gun, took aim briefly, and fired.

Butler came from nowhere, he seemed to fill the entire room, flinging himself in the bullet's path. From a greater distance, the Kevlar in his bulletproof vest might have held, but at point-blank range the Teflon-coated bullet drilled through the vest like a hot poker through snow. It entered Butler's chest half an inch below the heart. It was a fatal wound.

The bodyguard's own momentum combined with the force of the bullet sent Butler crashing into Artemis, pinning him to the dessert trolley. Nothing of the boy was visible, save one Armani loafer.

Butler's breathing was shallow and his vision gone, but he was not dead yet. Even though his brain's electricity was rapidly running out, the bodyguard held on to a single thought: *Protect the Principal*.

Arno Blunt drew a surprised breath and Butler fired six shots at the sound. He would have been disappointed with the spread had he been able to see it. But one of the bullets found its mark, clipping Blunt's temple. Unconsciousness was immediate, concussion inevitable. Arno Blunt joined the rest of his team, on the floor.

Butler ignored the pain squashing his torso like a giant fist. Instead he listened for movement. There was nothing locally, just the scratch of lobster claws on the tiles. And if one of the lobsters decided to attack, Artemis was on his own.

Nothing more could be done. Either Artemis was safe, or he was not. If not, Butler was in no condition to fulfill the terms of his contract. This realization brought tremendous calm. No more responsibility. Just his own life to live, for a few seconds at any rate. And anyway, Artemis wasn't just a Principal. He was his only true friend. Madam Ko might not have liked this attitude, but there wasn't much she could do about it now. There wasn't much anybody could do.

* * *

ᚠᚢᚦᚨᚱᚲ ᚷᚹᚺᚾᛁᛃᛇᛈ ᚦᛚᛗ ᛒᛖ

Artemis had never liked desserts. And yet, he found him-self submersed in éclairs, cheesecake, and pavlova. His suit would be absolutely destroyed. Of course Artemis's brain was only throwing up these facts so he could avoid thinking about what had happened. But a two-hundred-pound dead weight is a hard thing to ignore.

Luckily for Artemis, Butler's impact had actually driven him through to the trolley's second shelf, while the body-guard remained on the ice-cream ledge above. As far as Artemis could tell, the Black Forest Gâteau had cushioned his impact sufficiently to avoid serious internal injury. Still, he had no doubt that a visit to the chiropractor would be called for. Possibly for Butler too, though the man had the constitution of a troll.

Artemis struggled out from underneath his manservant. With each movement, malignant cream horns exploded over him.

"Really, Butler," grumbled the teenager. "I must begin choosing my business associates more carefully. Hardly a day goes by when we aren't the victims of some plot."

Artemis was relieved to see Arno Blunt unconscious on the restaurant floor.

"Another villain dispatched. Good shooting, Butler, as usual. And one more thing, I have decided to wear a bullet-proof vest to all future meetings. That should make your job somewhat easier, eh?"

It was at this point that Artemis noticed Butler's shirt.

The sight knocked the air from his chest like an invisible mallet. Not the hole in the material, but the blood leaking from it.

"Butler, you're injured. Shot. But the Kevlar?"

The bodyguard didn't reply, nor did he have to. Artemis knew science better than most nuclear physicists. Truth be told, he often posted Internet lectures on the subject under the pseudonym Emmsey Squire. Obviously the bullet's momentum had been too great for the jacket to withstand. Possibly it had been coated with Teflon for extra penetration.

A large part of Artemis wanted to drape his arms across the bodyguard's frame, and cry as he would for a brother. But Artemis repressed that instinct. Now was the time for quick thinking.

Butler interrupted his train of thought.

"Artemis . . . is that you?" he said, the words coming in short gasps.

"Yes, it's me," answered Artemis, his voice trembling. "Don't worry. Juliet will protect you. You'll be fine."

"Don't talk, Butler. Lie still. The wound is not serious."

Butler spluttered. It was as close as he could get to a laugh.

"Very well, it is serious. But I will think of something. Just stay still."

With his last vestige of strength, Butler raised a hand.

"Good-bye, Artemis," he said. "My friend."

Artemis caught the hand. The tears were streaming now. Unchecked.

"Good-bye, Butler."

The bodyguard's sightless eyes were calm. "Artemis, call me Domovoi."

The name told Artemis two things. First, his lifelong ally had been named for a Slavic guardian spirit. Second, graduates of the Madam Ko school were instructed never to reveal their first names to their Principals. It helped to keep things clinical. Butler would never have broken this rule . . . unless it no longer mattered.

"Good-bye, Domovoi," sobbed the boy. "Good-bye, my friend."

The hand dropped. Butler was gone.

"No!" shouted Artemis, staggering backward.

This wasn't right. This was not the way things should end. For some reason, he had always imagined that they would die together. Perhaps facing insurmountable odds in some exotic location. On the lip of Vesuvius perhaps, or the banks of the mighty Ganges. But together, as friends. After all they had been through, Butler could not simply be defeated at the hands of some grandstanding, second-rate muscleman.

Butler had almost died before. The year before last, he had been mauled by a troll from the deep tunnels below Haven City. Holly Short had saved him then, using her fairy

𝒽 • ⚮ • ⟑ ⚶ ⟩ ⓑ ⚷ ☺ • ⚮ ⟨ ⚶ 𝄽 ☺ ·· ⚮ •

magic. But now there were no fairies around to save his bodyguard.

Time was the enemy here. If Artemis had more of it, he could figure out how to contact the LEP and persuade Holly to use her magic once again. But time was running out. Butler had perhaps four minutes before his brain shut down. Not long enough, even for an intellect such as his. Artemis needed to buy some more time. Or steal some.

Think, boy, think. Use what the situation provides. Artemis shut off the wellspring of tears. He was in a restaurant, a fish restaurant. Useless! Worthless! Perhaps in a medical facility he could do something. But here? What was here? An oven, sinks, utensils. Even if he did have the proper tools, he had not yet completed his medical studies. It was too late for conventional surgery at any rate, unless there was a method of heart transplant that took less than four minutes.

The seconds were ticking by. Artemis was growing angry with himself. Time was against them. Time needed to be stopped. The idea sparked in Artemis's brain in a flash of neurons. Perhaps he couldn't stop time, but he could halt Butler's passage through it. The process was risky certainly, but it was the only chance they had.

Artemis popped the dessert trolley's brake with his foot, and began hauling the contraption toward the kitchen. He had to pause several times to drag moaning assassins from the vehicle's path. Emergency vehicles were approaching, making their way down Knightsbridge. Obviously the sonic grenade's detonation would have attracted attention. There were only moments left before he would have to fabricate some plausible story for the authorities. Better not to be here. Fingerprints wouldn't be a problem, as the restaurant would have had dozens of customers. All he had to do was get out of here before London's finest arrived.

The kitchen was forged from stainless steel. Hobs, hoods, and work surfaces were littered with fallout from the sonic grenade. Fish flapped in the sink, crustaceans clicked across the tiles, and caviar dripped from the ceiling.

There! At the back, a line of freezers, essentials in any seafood bistro. Artemis put his shoulder against the trolley, steering it to the rear of the kitchen.

The largest of the freezers was of the custom built pull-out variety often found in large restaurants. Artemis hauled open the drawer, quickly evicting the salmon, sea bass, and hake that were encrusted in the ice shavings.

Cryogenics. It was their only chance. The science of freezing a body until medicine had evolved sufficiently to revive it. Generally dismissed by the medical community, it nevertheless made millions each year from the estates of rich eccentrics who needed more than one lifetime to spend their money. Cryogenic chambers were generally built to very exact specifications, but there was no time for Artemis's usual standards now. This freezer would have to do as a temporary solution. It was imperative that

Butler's head be cooled to preserve the brain cells. So long as his brain functions were intact, he could theoretically be revived, even if there were no heartbeat.

Artemis maneuvered the trolley until it overhung the open freezer, then with the help of a silver platter, he levered Butler's body into the steaming ice. It was tight, but the bodyguard fit with barely a bend of the legs. Artemis heaped loose ice on top of his fallen comrade, and then adjusted the thermostat to four degrees below freezing, to avoid tissue damage. Butler's blank eyes stared at him through a layer of ice.

"I'll be back," the boy said. "Sleep well."

The sirens were close now. Artemis heard the screech of tires.

"Hold on, Domovoi," whispered Artemis, closing the freezer drawer.

Artemis left through the back door, mingling with the crowds of locals and sightseers. The police would have someone photographing the crowd, so he did not linger, or even glance back toward the restaurant. Instead, he made his way to Harrods, and found himself a table at the gallery café.

Once he had assured the waitress that he was not looking for his mommy, and produced sufficient cash to pay for his pot of Earl Grey tea, Artemis pulled out his cell phone, selecting a number from the speed-dial menu.

• ⊡⏃⏁⋔ • ⏚⟒⟒⟟ ⟟ ⟒⟒⊡ ⏚ • ⟟ ⟒⟒⏃⏁⟒ •

A man answered on the second ring. "Hello. Make it quick, whoever you are. I'm very busy at the moment."

The man was Detective Inspector Justin Barre of New Scotland Yard. Barre's gravelly tones were caused by a hunting knife across the gullet during a bar fight in the nineties. If Butler hadn't been on hand to stop the bleeding, Justin Barre would never have risen beyond sergeant. It was time to call in the debt.

"Detective Barre. This is Artemis Fowl."

"Artemis, how are you? And how's my old partner, Butler?"

Artemis kneaded his forehead. "Not well at all, I'm afraid. He needs a favor."

"Anything for the big man. What can I do?"

"Did you hear something about a disturbance in Knightsbridge?"

There was a pause. Artemis heard paper rip as a fax was torn off the roll.

"Yes, it just came in. A couple of windows were shattered in some restaurant. Nothing major. Some tourists got a bit shell-shocked. Preliminary reports say it was some kind of localized earthquake, if you can believe that. We've got two cars there right now. Don't tell me Butler was behind it?"

Artemis took a breath. "I need you to keep your men away from the freezers."

"That's a strange request, Artemis. What's in the freezers that I shouldn't see?"

꙰ ꙰ ꙰ • ꙰ ꙰ ꙰ ꙰ • ꙰ ꙰ • ꙰ ꙰ ꙰ ꙰ ꙰ ꙰ ꙰ ꙰

"Nothing illegal," promised Artemis. "Believe me when I say, this is life or death for Butler."

Barre didn't hesitate. "This is not exactly in my jurisdiction, but consider it done. Do you need to get whatever I'm not supposed to see out of the freezers?"

The detective had read his mind. "As soon as possible. Two minutes are all I need."

Barre chewed it over. "Okay. Let's synchronize schedules. The forensics team is going to be in there for a couple of hours. Nothing I can do about that. But by six-thirty, I can guarantee there won't be anyone on duty. You have five minutes."

"That will be more than sufficient."

"Good. And tell the big man that we're even."

Artemis kept his voice even. "Yes, Detective Barre. I'll tell him." *If I get the opportunity,* he thought.

The Ice Age Cryogenics Institute was not actually on London's Harley Street. Technically, it was tucked away in Dickens Lane, a side alley on the famous medical boulevard's southern end. But this did not stop the facility's MD, one Dr. Constance Lane, from putting Harley Street on all Ice Age stationery. You couldn't buy credibility like that. When the upper classes saw those magic words on a business card, they fell over themselves to have their frail frames frozen.

Artemis Fowl was not so easily impressed. But then, he had little choice. Ice Age was one of three cryogenic centers in the city, and the only one with free units. Though Artemis did consider the neon sign a bit much. PODS TO RENT. Honestly.

The building itself was enough to make Artemis squirm. The façade was clad in brushed aluminum, obviously designed to resemble a spaceship, and the doors were of the whoosh *Star Trek* variety. Where was culture? Where was art? How did a monstrosity like this get planning permission in historic London?

A nurse complete with white uniform and three-cornered hat was supervising the reception. Artemis doubted she was an actual nurse—it must have been the cigarette between her false nails.

"Excuse me, miss?"

The nurse barely glanced up from her gossip magazine.

"Yes? Are you looking for someone?"

Artemis clenched his fists behind his back.

"Yes, I would like to see Dr. Lane. She is the surgeon, is she not?"

The nurse ground out her cigarette in an overflowing ashtray.

"This is not another school project, is it? Dr. Lane says, no more projects."

"No. Not another school project."

"You're not a lawyer, are you?" asked the nurse suspiciously. "One of those geniuses who gets a degree while they're still in diapers?"

Artemis sighed. "A genius, yes. A lawyer, hardly. I am, mademoiselle, a customer."

And suddenly the nurse was all charm.

"Oh, a customer, why didn't you say so? I'll show you right in. Would sir care for tea, coffee, or perhaps something stronger?"

"I am thirteen years old, mademoiselle."

"A juice?"

"Tea would be fine. Earl Grey if you have it. No sugar obviously. It might make me hyperactive."

The nurse was quite prepared to accept sarcasm from an actual paying customer, and directed Artemis to a lounge where the style was again, space age. Plenty of shining velour and eternity mirrors. He had half finished a cup of something that most definitely was not Earl Grey when Dr. Lane's door swung open.

"Do come in," said a tall woman uncertainly.

"Shall I walk?" asked Artemis. "Or will you beam me up?"

The office walls were lined with frames. Along one side were the doctor's degrees and certificates. Artemis suspected that many of these certificates could be obtained over the weekend. Along the wall were several photographic portraits. Above these read the legend LOVE LIES SLEEPING. Artemis almost left then, but he was desperate.

Dr. Lane sat behind her desk. She was a very glamorous woman with flowing red hair and the tapered fingers of an artist. Even her smock was Dior. Constance Lane's smile was perfect. Too perfect. Artemis looked closer and realized that her entire face was the handiwork of a plastic surgeon. Obviously this woman's life was all about cheating time. He had come to the right place.

"Now, young man, Tracy says you wish to become a customer?" The doctor tried to smile, but the stretching made her face shine like a balloon.

"Not personally, no," replied Artemis. "But I do wish to rent one of your units. Short term."

Constance Lane pulled a company pamphlet from the drawer, ringing some figures in red. "Our rates are quite steep."

Artemis did not even glance at the numbers. "Money is no object. We can set up a wire transfer right now from my Swiss bank. In five minutes you can have a hundred thousand pounds sitting in your personal account. All I need is a unit for a single night."

The figure was impressive. Constance thought of all the nips and tucks it would buy, but she was reluctant. "Generally minors are not allowed to commit relatives to our chambers. It's the law actually."

Artemis leaned forward.

"Dr. Lane. Constance. What I'm doing here is not exactly legal, but no one is being hurt either. One night and you're a rich woman. This time tomorrow and I was never here. No bodies, no complaints."

⅃ ⌘⚬ • ⚔⟩⟨ • ⟩⟨⚭⚭ • ⚚⅃" • ⚔⅊⚬ • ⚘ ⚭⚭⚬ • ⚶

The doctor's hand flew to her jaw line.

"One night?"

"Just one. You won't even know we're here."

Constance took a hand mirror from her desk drawer, studying her reflection closely.

"Call your bank," she said.

Stonehenge, southern England

Two LEP chutes emerged in the south of England. One in London itself, but that was closed to the People because the Chelsea Football Club had built their grounds five hundred yards above the shuttleport.

The other port was in Wiltshire, beside what humans referred to as Stonehenge. Mud People had several theories as to the origins of the structure. Hypotheses ranged from spaceship landing port to pagan center of worship. The truth was far less glamorous. Stonehenge had actually been an outlet for a flat, bread-based food. Or in human terms, a pizza parlor.

A gnome called Bog had realized how many tourists forgot their sandwiches on aboveground jaunts, and so had set up shop beside the terminal. It was a smooth operation. You drove up to the one of the windows, named your toppings, and ten minutes later you were stuffing your face. Of course, Bog had to shift his operation belowground once humans began talking in full sentences. And anyway, all that cheese was making the ground soggy. A couple of the service windows had even collapsed.

It was difficult for civilians to get visas to visit Stonehenge because of the constant activity on the surface. Then again, hippies saw fairies every day and it never made the front page. As a police officer, Holly didn't have a visa problem; one flash of the Recon badge opened a hole right through to the surface.

But being a Recon officer didn't help if there was no magma flare scheduled. And the Stonehenge chute had been dormant for over three centuries. Not a spark. In the absence of a hotshot to ride, Holly was forced to travel aboard a commercial shuttle.

The first available shuttle was heavily booked, but luckily there was a late cancellation, so Holly wasn't forced to bump a passenger.

The shuttle was a fifty-seater luxury cruiser. It had been commissioned especially by the Brotherhood of Bog to visit their patron's site. These fairies, mostly gnomes, dedicated their lives to pizza, and every year on the anniversary of Bog's first day in business, they chartered a shuttle and took a picnic aboveground. The picnic consisted of pizza, tuber beer, and pizza-flavored ice cream. Needless to say, they did not remove their rubber pizza bonnets for the entire day.

So, for sixty-seven minutes, Holly sat wedged between two beer-swilling gnomes singing the pizza song:

ꗇ • ꛤ • ꛰ꚉꙶꚕ • ꛱ꛤꚅꚕ • ꗄꙵꚍꙮ • ꚿ

Pizza, pizza,
Fill up your face!
The thicker the pastry,
The better the base!

There were a hundred and fourteen verses. And it didn't get any better. Holly had never been happier to see the Stonehenge landing lights.

The actual terminal was pretty comprehensive, boasting a three-lane visa clearance booth, entertainment complex, and duty-free shopping. The current souvenir craze was a Mud Man hippie doll that said "Peace, man" when you pressed its tummy.

Holly badged her way through the customs line, taking a security elevator to the surface. Stonehenge had become easier to exit recently, because the Mud Men had put up fencing. The humans were protecting their heritage, or so they thought. Strange that Mud Men seemed more concerned about the past than the present.

Holly strapped on her wings, and once the control booth had given her the go-ahead, she cleared the air lock, soaring to a height of seven thousand feet. There was plenty of cloud cover, but nevertheless she activated her shield. Nothing could spot her now, she was invisible to human and mechanical eyes. Only rats and two species of monkey could see through a fairy shield.

Holly switched on the onboard navigator in the wings' computer and let the rig do the steering for her. It was

nice to be aboveground again, and at sunset too. Her favorite time of day. A slow smile spread across her face. In spite
of the situation, she was content. This was what she was
born to do. Recon. With the wind against her visor and a
challenge between her teeth.

Knightsbridge

It had been almost two hours since Butler had been shot.
Generally the grace period between heart failure and brain
damage is about four minutes, but that period can be
extended if the patient's body temperature is lowered sufficiently. Drowning victims, for example, can be resuscitated for
up to an hour after their apparent death. Artemis could only
pray that his makeshift cryogenic chamber could hold Butler
in stasis until he could be transferred to one of Ice Age's pods.

Ice Age Cryogenics had a mobile unit for transporting
clients from the private clinics where they expired. The
van was equipped with its own generator and full surgery.
Even if cryogenics was considered crackpot medicine by
many physicians, the vehicle itself would meet the strictest
standards of equipment and hygiene.

"These units cost almost a million pounds apiece," Dr.
Constance Lane informed Artemis, as they sat in the stark-
white surgery. A cylindrical cryo pod was strapped to a
gurney between them.

"The vans are custom made in Munich, specially armored,

too. This thing could drive over a land mine and come out smiling."

For once, Artemis was not interested in gathering information.

"That's very nice, Doctor, but can it go any faster? My associate's time is running out. It has already been one hundred and twenty-seven minutes."

Constance Lane tried to frown, but there wasn't enough slack skin across her brow.

"Two hours. Nobody has ever been revived after that long. Then again, no one has *ever* been revived from a cryogenic chamber."

The Knightsbridge traffic was, as usual, chaotic. Harrods was running a one-day sale, and the block was besieged by droves of eager customers lining up for access to the luxury store. It took a further seventeen minutes to reach En Fin's delivery entrance.

Just as promised, there were no policemen present, except one. Detective Justin Barre himself was standing sentry at the rear door. The man was huge, a descendant of the Zulu nation, according to Butler. It was not difficult to imagine him at Butler's side in some faraway land.

Incredibly, they found a parking space, and Artemis climbed down from the van.

"Cryogenics," said Barre, noting the vehicle's inscription. "Do you think you can do anything for him?"

"You looked in the freezer, then?" said Artemis.

⦿⦾⦿⚏ • ⚏⚏⊟ • ⋇⟫⟨ • ⟃⊟⟨⟩⟩⟩⚏⚏ • ⩍⟫⟨

The detective nodded. "How could I resist? Curiosity is my business. I'm sorry I checked now. He was a good man."

"*Is* a good man," insisted Artemis. "I am not ready to give up on him yet."

Barre stood aside to admit two uniformed Ice Age paramedics.

"According to my men, a group of armed bandits attempted to rob the establishment, but they were interrupted by an earthquake. And if that's what really happened, I'll eat my badge. I don't suppose you can throw any light on the situation?"

"A competitor of mine disagreed with a business strategy. It was a violent disagreement."

"Who pulled the trigger?"

"Arno Blunt. A New Zealander. Bleached hair, tattoos on his body and neck. Most of his teeth are missing."

Barre took a note. "I'll circulate the description to the airports. You never know, we might catch him."

Artemis rubbed his eyes. "Butler saved my life. The bullet was meant for me."

"That's Butler all right." Barre nodded. "If there's anything I can do?"

"You'll be the first to know," said Artemis. "Did your officers find anyone on the scene?"

Barre consulted his notebook. "Some customers and staff. They all checked out, so we let them go. The thieves escaped before we arrived."

• ⚷⚶⚳ • ⚸⚴⚹⚺⚻⚼ • ⚽⚾⚿⛀ • ⛁⛂

"No matter. Better I deal with the culprits myself."

Barre made a concerted effort to ignore the activity in the kitchen behind him.

"Artemis, can you guarantee this is not going to come back to haunt me? Technically, we're looking at a homicide."

Artemis looked Barre in the eye, which was quite an effort.

"Inspector Barre, no body, no case. And I guarantee that by tomorrow Butler will be alive and kicking. I shall instruct him to call you, if that would set your mind at rest."

"It would."

The paramedics rolled Butler past on a gurney, a frosting of ice covered his face. Tissue damage was already turning his fingers blue.

"Any surgeon who could fix this would have to be a real magician."

Artemis glanced downward.

"That's the plan, Inspector Barre. That's the plan."

Dr. Lane administered glucose injections in the van.

"These are to stop the cells collapsing," she informed Artemis, massaging Butler's chest to circulate the medication. "Otherwise, the water in his blood will freeze in spikes and puncture the cell walls."

Butler was lying in an open cryo unit with its own gyroscopes. He had been dressed in a special silver freezer suit, and cold packs were heaped on his body like sachets of sugar in a bowl.

Constance was unaccustomed to people actually paying attention when she explained the process, but this pale youth absorbed facts faster than she could present them.

"Won't the water freeze anyway? Glucose can't prevent that."

Constance was impressed. "Why, yes, it will. But in small pieces, so it can float safely between cells."

Artemis jotted a note in his handheld computer. "Small pieces, I understand."

"The glucose is only a temporary measure," continued the doctor. "The next step is surgery—we need to completely wash out his veins, and replace the blood with a preservative. Then we can lower the patient's temperature to minus thirty degrees. We'll have to do that back at the institute."

Artemis shut down his computer. "No need for that. I just need him held in stasis for a few hours. After that it won't make any difference."

"I don't think you understand, young man," said Dr. Lane. "Current medical practices have not evolved to the point where this kind of injury can be healed. If I don't do a complete blood substitute soon, there will be severe tissue damage."

The van jolted as a wheel crashed into one of London's numerous potholes. Butler's arm jerked, and for a moment Artemis could pretend he was alive.

"Don't worry about that, Doctor."

"But . . ."

"A hundred thousand pounds, Doctor. Just keep repeating that figure to yourself. Park the mobile unit outside and forget all about us. In the morning we'll be gone. Both of us."

Dr. Lane was surprised.

"Park outside? You don't even want to come in?"

"No, Butler stays outside," said Artemis. "My . . . ah . . . surgeon, has a problem with dwellings. But I may enter for a moment, to use your phone. I need to make a rather special phone call."

London airspace

The lights of London were spread out below Holly like the stars of some turbulent galaxy. England's capital was generally a no-fly area for Recon officers, because of the four airports feeding planes into the sky. Five years ago, Captain Trouble Kelp had narrowly missed being impaled by a Heathrow–JFK Airbus. Since then, all flight plans involving cities with airports had to be cleared personally by Foaly.

Holly spoke into her helmet mike.

"Foaly. Any flights coming in I should know about?"

"Let me just bring up the radar. Okay, let's see. I'd drop down to five hundred feet if I were you. There's a 747 coming in from Malaga in a couple of minutes. It won't hit you, but your helmet computer could interfere with its navigation systems."

Holly dipped her flaps until she was at the correct altitude. Overhead the giant jet screamed across the sky. If it hadn't been for Holly's sonic filter sponges, both her eardrums would have popped.

"Okay. One jet full of tourists successfully avoided. What now?"

"Now we wait. I won't call again unless it's important."

They didn't have to wait long. Less than five minutes later, Foaly broke radio silence.

"Holly. We got something."

"Another probe?"

"No. Something from Sentinel. Hold on, I'm sending the file to your helmet."

A sound file appeared in Holly's visor. Its wave resembled a seismograph's readout.

"What is it, a phone tap?"

"Not exactly," said Foaly. "It's one of a billion throwaway files that Sentinel sends us every day."

The Sentinel system was a series of monitoring units that Foaly had piggybacked onto obsolete U.S. and Russian satellites. Their function was to monitor all human telecommunications. Obviously, it would be impossible to review every phone call made each day. So the computer was programmed to pick up on certain key words. If, for example, the words *fairy*, *haven*, and *underground* appeared in a conversation, this call would be flagged by the computer. The more People-related phrases that appeared, the more urgent the rating.

"This call was made in London minutes ago. It's loaded with key words. I've never heard anything like it."

"Play," said Holly clearly, using voice command. A vertical line cursor began scrolling across the sound wave.

"People," said a voice hazy with distortion. "LEP, magic, Haven, shuttleports, sprites, B'wa Kell, trolls, time stop, Recon, Atlantis."

"That's it?"

"That's not enough? Whoever made that call could be writing our biography."

"But it's just a string of words. It makes no sense."

"Hey, there's no point arguing with me," said the centaur. "I just collect information. But there has to be a connection to the probe. Two things like this don't just happen on the same day."

"Okay. Do we have an exact location?"

"The call came from a cryogenics institute in London. Sentinel quality is not enough to run a voice-recognition scan. We just know it came from inside the building."

"Who was our mystery Mud Man calling?"

"Strange thing. He was calling the *Times* newspaper crossword hotline."

"Maybe those words were the answers to today's crossword?" said Holly hopefully.

⚱⚵⚭⚰⚬⚩ • ⚲⚵⚰⚳⚴⚬⚯⚲⚵⚭⚯⚯ •

"No. I checked the correct solution. Not a fairy-related word in sight."

Holly set her wings to manual. "Okay. Time to find out what our caller is up to. Send me the institute's coordinates."

Holly suspected that it was a false alarm. Hundreds of these calls came in every year. Foaly was so paranoid that he believed the Mud Men were invading every time someone mentioned the word *magic* on a phone line. And with the recent trend for human fantasy movies and video games, magical phrases cropped up quite a lot. Thousands of police hours were wasted staking out the residents of dwellings where these phone calls originated, and it usually turned out to be some kid playing on his PC.

More than likely this phantom phone call was the result of a crossed line, or some Hollywood hack pitching a screenplay, or even an undercover LEP operative trying to phone home. But then, today of all days, everything had to be checked.

Holly kicked up her legs behind her, dropping into a steep dive. Diving was against Recon regulations. All approaches were supposed to be controlled and gradual. But what was the point of flying if you couldn't feel the slipstream tugging at your toes?

Ice Age Cryogenics Institute, London

Artemis leaned against the cryogenics mobile unit's rear bumper. It was funny how quickly a person's priorities could change. That morning he had been worried about which loafers to wear with his suit, and now his dearest friend's life hung in the balance. And the balance was rapidly shifting.

Artemis wiped a coating of frost from the spectacles he'd retrieved from his bodyguard's jacket. These were no ordinary spectacles—Butler had twenty-twenty vision. These particular eyeglasses had been specially tooled to accommodate filters taken from an LEP helmet. Anti-shield filters. Butler had carried them since the time when Holly Short almost got the jump on him at Fowl Manor. You never know, he'd said. We're a threat to LEP security, and someday Commander Root could be replaced with someone who isn't quite so fond of us.

Artemis wasn't convinced. The fairies were by and large a peaceful people. He couldn't believe they would harm anyone, even a Mud Man, on the basis of past crimes. After all, they had parted friends. Or at least not enemies.

That was presuming the call worked. But there was no reason to believe it wouldn't. Several government security agencies monitored phone lines using the keyword system, recording conversations that could compromise national security. And if humans were doing it, it was a safe bet that Foaly was two steps ahead.

Artemis donned the glasses, climbing into the vehicle's cabin. He had placed the call ten minutes ago. Presuming Foaly got working on a trace straightaway, it could still be another two hours before the LEP could get an operative on the surface. That would make it almost five hours since Butler's heart had stopped. The record for a revival was two hours and fifty minutes for an Alpine skier frozen in an avalanche. There had never been a revival after three hours. Maybe there shouldn't be.

Artemis glanced at the tray of food sent out by Dr. Lane. On another day he would have complained about just about everything on the plate. But now the meal was simply sustenance to keep him awake until the cavalry arrived. Artemis took a long drink from a polystyrene cup of tea. It sloshed audibly around in his empty stomach. Behind him in the van's surgery, Butler's cryo unit hummed like a common household freezer. Occasionally the computer emitted electronic beeps and whirrs as the machine ran self-diagnostics. Artemis was reminded of the weeks spent in Helsinki waiting for his father to regain consciousness. Waiting to see what the fairy magic would do for him . . .

Excerpt from Artemis Fowl's diary, disk 2 (encrypted)

Today my father spoke to me. For the first time in over two years I heard his voice, and it is exactly as I remembered it. But not everything is the same.

It had been over two months since Holly Short used her healing magic on his battered body, and still he lay in his Helsinki hospital bed. Immobile, unresponsive.

· ⚶ ☺ · ⒉⒊⒐⚱ · ⅀⒉⒊⒊ · 𝍖⚱ · ⅀⚽⚇ · ⅀

The doctors could not understand it. He should be awake, they informed me. His brain waves are strong, exceptionally so. And his heart beats like a horse. It is incredible, this man should be at death's door, yet he has the muscle tone of a twenty-year-old.

Of course it is no mystery to me. Holly's magic has overhauled my father's entire being, with the exception of his left leg, which was lost when his ship went down off the coast of Murmansk. He has received an infusion of life, in body and mind.

The effect of the magic on his body does not worry me, but I cannot help but wonder what effect this positive energy will have on my father's mind. For my father, a change like this could be traumatic. He is the Fowl patriarch, and his life revolves around moneymaking.

For sixteen days we sat in my father's hospital room, waiting for some sign of life. I had, by then, learned to read the instruments and noticed immediately the morning that my father's brain waves began spiking. My diagnosis was that he would soon regain consciousness, and so I called the nurse.

We were ushered from the room, to admit a medical team of at least a dozen. Two heart specialists, an anesthesiologist, a brain surgeon, a psychologist, and several nurses.

In fact, my father had no need of medical attention. He simply sat up, rubbed his eyes, and uttered one word: "Angeline."

Mother was admitted. Butler, Juliet, and I were forced to wait for several more agonizing minutes until she reappeared at the door. "Come in, everyone," she said. "He wants to see you."

And suddenly I was afraid. My father, the man whose shoes

I had been trying to fill for two years, was awake. Would he still live up to my expectations? Would I live up to his?

I entered hesitantly. Artemis Fowl I was propped up by several pillows. The first thing that I noticed was his face. Not the scar traces, which were already almost completely healed, but the expression. My father's brow, usually a thunderhead of moody contemplation, was smooth and carefree.

After such a long time apart, I did not know what to say. My father had no such doubts.

"Arty," he cried, stretching his arms toward me. "You're a man now. A young man."

I ran into his embrace, and while he held me close all plots and schemes were forgotten. I had a father again.

Ice Age Cryogenics

Artemis's memories were interrupted by a sly movement on the wall above. He fixed his gaze on the spot, watching through filtered eyes. There was a fairy crouching on a third-story windowsill. A Recon officer complete with wings and helmet. After only fifteen minutes? His ruse had worked. Foaly had intercepted the call, and sent someone to investigate. Now all that remained was to hope this particular fairy was full to the brim with magic and willing to help.

This had to be handled sensitively. The last thing he wanted to do was to spook the Recon officer. One wrong move and he'd wake up in six hours, with absolutely no recollection of the day's events. And that would be fatal for Butler.

Artemis opened the van door slowly, stepping down into the yard. The fairy cocked its head, following his movements. To his dismay, Artemis saw the creature draw a platinum handgun.

"Don't shoot," said Artemis, raising his hands. "I am unarmed. And I need your help."

The fairy activated its wings, descending slowly until its visor was level with Artemis's eyes.

"Do not be alarmed," continued Artemis. "I am a friend to the People. I helped to defeat the B'wa Kell. My name is . . ."

The fairy unshielded, her opaque visor sliding up.

"I know what your name is, Artemis," said Captain Holly Short.

"Holly," said Artemis, grasping her by the shoulders. "It's you."

Holly shrugged off the human's hands. "I know it's me. What's going on here? I presume you made the call?"

"Yes, yes. No time for that now. I can explain later."

Holly opened the throttle on her wings, rising to a height of ten feet.

"No, Artemis. I want an explanation now. If you needed help, why didn't you call on your own phone?"

Artemis forced himself to answer the question. "You told

me that Foaly had pulled surveillance on my communications, and anyway I wasn't sure you'd come."

Holly considered it. "Okay. Maybe I wouldn't have." She noticed something. "Where's Butler? Watching our backs, as usual, I suppose."

Artemis didn't answer, but his expression told Holly exactly why the Mud Boy had summoned her.

Artemis pressed a button, and a pneumatic pump opened the cryo pod's lid. Butler lay inside, encased in an inch of ice.

"Oh, no," sighed Holly. "What happened?"

"He stopped a bullet that was meant for me," replied Artemis.

"When are you going to learn, Mud Boy?" snapped the fairy. "Your little schemes have a tendency to get people hurt. Usually the people who care about you."

Artemis didn't answer. The truth was the truth after all.

Holly peeled back a cold pack from the bodyguard's chest. "How long?"

Artemis consulted the clock on his cell phone. "Three hours. Give or take a few minutes."

Captain Short wiped off the ice, laying her hand flat on Butler's chest. "Three hours. I don't know, Artemis. There's nothing here. Not a flicker."

Artemis faced her across the cryo pod. "Can you do it, Holly? Can you heal him?"

ꕉꙮꗇꗩꗡ • ꖦꗇꖷꕉꗩ • ꗡꖝ • ꗧꗲꕤꗲ

Holly stepped back. "Me? I can't heal him. We need a professional warlock to even attempt something like this."

"But you healed my father."

"That was different. Your father wasn't dead. He wasn't even critical. I hate to say it, but Butler is gone. Long gone."

Artemis pulled a gold medallion from a leather thong around his neck. The disk was perforated by a single circular hole. Dead center.

"Remember this. You gave it to me for ensuring that your trigger finger got reattached to your hand. You said it would remind me of the spark of decency inside me. I'm trying to do something decent now, Captain."

"It's not a question of decency. It just can't be done."

Artemis drummed his fingers on the gurney. Thinking. "I want to talk to Foaly," he said finally.

"I speak for the People, Fowl," said Holly testily. "We don't take orders from humans."

"Please, Holly," said Artemis. "I can't just let him go. It's Butler."

Holly couldn't help herself. After all, Butler had saved all their hides on more than one occasion.

"Very well," she said, fishing a spare com-set from her belt. "But he's not going to have any good news for you."

Artemis hooked the speaker over one ear, adjusting the mike stem so it wound across his mouth.

"Foaly? Are you listening?"

"Are you kidding?" came the reply. "This is better than human soap operas."

Artemis composed himself. He would have to present a convincing case, or Butler's last chance was gone.

"All I want is a healing. I accept that it may not work, but what does it cost to try?"

"It's not that straightforward, Mud Boy," replied the centaur. "Healing isn't a simple process. It requires talent and concentration. Holly is pretty good, I grant you, but for something like this, we need a trained team of warlocks."

"There's no time," snapped Artemis. "Butler has already been under too long. This has to be done now, before the glucose is absorbed into his bloodstream. There is already tissue damage to the fingers."

"Maybe his brain, too?" suggested the centaur.

"No. I got his temperature down in minutes. The cranium has been frozen since the incident."

"Are you sure about that? We don't want to bring Butler's body back, and not his mind."

"I'm sure. The brain is fine."

Foaly didn't speak for several moments.

"Artemis, if we agree to try this, I have no idea what the results would be. The effect on Butler's body could be catastrophic, not to mention his mind. An operation of this kind has never been attempted on a human."

"I understand."

"Do you, Artemis? Do you really? Are you prepared to

accept the consequences of this healing? There could be any number of unforeseeable problems. Whatever emerges from this pod is yours to care for. Will you accept this responsibility?"

"I will," said Artemis, without hesitation.

"Very well, then it's Holly's decision. Nobody can force her to use her magic, it's up to her."

Artemis lowered his eyes. He could not bring himself to look at the LEP elf.

"Well, Holly. Will you do it? Will you try?"

Holly brushed the ice from Butler's brow. He had been a good friend to the People. "I'll try," she said. "No guarantees, but I'll do what I can."

Artemis's knees almost buckled with relief, then he was in control again. Time enough for weak knees later. "Thank you, Captain. I realize this could not be an easy decision to make. Now, what can I do?"

Holly pointed to the rear doors. "You can get out. I need a sterile environment. I'll come get you when it's over. And whatever happens, whatever you hear, don't come in until I call."

Holly unclipped her helmet camera, suspending it from the cryo pod's lid to give Foaly a better view of the patient. "How's that?"

"Good," replied Foaly. "I can see the whole upper body. Cryogenics. That Fowl is a genius, for a human. Do you realize that he had less than a minute to come up with this plan? That's one smart Mud Boy."

Holly scrubbed her hands thoroughly in the medi-sink. "Not smart enough to keep himself out of trouble. I can't believe I'm doing this. A three-hour healing. This has got to be a first."

"Technically it's only a two-minute healing, if he got the brain down to below zero straightaway. But . . ."

"But what?" asked Holly, rubbing her fingers briskly with a towel.

"But the freezing interferes with the body's own biorhythms and magnetic fields, things even the People don't understand fully. There's more than skin and bone at stake here. We have no idea what a trauma like this could do to Butler."

Holly stuck her head under the camera. "Are you sure this is a good idea, Foaly?"

"I wish we had time for discussion, Holly, but every second costs our old friend a couple of brain cells. I'm going to talk you through it. The first thing we need to do is take a look at the wound."

Holly peeled off several cold packs, unzipping the foil suit. The entry wound was small and black. Hidden in the center of a pool of blood, like a flower's bud. "He never had a chance. Right under the heart. I'm going to zoom in."

Holly closed her visor, using the helmet's filters to magnify Butler's wound. "There are fibers trapped in there. Kevlar, I'd say."

76

Foaly groaned over the speakers. "That's all we need. Complications."

"What difference do fibers make? And this really is not the time for jargon. I need plain Gnommish."

"Okay. Surgery for morons it is. If you poke your fingers into that wound, the magic will reproduce Butler's cells, complete with their new strands of Kevlar. He'll be dead, but completely bulletproof."

Holly could feel the tension creeping up her back. "So, I need to do what?"

"You need to make a new wound, and let the magic spread from there."

Oh great, thought Holly. A new wound. Just slice him open. "But he's as hard as rock."

"Well then, you're going to have to melt him down a little. Use your Neutrino 2000, low setting, but not too much. If that brain wakes up before we want it to, he's finished."

Holly drew her Neutrino, adjusting the output to minimum. "Where do you suggest I melt?"

"The other pectoral. Be ready to heal—that heat is going to spread rapidly. Butler needs to be healed before oxygen gets to his brain."

Holly pointed the laser at the bodyguard's chest. "Just say the word."

"In a bit closer. Six inches approximately. A two-second burst."

Holly raised her visor, taking several deep breaths. A

Neutrino 2000 being used as a medical instrument. Who would have thought it? Holly pulled her trigger to the first click. One more click would activate the laser. "Two seconds."

"Okay. Go."

Click. An orange beam of concentrated heat spilled from the Neutrino's snout, blossoming across Butler's chest. Had the bodyguard been awake, he would have been knocked unconscious. A neat circle of ice evaporated, rising to condense on the surgery's ceiling.

"Now," said Foaly, his voice high-pitched with urgency. "Narrow the beam and focus it."

Holly manipulated the gun controls expertly with her thumb. Narrowing the beam would intensify its power, but the laser would have to be focused at a certain range to avoid slicing right through Butler's body. "I'm setting it for six inches."

"Good, but hurry, that heat is spreading."

The color had returned to Butler's chest and the ice was melting across his body. Holly pulled the trigger again, this time carving a crescent-shaped slit in Butler's flesh. A single drop of blood oozed from between the wound's edges.

"No steady flow," said Foaly. "That's good."

Holly holstered her weapon. "Now what?"

"Now get your hands in deep, and give it every drop of magic you've got. Don't just let it flow, push the magic out."

Holly grimaced. She never liked this bit. No matter how

many healings she performed, she could never get used to sticking her fingers into other people's insides. She lined her thumbs up, back to back, and slid them into the incision.

"Heal," she breathed, and the magic scurried down her fingers. Blue sparks hovered over Butler's wound, then disappeared inside like shooting stars diving behind the horizon.

"More, Holly," urged Foaly. "Another shot."

Holly pushed again, harder. The flow was thick at first, a roiling mass of blue streaks, then as her magic ebbed, the flow grew weaker. "That's it," she panted. "I have barely enough left to shield on the way home."

"Well, then," said Foaly. "Stand back until I tell you. Because all hell is about to break loose."

Holly backed up to the wall. Nothing much happened for several moments, then Butler's back arched, throwing his chest into the air. Holly heard a couple of vertebrae groaning.

"That's the heart started," noted Foaly. "The easy bit."

Butler flopped back into the pod, blood flowing from his most recent wound. The magical sparks knitted together, forming a vibrating lattice over the bodyguard's torso. Butler hopped on the gurney like a bead in a rattle, as the magic reshaped his atoms. His pores vented mist as toxins were expelled from his system.

The coating of ice dissolved instantly, causing clouds of

steam and then rain as the water particles condensed on the metal ceiling. Cold packs popped like balloons, sending crystals ricocheting around the surgery. It was like being in the center of a multicolored storm.

"You need to get in there now!" said Foaly in Holly's ear.

"What?"

"Get in there. The magic is spreading up his spinal column. Hold his head still for the healing, or any damaged cells could be replicated. And once something's been healed, we can't undo it."

Great, thought Holly. Hold Butler still. No problem. She battled her way through the debris, cold-pack crystals popping against her visor. The human's frame continued thrashing in the cryo pod, shrouded by a cloud of steam.

Holly clamped a hand on either side of Butler's head. The vibrations traveled the length of her arms and through her body.

"Hold him, Holly. Hold him!"

Holly leaned across the pod, placing the weight of her body on the bodyguard's head. In all the confusion, she couldn't tell if her efforts were having any effect whatsoever.

"Here it comes!" said Foaly in her ear. "Brace yourself!"

The magical lattice spread along Butler's neck and across his face. Blue sparks targeted the eyes, traveling along the optic nerve, into the brain itself. Butler's eyes flew open, rolling in their sockets. His mouth was reactivated too, spewing out long strings of words in various languages. None of which made any sense.

"His brain is running tests," said Foaly. "Just to check that everything's working."

Each muscle and joint was tested to its limit; rolling, swiveling, and stretching. Hair follicles grew at an accelerated rate, covering Butler's normally shaven dome with a thick growth of hair. Nails shot out of his fingers like tiger claws and a raggedy beard snaked from his chin.

Holly could only hang on. She imagined that this was how it must feel to be a rodeo cowboy straddling a particularly bad-tempered bull.

Eventually the sparks dissipated, spiraling into the air like the embers on a breeze. Butler calmed and settled, his body sinking into six inches of water and coolant. His breathing was slow and deep.

"We did it," said Holly, sliding off the pod onto her knees. "He's alive."

"Don't start celebrating just yet," said Foaly. "There's still a long way to go. He won't regain consciousness for a couple of days at least, and even then who knows what shape his mind will be in. And of course, there's the obvious problem."

Holly raised her visor. "What obvious problem?"

"See for yourself."

Captain Short was almost afraid to look at whatever lay in the pod. Grotesque images crowded her imagination.

What kind of misshapen mutant human had they created? The first thing she noticed was Butler's chest. The bullet hole itself had completely disappeared, but the skin had darkened, with a red line amid the black. It looked like a capital *I*.

"Kevlar," explained Foaly. "Some of it must have replicated. Not enough to kill him, thankfully, but enough to slow down his breathing. Butler won't be running any marathons with those fibers clinging to his ribs."

"What's the red line?"

"At a guess, I'd say dye. There must have been writing on the original bulletproof jacket."

Holly glanced around the surgery. Butler's vest lay discarded in a corner. The letters *FBI* were printed in red across the chest. There was a small hole in the center of the *I*.

"Ah, well," said the centaur. "It's a small price to pay for his life. He can pretend it's a tattoo. They're very popular among Mud Men these days."

Holly had been hoping the Kevlar-reinforced skin was the "obvious problem" Foaly had been referring to. But there was something else. The something else became immediately apparent when her gaze landed on the bodyguard's face. Or more accurately, the hair sprouting from his face.

"Oh, gods," she breathed. "Artemis is not going to like this."

• ⚏⚏⚏⚏⚏ • ⚏⚏ • ⚏⚏⚏⚏ ⚏⚏ ⚏⚏ • ⚏⚏ • ⚏⚏⚏⚏ ⚏⚏

* * *

Artemis paced the yard while his bodyguard underwent magical surgery. Now that his plan was actually in progress, doubts began to chew at the edges of his mind like slugs on a leaf. Was this the right thing to do? What if Butler wasn't himself? After all, his father had been undeniably different on the day he had finally come back to them. He would never forget that first conversation. . . .

Excerpt from Artemis Fowl's diary, disk 2 (encrypted)

The doctors in Helsinki were determined that they would pump my father full of vitamin supplements. He was just as determined that they wouldn't. And a determined Fowl usually gets his way.

"I am perfectly fine," he insisted. "Please allow me some time to reacquaint myself with my family."

The doctors withdrew, disarmed by his personality. I was surprised by this approach. Charm had never been my father's weapon of choice. He had previously achieved his aims by bulldozing over anybody stupid enough to stand in his way.

Father sat in the hospital room's only armchair, his shortened leg resting on a footstool. My mother was perched on the armrest, resplendent in white Armani faux fur.

Father caught me looking at his leg. "Don't worry, Arty," he said. "I'm being measured for a prosthesis tomorrow. Dr. Hermann Gruber is being flown in from Dortmund."

I had heard of Gruber. He worked with the German Special Olympics squad. The best.

"I'm going to ask for something sporty. Maybe with speed stripes."

A joke. That wasn't like my father.

Angeline ruffled her husband's hair.

"Stop teasing, darling. This is difficult for Arty, you know. He was only a baby when you left."

"Hardly a baby, Mother," I said. "I was eleven, after all."

My father smiled at me fondly. Perhaps now would be an appropriate time for us to talk, before his good mood wore off to be replaced by the usual gruffness.

"Father. Things have changed, since your disappearance. I have changed."

Father nodded solemnly.

"Yes, you are right. We need to talk about the business."

Ah, yes. Back to business. This was the father I remembered.

"I think you will find that the family bank accounts are healthy, and I trust you will approve of the stock portfolio. It has yielded an eighteen-percent return in the past financial year. Eighteen percent is quite exemplary in the current market. I haven't failed you."

"I have failed you, son," said Artemis senior, "if you think bank accounts and stocks are all that's important. You must have learned that from me."

He pulled me close to him.

"I haven't been the perfect father, Arty, far from it. Too busy

with the family business. I was always taught that it was my duty to carry on the Fowl empire. A criminal empire, as we both know. If any good has come out of my abduction, it's that I have reassessed my priorities. I want a new life for us all."

I could not believe what I was hearing. One of my most persistent memories was of Father repeatedly quoting the family motto, Aurum Est Potestas: "Gold Is Power." And now, here he was, turning his back on Fowl principles. What had the magic done to him?

"Gold isn't all-important, Arty," he continued. "Neither is power. We have everything we need right here. The three of us."

I was utterly surprised. But not unpleasantly so.

"But, Father. You have always said . . . This isn't you. You're a new man."

Mother joined the conversation. "No, Arty. Not a new man. An old one. The one I fell in love with and married, before the Fowl empire took over. And now I have him back, we're a family again."

I looked at my parents, how happy they were together. A family? Was it possible that the Fowls could be a normal family?

Ice Age Cryogenics

Artemis was yanked back to the present by a commotion from inside the Ice Age mobile unit. The mobile unit began to rock on its axles, blue light crackling from beneath the door.

Artemis did not panic. He had seen healings before. Last year, when Holly had reattached her index finger, the magical fallout had shattered half a ton of ice. And that was for one little finger. Imagine the damage Butler's system could do, repairing a critical injury.

The pandemonium continued for several minutes, popping two of the van's tires and completely wrecking the suspension. Luckily, the institute was locked up for the night, or Dr. Lane would certainly be adding automobile repairs to her bill.

Eventually the magical storm subsided, and the vehicle settled like a roller-coaster car after the ride. Holly opened the rear door, leaning heavily against the frame. She was exhausted, drained. A sickly pallor glowed through her coffee-colored complexion.

"Well?" demanded Artemis. "Is he alive?"

Holly didn't answer. A strenuous healing often resulted in nausea and fatigue. Captain Short took several deep breaths, resting on the rear bumper.

"Is he alive?" repeated the youth.

Holly nodded. "Alive. Yes, he's alive. But . . ."

"But what, Holly. Tell me!"

Holly tugged off her helmet. It slipped from her fingers, rolling across the yard. "I'm sorry, Artemis. I did the best I could."

It was possibly the worst thing she could have said.

Artemis climbed into the van. The floor was slick with water and colored crystals. Smoke leaked from the fractured grille of the air-conditioning system, and the overhead neon strip flickered like lightning in a bottle.

The cryo pod lay off-kilter in one corner, its gyroscopes leaking fluid. One of Butler's arms flopped over the unit's edge, throwing a monster shadow on the wall.

The cryo pod's instruments' panel was still operating. Artemis was relieved to see the heartbeat icon blipping gently in the display. Butler was alive. Holly had done it again. But something had been worrying the fairy captain. There was a problem.

As soon as Artemis looked inside the pod, it became immediately apparent what that problem was. The newly grown hair was heavily streaked with gray. Butler had gone into the cryo chamber forty years of age. The man before him now was at least fifty. Possibly older. In the space of three hours, Butler had grown old.

Holly appeared at Artemis's shoulder.

"He's alive, at least," said the fairy.

Artemis nodded. "When will he wake up?"

"A couple of days. Maybe."

"How did this happen?" asked the boy, brushing a lock of hair from Butler's brow.

Holly shrugged. "I'm not exactly sure. That's Foaly's area."

Artemis took the spare headset from his pocket, hooking the speaker wire over his ear.

"Any theories, Foaly?"

"I can't be sure," the centaur replied. "But I'm guessing that Holly's magic wasn't enough. Some of Butler's own

life force was needed for the healing. About fifteen years'
worth, by the looks of it."

"Can anything be done?"

"Afraid not. A healing can't be undone. If it's any consola-
tion, he'll probably live longer than he would have naturally.
But there's no reclaiming his youth, and what's more, we
can't be sure about the state of his mind. The healing could
have wiped his brain cleaner than a magnetized disk."

Artemis sighed deeply. "What have I done to you, old
friend?"

"No time for that," said Holly briskly. "You both should
get out of here. I'm sure all the commotion will have
attracted attention. Do you have transport?"

"No. We flew over on a public flight. Then took a taxi
from Heathrow."

Holly shrugged. "I'd like to help, Artemis. But I've already
given up enough time here. I'm on a mission. An extremely
important mission, and I have to get back to it."

Artemis stepped away from the cryo unit.

"Holly, about your mission . . ."

Captain Short turned slowly.

"Artemis . . ."

"You were probed, weren't you? Something got past
Foaly's defenses?"

Holly pulled a large sheet of camouflage foil from her
surveillance backpack. "We need to go somewhere to talk.
Somewhere private."

* * *

The following forty-five minutes were something of a blur to Artemis. Holly wrapped both humans in camouflage foil from her surveillance pack and clipped them onto a Moonbelt. The belt effectively reduced their weight to one sixth of Earth's norm.

Even then it was a struggle for her mechanical wings to hoist the three of them into the night sky. Holly had to open the throttle wide just to bring them five hundred feet above sea level.

"I'm going to shield now," she said into her mike. "Try not to thrash about too much. I don't want to have to cut one of you loose."

Then she was gone, and in her place hovered a slightly shimmering Holly-shaped patch of stars. The vibration rattled through the belt links, shaking Artemis's teeth in his head.

Artemis felt like a bug in a cocoon, trussed up in foil with only his face exposed to the night air. Initially the experience was almost enjoyable; riding high above the city watching the cars flicker along the motorways. Then Holly picked up a westerly wind and threw them into the air currents over the English Channel.

Suddenly, Artemis's universe was a maelstrom of cutting wind, buffeted passengers, and startled birds. Beside him, Butler hung limply in his makeshift foil truss. The foil absorbed the local colors, reflecting the dominant hues.

It was by no means a perfect re-creation of the surroundings, but certainly good enough for a night flight across the channel to Ireland.

"Is this foil invisible to radar?" said Artemis into the headset. "I don't want to be mistaken for a UFO by some eager Harrier jump-jet pilot."

Holly considered it. "You're right. Maybe I should take us down a bit, just in case."

Two seconds later, Artemis deeply regretted breaking radio silence. Holly tilted her wing rig into a steep dive, sending the three of them hurtling toward the midnight waves below. She pulled up at the last moment, when Artemis could have sworn the skin was about to peel from his face.

"Low enough for you?" asked Holly, with the barest hint of humor in her voice.

They skimmed the wave tops, spray sparking against the camouflage foil. The ocean was rough that night, and Holly followed the water patterns, dipping and climbing to match the swell's curve. A school of humpback whales sensed Holly's presence and broke through the storm foam, leaping fully thirty meters across a trough before disappearing beneath the black water. There were no dolphins. The small mammals were taking shelter from the elements in the inlets and coves along the Irish coast.

Holly skirted the hull of a passenger ferry, flying close enough to feel the engine's pulse. On deck, scores of passengers vomited over the railings, narrowly missing the invisible travelers below.

"Charming," muttered Artemis.

"Don't worry," said Holly's voice, out of thin air. "Almost there."

They passed Rosslare's ferry terminal, following the coastline northward, over the Wicklow Mountains. Even in his disoriented state, Artemis could not help but marvel at their speed. Those wings were a fantastic invention. Imagine the money that could be made for a patent like that. Artemis stopped himself. Selling fairy technology was what had got Butler hurt in the first place.

They slowed sufficiently for Artemis to make out individual landmarks. Dublin squatted to the east, an aura of yellow light buzzing over its highway system. Holly skirted the city, heading for the less populated north of the county. In the center of a large dark patch sat a single building, painted white by external spotlights: Artemis's ancestral home. Fowl Manor.

Fowl Manor, Ireland

"Now, explain yourself," said Holly, once they had floated Butler safely to bed.

She sat on the great stairway's bottom step. Generations of Fowls glared down at her from oil portraits. The LEP captain activated her helmet mike. "Foaly, record this, would you? I have a feeling we're going to want to hear it again."

"This entire incident began at a business meeting this afternoon," began Artemis.

"Go on."

"I was meeting Jon Spiro, an American industrialist."

Holly heard keys being tapped in her ear. Undoubtedly, Foaly was running a background check on this Spiro character.

"Jon Spiro," said the centaur, almost immediately. "A shady character, even by human standards. Mud Man security agencies have been trying to put this guy away for thirty years. His companies are ecodisasters. And that's only the tip of the pyramid: industrial espionage, pollution, abduction, blackmail, Mob connections. You name it, he's gotten away with it."

"That's the guy," said Artemis. "I set up a rendezvous with Mr. Spiro."

"What were you selling?" interrupted Foaly. "A man like Spiro doesn't cross the Atlantic for tea and muffins."

Artemis frowned. "I wasn't actually selling him anything. But I did offer to suppress some revolutionary technology, for a price, of course."

Foaly's voice was cold in his ear. "What revolutionary technology?"

Artemis hesitated for a beat. "Do you remember those helmets Butler took from the retrieval squad?"

Holly groaned. "Oh, no."

"I deactivated the helmets' auto-destruct mechanisms and constructed a cube from the sensors and chips. The C Cube, a mini computer. It was a simple matter to install a fiber-optic blocker so you couldn't take control of the Cube if you detected it."

"You gave fairy technology to a man like Jon Spiro?"

"I quite obviously didn't give it to him," snapped Artemis. "He took it."

Holly pointed a finger at the youth. "Don't bother playing the victim, Artemis. It doesn't suit you. What did you think? That Jon Spiro was going to walk away from technology that could make him the richest man on the face of the planet?"

"So it was your computer that pinged us?" said Foaly.

"Yes," admitted Artemis. "Unintentionally. Spiro asked for a surveillance scan, and the Cube's fairy circuits picked up LEP satellite beams."

"Can't we block any future probes?" asked the LEP captain.

"Haven's deflectors will be useless against our own technology. Sooner or later, Spiro will find out about the People. And if that happens, I can't see a man like him just allowing us to live in harmony."

Holly glared pointedly at Artemis. "Remind you of anyone?"

"I am nothing like Jon Spiro," objected the boy. "He's a cold-blooded killer!"

"Give yourself a few years," said Holly. "You'll get there."

Foaly sighed. Put Artemis Fowl and Holly Short together in a room, and sooner or later there was bound to be a fight.

"Okay, Holly," said the centaur. "Let's try to act like professionals. Step one is to call off the lockdown. Our next priority is to retrieve the Cube before Spiro can unlock its secrets."

"We do have some time," said Artemis. "The Cube is encrypted."

"How encrypted?"

"I built an eternity code into its hard drive."

"An eternity code," said Foaly. "I'm impressed."

"It wasn't that difficult. I invented an entirely new base language, so Spiro will have no frame of reference."

Holly was feeling a bit left out. "And how long will it take to crack this eternity code?"

Artemis couldn't resist raising an eyebrow.

"Eternity," he said, "in theory. But with Spiro's resources, quite a bit less."

Holly ignored the tone. "Okay, then, we're safe. No need to go hunting Spiro if all he has is a box of useless circuits."

"Far from useless," countered Artemis. "The chip design alone will lead his research-and-development team in interesting directions. But you are right about one thing, Holly, there is no need to go hunting Spiro. Once he realizes that I am still alive, he will come looking for me. After all, I am the only one who can unlock the full potential of the C Cube."

Holly dropped her head into her hands. "So, any moment now a team of hit men could come blasting in here, looking for the key to your eternity code. It's at times like these, we could do with someone like Butler."

Artemis plucked the wall phone from its cradle. "There's more than one Butler in the family," he said.

⟂🜚⚏🝪 • 🝩 ⚘🝮⟫ • 🜚⚏🝪 • ⚘⥾🝮🜸🝪 ⟅

CHAPTER 4
RUNNING IN THE FAMILY

Sfax, Tunisia, North Africa

For her eighteenth birthday, Juliet Butler asked for, and received, a ribbed judo crash vest, two weighted throwing knives, and a World Wrestling Grudge Match video. Items that did not generally feature on the average teenage girl's wish list. Then again, Juliet Butler was not the average teenage girl.

Juliet was extraordinary in many ways. For one thing she could hit a moving target with any weapon you cared to name, and for another she could throw most people a lot further than she trusted them.

Of course, she didn't learn all of this by watching wrestling videos. Juliet's training began at age four. After kindergarten each day, Domovoi Butler would escort his little sister to the Fowl Estate dojo, where he instructed her in

•)(꘏ꘒꘔ • ꘉ꘎ꘈꘓꘔꘑ(꘏)(• ꗞ)(꘏ꗞ ꖰꙏꘔꘒ •

the various forms of martial arts. By the time she was eight, Juliet was a third-dan black belt in seven disciplines. By ten years of age, she was beyond belts.

Traditionally all Butler males enrolled in Madam Ko's Personal Protection Academy on their tenth birthday, spending six months of every year learning the bodyguard's craft, and the other six guarding a low-risk Principal. The female Butlers generally went into service for various wealthy families around the world. Juliet decided she would combine both roles, spending half the year with Angeline Fowl, and the other half honing her martial arts skills in Madam Ko's camp. She was the first Butler female to have enrolled in the academy, and only the fifth female ever to make it past the physical exam. The camp was never located in the same country for more than five years. Butler had done his training in Switzerland and Israel, but his younger sister received her instruction in the Utsukushigahara Highlands in Japan.

Madam Ko's dormitory was a far cry from the luxurious accommodations in Fowl Manor. In Japan, Juliet slept on a straw mat, owned nothing apart from two rough cotton robes, and consumed only rice, fish, and protein shakes.

The day began at five-thirty when Juliet and the other acolytes ran four miles to the nearest stream, and caught fish with their bare hands. Having cooked and presented the fish to their sensei, the acolytes strapped empty twenty-gallon barrels to their backs and climbed to the snowline.

When their barrels were filled with snow, the acolytes would roll them back to base camp, and then pound the snow with bare feet until it melted, and could be used by the sensei to bathe. Then the day's training could begin.

Lessons included Cos Ta'pa, a martial art developed by Madam Ko herself, specially tailored for bodyguards, whose primary aim was not self-defense, but defense of the Principal. Acolytes also studied advanced weaponry, information technology, vehicular maintenance, and hostage negotiation techniques.

By her eighteenth birthday, Juliet could break down and reassemble ninety percent of the world's production weapons blindfolded, operate any vehicle, do her makeup in under four minutes, and, in spite of her stunning Asian and European gene mix, blend into any crowd like a native. Her big brother was very proud.

The final step in her training was a field simulation in a foreign environment. If she passed this test, Madam Ko would have Juliet's shoulder marked with a blue diamond tattoo. The tattoo, identical to the one on Butler's shoulder, symbolized not only the graduate's toughness but the multifaceted nature of his training. In personal protection circles, a bodyguard bearing the blue diamond needed no further reference.

Madam Ko had chosen the city of Sfax in Tunisia for Juliet's final assessment. Her mission was to guide the Principal through the city's tumultuous market, or medina.

Generally, a bodyguard would advise his Principal against venturing into such a densely populated area. But Madam Ko pointed out that Principals rarely listened to advice, and it was best to be prepared for every eventuality. And as if Juliet wasn't under enough pressure, Madam Ko herself had decided to act as surrogate Principal.

It was exceptionally hot in North Africa. Juliet squinted through her wraparound sunglasses, concentrating on following the diminutive figure bobbing through the crowd before her.

"Hurry," snapped Madam Ko. "You will lose me."

"In your dreams, Madam," replied Juliet, unperturbed.

Madam Ko was simply trying to distract her with conversation. And there were already enough distractions in the local environment. Gold hung in shimmering ropes from a dozen stalls, Tunisian rugs flapped from wooden frames, the perfect cover for an assassin. Locals pressed uncomfortably close, eager for a look at this attractive female, and the terrain was treacherous, one false step could lead to a twisted ankle, and failure.

Juliet processed all this information automatically, factoring it into every move. She placed a firm hand on the chest of a teenager grinning at her, skipped over an oily puddle reflecting rainbow patterns, and followed Madam Ko down yet another alley in the medina's endless maze. Suddenly, there was a man in her face. One of the market traders.

•)(⊃ ≷ • ⽊⽊ ⻤ ⼁ ≷ (⼁))(• ⽊ ⻤ •)(⽊⽊ • ≷ ⻤ ⽊

"I have good carpets," he said, in broken French. "You come with me. I show you!"

Madam Ko kept going. Juliet attempted to follow her, but the man blocked her path.

"No, thank you. I am so not interested. I live outdoors."

"Very funny, mademoiselle. You make good joke. Now come and see Ahmed's carpets."

The crowd began to take notice. Swirling to face her, like the tendrils of a giant organism. Madam Ko was drawing further away. She was losing the Principal.

"I said no. Now back off, Mr. Carpet Man, don't make me break a nail."

The Tunisian man was unaccustomed to taking orders from a female, and now his friends were watching.

"I give good bargain," he persisted, pointing at his stall. "Best rugs in Sfax."

Juliet dodged to one side, but the crowd moved to cut her off.

It was at this point Ahmed lost all sympathy Juliet may have had for him. Up to now, he had simply been an innocent local in the wrong place at the wrong time. But now . . .

"Let's go," said the Tunisian, wrapping an arm around the blond girl's waist. Not an idea that would make his top ten of good ideas.

"Oh, bad move, carpet man!"

Faster than the eye could blink, Ahmed was wrapped in

the folds of a nearby carpet, and Juliet was gone. Nobody had a clue what had happened until they replayed the incident on the screen of Kamal the chicken man's camcorder. In slow motion the traders saw the girl hoist Ahmed by the throat and belt, and lob him bodily into a carpet stall. It was a move that one of the gold merchants recognized as a *slingshot*. A maneuver made popular by the American wrestler Papa Hog. The traders laughed so much that several of them became dehydrated. It was the funniest thing to happen all year. The clip even won a prize on Tunisia's version of the *World's Funniest Home Videos*. Three weeks later, Ahmed moved to Egypt.

Back to Juliet. The bodyguard-in-training ran like a sprinter out of the blocks, dodging around stunned merchants and hanging a hard right down the alley. Madam Ko couldn't have gone far. She could still complete her assignment.

Juliet was furious with herself. This was exactly the kind of stunt her brother had warned her about.

Watch out for Madam Ko, Butler had advised. *You never know what she'll cook up for a field assignment. I heard that she once stampeded a herd of elephants in Calcutta, just to distract an acolyte.*

The trouble was that you couldn't be sure. That carpet merchant may have been in Madam Ko's employ, or he may have been an innocent civilian who happened to stick his nose in where it didn't belong.

⚷⚸⚹⚺⚻ · ◐⚸♋⊕ · ⟩⚸⚛⚜⚝⚞⚟⚺⚻ "

The alley narrowed so the human traffic ran single file. Makeshift clotheslines zigzagged at head height, *gutras* and *abayas* hung limp and steaming in the heat. Juliet ducked below the laundry, dodging around dawdling shoppers. Startled turkeys hopped as far out of the way as their string leads would allow.

And suddenly she was in a clearing. A dim square surrounded by three-story houses. Men lounged in the upper balconies puffing on fruit-flavored water pipes. Underfoot was a priceless chipped mosaic, depicting a Roman bath scene.

In the center of the square, lying with her knees hugged to her chest, was Madam Ko. She was being assaulted by three men. These were no local traders. All three wore special-forces black, and attacked with the assuredness and accuracy of trained professionals. This was no test. These men were actually trying to kill her sensei.

Juliet was unarmed, this was one of the rules. To be caught smuggling arms into the African country would automatically mean life imprisonment. Luckily, it seemed as though her adversaries were also without weapons, though hands and feet would certainly be sufficient for the job they had in mind.

Improvisation was the key to survival here. There was no point in attempting a straight assault. If these three had subdued Madam Ko, then they would be more than a match for her in regular combat. Time to try something a bit unorthodox.

Juliet leapt on the run, snagging a clothesline on her way past. The ring resisted for a second, then popped out of the dry plaster. The cable played out behind her, sagging with its load of rugs and head scarves. Juliet veered left as far as the line's other anchor would allow, and then swung around toward the men. "Hey, boys!" she yelled, not from bravado, but because her maneuver would work better head-on.

The men looked up just in time to get a faceful of sopping camel-hair. The heavy rugs and garments wrapped themselves around their flailing limbs, and the nylon cable caught them below the chins. In less than a second the three were down.

Juliet made certain they stayed down with pinches to the nerve clusters at the base of the neck.

"Madam Ko," she cried, searching the laundry for her sensei.

The old woman lay shuddering in an olive dress, a plain head scarf covering her face.

Juliet helped the woman to her feet. "Did you see that move, Madam? I totally decked those morons. I bet they never saw anything like that before. Improvisation. Butler always says it's the key. You know, I think my eye shadow distracted them. Glitter green. Never fails . . ."

Juliet stopped talking because there was a knife at her throat. The knife was wielded by Madam Ko herself, who was in fact not Madam Ko, but some other tiny Asian lady, in an olive dress. A decoy.

"You are dead," said the lady.

"Yes," agreed Madam Ko, stepping from the shadows. "And if you are dead, then the Principal is dead. And you have failed."

Juliet bowed low, joining her hands. "That was a sly trick, Madam," she said, trying to sound respectful.

Her sensei laughed. "Of course. That is the way of life. What did you expect?"

"But those assassins, I completely kicked their b—I defeated them comprehensively."

Madam Ko dismissed the claim with a wave. "Luck. Fortunately for you, these were not assassins, but three graduates of the academy. What was that nonsense with the wire?"

"It's a wrestling trick," said Juliet. "It's called the clothesline."

"Unreliable," said the Japanese lady. "You succeeded because fortune was with you. Fortune is not enough in our business."

"It wasn't my fault," protested Juliet. "There was this guy in the market. Totally in my face. I had to put him to sleep for a while."

Madam Ko tapped Juliet between the eyes. "Quiet, girl. Think for once. What should you have done?"

Juliet bowed an inch lower. "I should have incapacitated the merchant immediately."

"Exactly. His life means nothing. Insignificant, compared to the Principal's safety."

ᘔᙅᚐ᚛ᚊ • ᚈᚋ ᚑ ᙏᚐ᚜ᚔᘔ • ᚗᚌ ᚘᚕᚙ ᚈᚕ • ᙏᚐ ᚈ

"I can't just kill innocent people," protested Juliet.

Madam Ko sighed. "I know, child. And that is why you are not ready. You have all the skill, but you lack focus and resolve. Perhaps next year."

Juliet's heart plummeted. Her brother had earned the blue diamond at eighteen years of age. The youngest graduate in the academy's history. She had been hoping to equal that feat. Now she would have to try again in twelve months. It was pointless to object any further. Madam Ko never reversed a decision.

A young woman in acolyte's robes emerged from the alley, holding a small briefcase.

"Madam," she said, bowing. "There is a call for you on the satellite phone."

Madam Ko took the offered handset, listening intently for several moments. "A message from Artemis Fowl," she said eventually.

Juliet itched to straighten from her bow, but it would be an unforgivable breach of protocol. "Yes, Madam?"

"The message is: Domovoi needs you."

Juliet frowned. "You mean, Butler needs me."

"No," said Madam Ko without a trace of emotion. "I mean Domovoi needs you. I am just repeating what was told to me."

And suddenly Juliet could feel the sun pounding on her neck, and she could hear the mosquitoes whining in her ear like dentists' drills, and all she wanted to do was straighten up and run all the way to the airport. Butler would never have revealed his name to Artemis. Not unless . . . No, she couldn't believe it. She couldn't even allow herself to think it.

Madam Ko tapped her chin thoughtfully. "You are not ready. I should not let you leave. You are too emotionally involved to be an effective bodyguard."

"Please, Madam," said Juliet.

Her sensei considered it for two long minutes. "Very well," she said. "Go."

Juliet was gone before the word finished echoing around the square, and heaven help any carpet merchant who blocked her path.

CHAPTER 5

THE METAL MAN AND THE MONKEY

The Spiro Needle, Chicago

Jon Spiro took the Concorde from Heathrow to O'Hare International Airport in Chicago. A stretch limousine ferried him downtown to the Spiro Needle, a sliver of steel and glass rising eighty-six stories above the Chicago skyline. Spiro Industries was located on floors fifty through eighty-five. The eighty-sixth floor was Spiro's personal residence, accessible either by private elevator or helipad.

Jon Spiro hadn't slept for the entire journey, too excited by the little cube sitting in his briefcase. The head of his technical staff was equally excited when Spiro informed him what this harmless-looking box was capable of, and immediately scurried off to unravel the C Cube's secrets. Six hours later he scurried back to the conference room for a midnight meeting.

ᗺ•ᜤᗡ૨•ᚐᗉᗷᚼᚽᛉ•ᚼᚼ•ᚐᜤᚭᗺᛁᚿ

"It's useless," said the scientist, whose name was Dr. Pearson.

Spiro swirled an olive in his martini glass. "I don't think so, Pearson," he said. "In fact, I know that little gizmo is anything but useless. I think that maybe you're the useless one in this equation."

Spiro was in a terrible mood. Arno Blunt had just called to inform him of Fowl's survival. When Spiro was in a dark mood, people had been known to disappear off the face of the earth, if they were lucky.

Pearson could feel the stare of the conference room's third occupant bouncing off his head. This was not a woman you wanted angry with you. Pearson knew that if Jon Spiro decided to have him thrown out the window, this particular individual would have no problem signing an affidavit swearing that he had jumped.

Pearson chose his words carefully. "This device . . ."

"The C Cube. That's what it's called. I told you that, so use the name."

"The C Cube undoubtedly has enormous potential. But it's encrypted."

Spiro threw the olive at his head scientist. It was a humiliating experience for a Nobel Prize winner.

"So break the encryption. What do I pay you guys for?"

Pearson could feel his heart speeding up. "It's not that simple. This code. It's unbreakable."

"Let me get this straight," said Spiro, leaning back in his

oxblood leather chair. "I'm putting two hundred million a year into your department, and you can't break one lousy code, set up by a kid?"

Pearson was trying not to think about the sound his body would make hitting the pavement. His next sentence would save him or damn him.

"The Cube is voice activated, and coded to Artemis Fowl's voice patterns. Nobody can break the code. It's not possible."

Spiro did not respond, it was a signal to continue.

"I've heard of something like this. We scientists theorize about it. An eternity code, it's called. The code has millions of possible permutations, and not only that, but it's based on an unknown language. It seems as though this boy has created a language that is spoken only by him. We don't even know how it corresponds to English. A code like this is not even supposed to exist. If Fowl is dead, then I'm sorry to say, Mr. Spiro, but the C Cube died with him."

Jon Spiro stuck a cigar into the corner of his mouth. He did not light it. His doctors had forbidden it. Politely.

"And if Fowl were alive?"

Pearson knew a lifeline when it was being thrown to him.

"If Fowl were alive, he would be a lot easier to break than an eternity code."

"Okay, Doc," said Spiro. "You're dismissed. You don't want to hear what's coming next."

𝕃 2 𝔈𝕝 𝟓 • 𝕆)(2)(𝟓)(2 𝕤 • 𝟪𝟪 𝕌 • 𝕤 𝕐 • 𝔸𝔸 •

Pearson gathered his notes and hurried for the door. He tried not to look at the face of the woman at the table. If he didn't hear what came next, he could kid himself that his conscience was clear. And if he hadn't actually seen the woman at the conference table, then he couldn't pick her out of a lineup.

"It looks like we have a problem," said Spiro to the woman in the dark suit.

The woman nodded. Everything she wore was black. Black power suit, black blouse, black stilettos. Even the Rado watch on her wrist was jet black.

"Yes. But it's my kind of problem."

Carla Frazetti was goddaughter to Spatz Antonelli, who ran the downtown branch of the Antonelli crime family. Carla operated as liaison between Jon Spiro and Antonelli, possibly the two most powerful men in Chicago. Spiro had learned early in his career that businesses allied to the Mob tended to flourish.

Carla checked her manicured nails. "It seems to me that you only have one option, you nab the Fowl kid, and squeeze him for this code."

Spiro sucked on his unlit cigar, thinking about it. "It's not that straightforward. The kid runs a tight operation. Fowl Manor is like a fortress."

Carla smiled. "This is a thirteen-year-old kid we're talking about, right?"

)(⟨⟩⊞⊗ ⟩⟩• ⟨⊠ ♡ ⟨⟩ ⟨• ⊞⊗ ⟩ • (⟨ ⊞⊗ ♧ ⟨⟩ ⟐⟨⟩ ⟨•

"He'll be fourteen in six months," said Spiro defensively. "Anyway, there are complications."

"Such as?"

"Arno is injured. Somehow Fowl blew his teeth out."

"Ouch," said Carla, wincing.

"He can't even stand in a breeze, never mind head up an operation."

"That's a shame."

"In fact, the kid incapacitated all my best people. They're on a dental plan too. It's going to cost me a fortune. No, I need some outside help on this one."

"You want to contract the job to us?"

"Exactly. But it's got to be the right people. Ireland is an Old World kind of place. Wise guys are going to stick out a mile. I need guys who blend in and can persuade a kid to accompany them back here. Easy money."

Carla winked. "I read you, Mr. Spiro."

"So, you got guys like that? Guys who can take care of business without drawing attention to themselves?"

"The way I see it, you need a metal man and a monkey."

Spiro nodded, familiar with Mob slang. A metal man carried the gun, and a monkey got into hard-to-reach places.

"We have two such men on our books. I can guarantee they won't attract the wrong kind of attention in Ireland. But it won't be cheap."

"Are they good?" asked Spiro.

Carla smiled. One of her incisors was inset with a tiny ruby.

"Oh, they're good," she replied. "These guys are the best."

The Inkblot tattoo parlor, downtown Chicago

Loafers McGuire was having a tattoo done. A skull's head in the shape of the ace of spades. It was his own design, and he was very proud of it. So proud in fact, that he'd wanted the tattoo on his neck. Inky Burton, the tattooist, managed to change Loafers' mind, arguing that neck tattoos were better than a name tag when the cops wanted to ID a suspect. Loafers relented. *Okay,* he'd said. *Put it on my forearm.*

Loafers had a tattoo done after every job. There wasn't much skin left on his body that still retained its original color. That was how good Loafers McGuire was at his job.

Loafers' real name was Aloysius, and he hailed from the Irish town of Kilkenny. He'd come up with the nickname *Loafers* himself, because he thought it sounded more Moblike than Aloysius. All his life, Loafers had wanted to be a mobster, just like the guys in the movies. When his efforts to start a Celtic Mafia had failed, Loafers came to Chicago.

The Chicago Mob welcomed him with open arms. Actually, one of their enforcers grabbed him in a bear hug. Loafers sent that man and six of his buddies to the Mother of Mercy Hospital. Not bad for a guy five feet tall. Eight hours after stepping off the plane, Loafers was on the payroll.

And here he was, two years and several jobs later, already the Antonellis' top metal man. His specialties were robbery and debt collection. Not the usual line of work for five-footers. But then, Loafers was not the usual five-footer.

Loafers leaned back in the tattooist's adjustable chair.

"You like the shoes, Inky?"

Inky blinked sweat from his eyes. You had to be careful with Loafers. Even the most innocent question could be a trap. One wrong answer and you could find yourself making your excuses to Saint Peter.

"Yeah. I like 'em. What are they called?"

"Loafers!" snapped the tiny gangster. "Loafers, idiot. They're my trademark."

"Oh yeah, loafers. I forgot. Cool, havin' a trademark."

Loafers checked the progress on his arm. "You ready with that needle yet?"

"Just ready," replied Inky. "I'm finished painting on the guidelines. I just gotta put in a fresh needle."

"It's not gonna hurt, is it?"

Of course it is, moron, thought Inky, I'm sticking a needle in your arm. But out loud he said, "Not too much. I gave your arm a swab of anesthetic."

"It better not hurt," warned Loafers. "Or you'll be hurting shortly afterward."

Nobody threatened Inky except Loafers McGuire. Inky did all the Mob's tattoo work. He was the best in the state.

• ⊃⋔⏁)(⋇⋇⧠⋔⋈⊖⏁ •)(⋛⋗⋗ • ⊗⏁

Carla Frazetti pushed through the door. Her black-suited elegance seemed out of place in the dingy establishment.

"Hello, boys," she said.

"Hello, Miss Carla," said Inky, blushing deeply. You didn't get too many ladies in the Inkblot.

Loafers jumped to his feet. Even he respected the boss's goddaughter.

"Miss Frazetti. You could have beeped me. No need for you to come down to this dump."

"No time for that. This is urgent. You leave straightaway."

"I'm leaving. Where am I going?"

"Ireland. Your Uncle Pat is sick."

Loafers frowned. "Uncle Pat? I don't have an Uncle Pat."

Carla tapped the toe of one stiletto. "He's sick, Loafers. Real sick, if you catch my drift."

Loafers finally caught on. "Oh, I get it. So I gotta pay him a visit."

"That's it. That's exactly how sick he is."

Loafers used a rag to clean the ink off his arm.

"Okay, I'm ready. Are we going straight to the airport?"

Carla winked at the tiny gangster. "Soon, Loafers. But first we need to pick up your brother."

"I don't have a brother," protested Loafers.

"Of course you do. The one with the keys to Uncle Pat's house. He's a regular little monkey."

"Oh," said Loafers. "That brother."

* * *

Loafers and Carla took the limo out to the East Side. Loafers was still awed by the sheer size of American buildings. In Kilkenny there was nothing over five stories, and Loafers himself had lived all his life in a suburban bungalow. Not that he would ever admit that to his Mob friends. For their benefit he had reinvented himself as an orphan who had spent his youth in and out of various foster homes.

"Who's the monkey?" he asked.

Carla Frazetti was fixing her jet black hair in a compact mirror. It was short and slicked back.

"A new guy. Mo Digence. He's Irish, like you. It makes things very convenient. No visas, no papers, no elaborate cover story. Just two short guys home for the holidays."

Loafers bristled. "What do you mean, two short guys?"

Carla snapped the compact shut. "Who are you talking to, McGuire? Because you couldn't be talking to me. Not in that tone."

Loafers paled, his life flashing before him.

"I'm sorry, Miss Frazetti. It's just the short thing. I've been listening to it my whole life."

"What do you want people to call you? Lofty? You're short, Loafers. Get over it. That's what gives you your edge. My godfather always says; there's nothing more dangerous than a short guy with something to prove. That's why you've got a job."

"I suppose."

Carla patted him on the shoulder. "Cheer up, Loafers. Compared to this guy, you're a regular giant."

Loafers perked up considerably. "Really? Just how short is Mo Digence?"

"He's short," said Carla. "I don't know the exact inches, but any shorter and I'd be changing his diaper and stuffing him in a stroller."

Loafers grinned. He was going to enjoy this job.

Mo Digence had seen better days. Less than four months ago he had been living it up in a Los Angeles penthouse with more than a million dollars in the bank. Now his funds had been frozen by the Criminal Assets Bureau, and he was working for the Chicago Mob on a commission basis. And Spatz Antonelli was not known for the generosity of his commissions. Of course, Mo could always leave Chicago and go back to L.A., but there was a police task force there with his name on it, just waiting for him to return to the scene of the crime. In fact there was no safe haven for Mo aboveground or below it, because Mo Digence was actually Mulch Diggums, kleptomaniac dwarf and fugitive from the LEP.

Mulch was a tunnel dwarf who had decided that a life in the mines was not for him, and put his mining talents to another use. Namely, relieving Mud Men of their valuables and selling them on the fairy black market. Of course, entering another's dwelling without permission meant forfeiting your magic, but Mulch didn't care. Dwarfs didn't have much power anyway, and casting spells had always made him nauseous.

Dwarfs have several physical features that make them ideal burglars. They can dislocate their jaws, ingesting several kilos of dirt a second. This dirt is stripped of any beneficial minerals, then ejected at the other end. They have also developed the ability to drink through their pores, an attribute that can be very handy during cave-ins. It also transforms the pores into living suction cups, a convenient tool in any burglar's arsenal. Finally, dwarf hair is actually a network of living antennae, similar to feline whiskers, that can do everything from trap beetles to bounce sonar waves off a tunnel wall.

Mulch had been a rising star in the fairy underworld, until Commander Julius Root got hold of his file. Since then, he had spent more than three hundred years in and out of prison. He was currently on the run for stealing several gold bars from the Holly Short ransom fund. There was no safe haven belowground anymore, even among his own kind. So, Mulch was forced to pass himself off as human, and take whatever work he could get from the Chicago Mob.

There were hazards associated with impersonating a human. Of course, his size drew attention from everyone who happened to glance downward. But Mulch quickly discovered that Mud Men could find a reason to distrust almost anyone. Height, weight, skin color, religion. It was almost safer to be different in some way. The sun was a bigger problem. Dwarfs are extremely photosensitive, with a burn time of three minutes. Luckily, Mulch's job generally involved night work, but when he was forced to venture abroad in daylight hours, the dwarf made certain that every inch of exposed skin was covered with long-lasting sun block.

Mulch had rented a basement apartment in an early-twentieth-century brownstone. It was a bit of a fixer-upper, but this suited the dwarf just fine. He had stripped out the floorboards in the bedroom, dumping two tons of top-soil and fertilizer onto the rotten foundations. There was already mold and damp climbing the walls, so no need to remodel anything there. In a matter of hours, insect life was thriving in the room. Mulch would lie back in his pit and snag cockroaches with his beard hair. Home sweet home. Not only was the apartment beginning to resemble a tunnel cave, but if the LEP came a callin', he could be fifty yards belowground in the blink of an eye.

In the coming days, Mulch would come to regret not taking that route as soon as he heard the knock at the door.

There was a knock at the door. Mulch crawled out of his tunnel bed and checked the video buzzer. Carla Frazetti was checking her hair in the brass knocker.

The boss's goddaughter? In person? This must be a big job. Perhaps the commission would be enough to set him up in another state. He'd been in Chicago for nearly three months now, and it was only a matter of time before the

LEP picked up his trail. He would never leave the U.S. though. If you had to live aboveground, it might as well be somewhere with cable TV and a lot of rich people to steal from.

Mulch pressed the intercom panel.

"Just a minute, Miss Frazetti; I'm getting dressed."

"Hurry it up, Mo," snapped Carla, her voice crackly through the cheap speakers. "I'm getting old here."

Mulch threw on a robe he had fashioned from old potato sacks. He found the texture of the cloth, reminiscent of Haven Penitentiary pajamas, to be weirdly comforting. He gave his beard a quick comb to dislodge any straggling beetles, and answered the door.

Carla Frazetti swept past him into the lounge, settling into the room's only armchair. There was another person on the doorstep, hidden beneath the camera's field. Mulch made a mental note. *Redirect the CCTV lens.* A fairy could sneak right in under the lens, even if he wasn't shielded.

The man gave Mulch a dangerous squint. Typical Mob behavior. Just because these people were murdering gangsters didn't mean they had to be rude.

"Don't you have another chair?" asked the small human, following Miss Frazetti into the lounge.

Mulch closed the door. "I don't get many visitors. Actually, you're the first. Usually Bruno beeps me, and I come into the chop shop."

Bruno the Cheese was the Mob's local supervisor. He ran

his business from a local hot-car warehouse. Legend had it that he hadn't been out from behind his desk during work hours in fifteen years.

"Quite a look you've got going here," said Loafers sarcastically. "Mold and woodlice. I like it."

Mulch ran a fond finger along a green strip of damp. "That mold was just sitting behind the wallpaper when I moved in. Amazing what people cover up."

Carla Frazetti took a bottle of White Petals perfume from her bag, spraying the air around her person.

"Okay, enough conversation. I have a special job for you, Mo."

Mulch forced himself to stay calm. This was his big chance. Maybe he could find a nice damp hellhole and settle down for a while.

"Is this the kind of job where there's a big payoff if you do it right?"

"No," replied Carla. "This is the kind of job where there's a painful payoff if you do it wrong."

Mulch sighed. Didn't anyone ask nicely anymore?

"So why me?"

Carla Frazetti smiled, her ruby winking in the gloom. "I'm going to answer that question, Mo. Even though I'm not used to explaining myself to the hired help. Especially not a monkey like yourself."

Mulch swallowed. Sometimes he forgot how ruthless these people were. Never for long.

• (𝕂 ⚎ ⋙ • ⟩⟨ ᗡ ⦀ ᐰ • ⚉ ⚌⚌ ⟩⟨⟩⟨ ⚌⚌ ᐰ ⚏ •

"You've been chosen for this assignment, Mo, because of the outstanding job you did with that van Gogh."

Mulch smiled modestly. The museum alarm had been child's play. There hadn't even been any dogs.

"But also because you have an Irish passport."

A gnome fugitive hiding out in New York City had run him up Irish papers on a stolen LEP copier. The Irish had always been Mulch's favorite humans, so he had decided to become one. He should have known it would lead to trouble.

"This particular job is in Ireland, which might be a problem, generally. But for you two, it'll be like a paid holiday."

Mulch nodded at Loafers. "Who's the mutt?"

Loafers' squint narrowed. Mulch knew that if Miss Frazetti gave the word, the man would kill him on the spot.

"The mutt is Loafers McGuire, your partner. He's a metal man. It's a two-tier job. You open the doors. Loafers escorts the mark back here."

Escorting the mark. Mulch knew what that term meant, and he didn't want any part of it. Robbery was one thing, but kidnapping was another. Mulch knew that he couldn't actually turn down this assignment. What he could do was ditch the metal man at the first opportunity and head to one of the Southern states. Apparently Florida had some lovely swamps.

"So, who's the mark?" said Mulch, pretending that it mattered.

⚶☻⚇ • ☻⚭⚎ • ⚝⚲⚵ • ☻⚶⚴⚵ • ⚲⚶

"That's need-to-know information," said Loafers.

"And let me guess—I don't need to know."

Carla Frazetti pulled a photograph from her coat pocket. "The less you know, the less you have to feel guilty about. This is all you need. The house. This photograph is all we have for the moment, you can case the joint when you get there."

Mulch took the photo. What he saw on the paper hit him like a gas attack. It was Fowl Manor. Therefore, Artemis was the target. This little psychopath metal man was being sent to kidnap Artemis.

Frazetti sensed his discomfort. "Something wrong, Mo?"

Don't let it show on your face, thought Mulch. Don't let them see.

"No. It's . . . eh . . . that's quite a setup. I can see alarm boxes and outdoor spots. It's not going to be easy."

"If it was easy, I'd do it myself," said Carla.

Loafers took a step forward, looking down at Mulch.

"What's the matter, little man? Too tough for you?"

Mulch was forced to think on his feet. If Carla Frazetti thought he wasn't up to the job, then they would send somebody else. Somebody with no qualms about leading the Mob to Artemis's door. Mulch was surprised to realize that he couldn't let that happen. The Irish boy had saved his life during the goblin rebellion, and was the closest thing he had to a friend. Which was pretty pathetic when you thought about it. He had to take the job, if only to make sure that it didn't go according to plan.

"Hey, don't worry about me. The building hasn't been built that Mo Digence can't crack. I just hope Loafers is man enough for the job."

Loafers grabbed the dwarf by the lapels. "What's that supposed to mean, Digence?"

Mulch generally avoided insulting people who were likely to kill him, but it might be useful to establish Loafers as a hothead now. Especially if he was going to blame him for things going wrong later.

"It's one thing being a midget monkey, but a midget metal man? How good can you be at close quarters?"

Loafers dropped the dwarf, ripping open his own shirt. His chest was a rippling tapestry of tattoos. "That's how good I am, Digence. Count the tattoos. Count 'em."

Mulch shot Carla a loaded look. The look said, *You're going to trust this guy?*

"That's enough!" said Carla. "The testosterone in here is starting to stink worse than the walls. This is a very important job. If you two can't handle it, I'll bring in another team."

Loafers buttoned his shirt.

"Okay, Miss Frazetti. We can handle it. This job is as good as done."

Carla stood, brushing a couple of centipedes from the hem of her jacket. The insects didn't bother her unduly. She'd seen a lot worse in her twenty-five years. "Glad to hear it. Mo, put some clothes on and grab your monkey kit. We'll wait in the limo."

Loafers poked Mulch in the chest. "Five minutes. Then we're coming in to get you."

Mulch watched them go. This was his last chance to duck out. He could chew through the bedroom foundations, and be on a southbound train before Carla Frazetti knew he was gone.

Mulch thought about it seriously. This kind of thing was totally against his nature. It wasn't that the dwarf was a bad fairy, it was simply that he wasn't accustomed to helping other people. Not unless there was something in it for him. Deciding to help Artemis Fowl was a completely selfless act. Mulch shuddered. A conscience was the last thing he needed right now. Next thing you knew, he'd be selling cookies for the Girl Scouts.

CHAPTER 6
ASSAULT ON FOWL MANOR

Excerpt from Artemis Fowl's diary, disk 2 (encrypted)

My father had finally regained consciousness. I was, of course, relieved, but his last words to me that day were chasing themselves around my mind. "Gold isn't all-important, Arty," he had said. "Neither is power. We have everything we need right here. The three of us."

Was it possible that the magic had transformed my father? I had to know. I needed to speak to him alone. So, at 3 A.M. the following morning, I had Butler bring me back to Helsinki's University Hospital in the rented Mercedes.

Father was still awake, reading War and Peace *by lamplight. "Not many laughs," he commented. More jokes. I tried to smile, but my face just wasn't in the mood.*

Father closed the book. "I've been expecting you, Arty. We need to talk. There are a few things we have to straighten out."

I stood stiffly at the foot of the bed. "Yes, Father. I agree."

Father's smile was tinged with sadness. "So formal. I remember being the same with my own father. I sometimes think that he didn't know me at all, and I worry that the same thing will happen to us. So I want us to talk, son, not about bank accounts. Not stocks and shares. Not corporate takeovers. I don't want to talk business, I want to talk about you."

I had been afraid of this. "Me? You are the priority here, Father."

"Perhaps, but I cannot be happy until your mother's mind is put at rest."

"At rest?" I asked, as though I didn't know where this was going.

"Don't play the innocent, Artemis. I've called a few of my law enforcement contacts around Europe. Apparently, you have been active in my absence. Very active."

I shrugged, unsure whether I was being scolded or praised.

"Not so long ago I would have been very impressed by your antics. Such audacity, and still a minor. But now, speaking as a father, I am telling you that things have to change, Arty. You must reclaim your childhood. It is my wish, and your mother's, that you return to school after the holidays, and leave the family's business to me."

"But—Father!"

"Trust me, Arty. I've been in business a lot longer than you. I have promised your mother that the Fowls are on the straight and narrow from now on. All the Fowls. I have another chance, and I will not waste it on greed. We are a family now. A proper one.

From now on the Fowl name will be associated with honor and honesty. Agreed?"

"Agreed," I said, clasping his hand.

But what of my meeting with Chicago's Jon Spiro? I decided to proceed as planned. One last adventure, then the Fowls could be a proper family. After all, Butler would accompany me. What could go wrong?

Fowl Manor

Butler opened his eyes. He was home. Artemis was asleep on the armchair beside the bed. The boy looked a hundred years old. It wasn't surprising, after all he'd been through. That life was over now though, all of it.

"Anybody home?" said the manservant.

Artemis was instantly alert.

"Butler, you've come back to us."

Butler struggled onto his elbows. It was quite an effort.

"It's a surprise to me. I never expected to see you, or anyone, ever again."

Artemis poured a glass of water from the bedside jug.

"Here, old friend. Just rest."

Butler drank slowly. He was tired, but it was more than that. He had felt battle fatigue before, but this went deeper.

"Artemis, what has happened? I shouldn't be alive at all. And if I accept that I am alive, then I should be experiencing massive amounts of pain right about now."

Artemis crossed to the window, looking out over the estate.

"Blunt shot you. It was a fatal wound, and Holly wasn't around to help, so I froze you until she arrived."

Butler shook his head. "Cryogenics? Only Artemis Fowl. You used the fish freezers, I suppose?"

Artemis nodded.

"I trust I am not part freshwater trout now, eh?"

When Artemis turned to face his friend, he was not smiling.

"There were complications."

"Complications?"

Artemis took a breath. "It was a difficult healing, no way to predict the outcome. Foaly warned that it might be too much for your system, but I insisted we press on."

Butler sat up. "Artemis. It's all right. I'm alive. Anything is better than the alternative."

Artemis was not reassured. He took a pearl-handled mirror from the locker. "Prepare yourself, and take a look."

Butler took a deep breath and looked. He stretched his jaw, and pinched the bags beneath his eyes.

"Just how long was I out?" he asked.

Aboard a transatlantic Boeing 747

Mulch had decided that the best way to undermine the mission was to antagonize Loafers until he went crazy. Driving people crazy was a talent of his, and one that he did not get to exercise often enough.

The two diminutive individuals were seated side by side in a 747 watching the clouds shoot past below. First class. One of the perks of working for the Antonellis.

Mulch sipped delicately from a champagne flute.

"So, Slippers . . ."

"That's Loafers."

"Oh yes, *Loafers.* What's the story behind all the tattoos?"

Loafers rolled up his sleeve, revealing a turquoise snake with drops of blood for eyes. Another of his own designs. "I get one done after every job."

"Oh," said Mulch. "So if you paint a kitchen, then you get a tattoo?"

"Not that kind of job, stupid."

"What kind of job then?"

Loafers gritted his teeth. "Do I have to spell it out for you?"

Mulch swiped some peanuts from a passing tray.

"No point. I never got no schoolin'. Plain English will be fine."

"You can't be this stupid! Spatz Antonelli doesn't hire morons."

Mulch winked a smarmy wink. "You sure about that?"

Loafers patted his shirt, hoping to find a weapon of some kind.

"You wait until this is over, smart aleck. Me and you will settle our differences."

�᚜ᚎᚋ᚜ᚌᚎ • ᚁᚎᚒᚋᚌᚎᚈ •᚜• ᚈᚑᚉᚋ • ᚐᚋᚈᚈᚈ

"You keep telling yourself that, Boots."

"Loafers!"

"Whatever."

Mulch hid behind the airline magazine. This was too easy. The mobster was half-crazed already. A few more hours in Mulch's company should be enough to have Loafers McGuire foaming at the mouth.

Dublin Airport

Mulch and Loafers passed through Irish customs without incident. After all, they were simply citizens returning home for the holidays. It wasn't as if they were a Mob team up to no good. How could they be? Whoever heard of little people being involved in organized crime? Nobody. But maybe that was because they were very good at it.

Passport control provided Mulch with another opportunity to infuriate his partner. The officer was doing his best not to notice Mulch's height, or lack of it.

"So, Mr. Digence, home to visit the family?"

Mulch nodded. "That's right. My mother's folks are from Killarney."

"Oh, really?"

"O'Reilly, actually. But what's a vowel between friends?"

"Very good. You should be on the stage."

"It's funny you should mention that."

The passport officer groaned. Ten more minutes and

)(・⧊⧊⧋⧊⦵⧊⧫⧊⧓⧓・⦗⧊⧈⧇⧇⦶・⧊⧈⧓・

his shift would have been over. "I was being sarcastic, actually . . ."

"Because my friend, Mr. McGuire, and I are also doing a stint in the Christmas pantomime. It's *Snow White*. I'm Doc, and he's Dopey."

The passport officer forced a smile. "Very good. Next."

Mulch spoke for the entire line to hear. "Of course, Mr. McGuire there was born to play Dopey, if you catch my drift."

Loafers lost it right there in the terminal. "You little freak!" he screamed. "I'll kill you! You'll be my next tattoo. You'll be my next tattoo!"

Mulch tutted as Loafers disappeared beneath half a dozen security guards.

"Actors," he said. "Highly strung."

They released Loafers three hours later after a full search and several phone calls to the parish priest in his hometown. Mulch was waiting in the pre-ordered rental car, a specially modified model with elevated accelerator and brake pedals.

"Your temper is seriously jeopardizing this operation," commented the dwarf, straight-faced. "I'll have to phone Miss Frazetti if you can't control yourself."

"Drive," said the metal man hoarsely. "Let's get this over with."

"Okay, then. But you're on your very last chance. One

more episode like that, and I'm going to have to crush your head between my teeth."

Loafers noticed his partner's teeth for the first time. They were tombstone-shaped blocks of enamel, and there seemed to be an awful lot of them for just one mouth. Was it possible that Digence could actually do what he threatened? No, Loafers decided. He was just a bit spooked after the customs interrogation. Still, there was something about the dwarf's smile. A glint that spoke of hidden and frightening talents. Talents that the metal man would prefer to stay hidden.

Mulch took care of the driving, while Loafers made a couple of calls on his cell phone. It was a simple matter for him to contact a few old associates and arrange for a weapon, silencer, and two headsets to be left in a duffel bag behind the highway exit sign for Fowl Manor. Loafers' associates even took credit cards, so there was no need for the usual macho trade-off that generally accompanied black-market transactions.

Loafers checked the weapon's action and sights in the car. He felt in control again.

"So, Mo," said Loafers, chuckling as if that simple rhyme was the funniest joke he had ever made. (Sadly, it was.) "Have you put together a plan yet?"

Mulch didn't take his eyes from the road. "Nope. I thought you were the head honcho here. Plans are your department. I just break and enter."

"That's right. I am the head honcho, and believe me, Master Fowl is going to realize that too when I'm finished talking to him."

"*Master* Fowl?" said Mulch innocently. "We're here for some kid?"

"Not just some kid," revealed Loafers, against orders. "Artemis Fowl. Heir to the Fowl criminal empire. He has something in his head that Miss Frazetti wants. So we're supposed to impress upon the little brat how important it is that he come with us and spill the beans."

Mulch's grip tightened on the wheel. He should have made his move before now. But the trick was not to incapacitate Loafers, it was to convince Carla Frazetti not to send another team.

Artemis would know what to do. He had to get to the boy before Loafers did. A cell phone and a visit to the bathroom were all he needed. A pity he had never bothered purchasing a phone, but there had never been anybody to call before. Besides, you could never be too careful with Foaly. That centaur could triangulate a chirping cricket.

"We better stop for supplies," said Loafers. "It could take days to check this place out."

"No need. I know the layout. I burgled this place before in my youth. Piece of cake."

"And you didn't mention this before because . . ."

Mulch made a rude gesture at a truck driver hogging both lanes.

)|⚇⚌⚐)(⚒⚉⚏ • ⚏⊥)}⚒⚍)(• ⚒⚍⚌⚏ • ⚒⚍ •

"You know the way it is. I work on commission. The commission is calculated on a hardship basis. The second I say I turned this place over before, ten grand is cut off my fee."

Loafers didn't argue. It was true. You always exaggerated the difficulty of the job. Anything to squeeze a few more bucks out of your employer.

"So, you can get us in there?"

"I can get *me* in there. Then I come back out for you."

Loafers was suspicious. "Why don't I just come with you? It would be a lot easier than hanging around in broad daylight."

"First, I'm not going in until after dark. And second, sure you can come with me, if you don't mind crawling through the septic tank and up thirty feet of effluent pipe."

Loafers had to open a window at the thought of it.

"Okay. You come get me. But we stay in contact over the headsets. Anything goes wrong, you let me know."

"Yes, sir, boss," said Mulch, screwing the earpiece into a hairy ear and clipping the mike to his jacket. "Wouldn't want you to miss your appointment intimidating a kid."

The sarcasm made a slight whistling noise as it flew over Loafers' head.

"That's right," said the Kilkenny man. "I *am* the boss. And you *don't* want to make me late for my appointment."

Mulch had to concentrate to stop his beard hair curling. Dwarf hair is very mood sensitive, especially to hostility, which was flowing out of this man's every pore. Mulch's bristles had never been wrong yet. This little partnership was not going to end well.

Mulch parked in the shadow of the Fowl Estate's boundary wall.

"You certain this is the place?" asked Loafers.

Mulch pointed a stubby finger at the ornate iron gate.

"You see there where it says *Fowl Manor*?"

"Yes."

"I'd say this was probably the place."

Even Loafers couldn't miss a direct gibe like that.

"You better get me in there, Digence, or . . ."

Mulch showed him the teeth. "Or what?"

"Or Miss Frazetti will be extremely annoyed," completed Loafers lamely, well aware that he was losing the tough-guy banter battle. Loafers resolved to teach Mo Digence a lesson as soon as possible.

"We wouldn't want to annoy Miss Frazetti," said Mulch. He climbed down from the elevated seat and reclaimed his gear bag from the trunk. There were certain unorthodox burglary tools in the bag supplied by his fairy fence in New York. He hoped none of them would be needed. Not the way he intended to gain entrance to the manor.

Mulch rapped on the passenger window. Loafers buzzed it open.

"What?"

"Remember, you stay here until I come and get you."

"That sounds like an order, Digence. Are you giving me orders now?"

"Me?" said Mulch, revealing the full expanse of his teeth. "Giving orders? I wouldn't dream of it."

Loafers buzzed the window back up.

"You better not be," he said, as soon as there was a layer of reinforced glass between him and those teeth.

Inside Fowl Manor, Butler had just finished clipping and shaving. He was beginning to look like his old self again. His older self.

"Kevlar, you say?" he said, examining the darkened tissue on his chest.

Artemis nodded. "Apparently some fibers were trapped in the wound. The magic replicated them. According to Foaly, the new tissue will restrict your breathing, but it isn't dense enough to be bulletproof, except for a small-caliber bullet."

Butler buttoned his shirt. "Everything is different, Artemis. I can't guard you anymore."

"I won't need guarding. Holly was right. My grand schemes generally lead to people getting hurt. As soon as we have dealt with Spiro, I intend to concentrate on my education."

"As soon as we have dealt with Spiro? You make it sound like a foregone conclusion. Jon Spiro is a dangerous man, Artemis. I thought you would have learned that."

"I have, old friend. Believe me, I won't underestimate him again. I have already begun to formulate a plan. We should be able to retrieve the C Cube and neutralize Mr. Spiro, providing Holly agrees to help."

"Where is Holly? I need to thank her. Again."

Artemis glanced out of the window. "She has gone to complete the Ritual. You can guess where."

Butler nodded. They had first encountered Holly at a sacred fairy site in the southeast while she was conducting the power-restoring Ritual. Although *encountered* was not the term Holly would have used. *Abducted* would have been closer to the truth.

"She should be back within the hour. I suggest you rest until then."

Butler shook his head. "I can rest later. Right now, I have to check the grounds. It's unlikely that Spiro could put a team together so quickly. But you never know."

The bodyguard crossed to a wall panel that linked his room to the security system control booth. Artemis could see that each step was an effort. With Butler's new chest tissue, just climbing the stairs would seem like a marathon.

Butler split screened his monitor so he could view all the CCTVs simultaneously. One of the screens interested him more than the others, so he punched it up on the entire monitor.

"Well, well," he chuckled. "Look who's dropped in to say hello."

Artemis crossed to the security panel. There was a very small individual making rude gestures at the kitchen-door camera.

"Mulch Diggums," said Artemis. "Just the dwarf I wanted to see."

Butler transferred Mulch's image to the main screen. "Perhaps. But why does he want to see you?"

Melodramatic as always, the dwarf insisted on a sandwich before explaining the situation. Unfortunately for Mulch, it was Artemis who volunteered to prepare it for him. He emerged from the pantry with something that resembled nothing so much as an explosion on a plate.

"It's more difficult than it looks," explained the boy.

Mulch cranked open his massive jaws, pouring the whole pile down in one swallow. After several minutes' chewing, he reached an entire hand into his mouth, dislodging a chunk of roast turkey.

"Next time, more mustard," he said, brushing some crumbs from his shirt, and in the process inadvertently switching on the microphone clipped there.

"You're welcome," said Artemis.

"You should be thanking me, Mud Boy," said Mulch. "I came all the way from Chicago to save your life. Surely, that's worth one lousy sandwich. And when I say sandwich, I mean it in the loosest sense of the word."

"Chicago? Jon Spiro sent you?"

The dwarf shook his head. "Possibly, but not directly. I work for the Antonelli family. Of course, they have no idea that I am an actual fairy dwarf, they think I'm simply the best cat burglar in the business."

"Chicago's district attorney has linked the Antonellis to Spiro in the past. Or rather, he's tried to."

"Whatever. Anyway, the plan is that I break in here, and then my partner encourages you to accompany us to Chicago."

Butler was leaning against the table. "Where is your partner now, Mulch?"

"Outside the gate. He's the small, angry one. Glad to see you're alive by the way, big man. There was a rumor going round the underworld that you were dead."

"I was," said Butler, heading for the security booth. "But I'm better now."

Loafers took a small spiral pad from his breast pocket. In it he had recorded any quips that he felt had really worked in dangerous situations. Snappy dialogue, that was the trademark of a good gangster, according to the movies, at any rate. He flicked through the pages, smiling fondly.

It's time to close your account. Permanently. Larry Ferrigamo. Bent banker. August 9.

I'm afraid your hard drive has just been wiped. David Spinski. Computer hacker. September 23.

I'm doing this 'cause I knead the dough. Morty the Baker, July 17.

ᔑ°⌇• ⋔⁅• ⁅⧫⊸ • ⍑ᔑ • ⋔⊬ • ⍊⊸ᔑ • ⚶

It was good material. Maybe he would write his memoirs some day.

Loafers was still chuckling when he heard Mo talking in his earpiece. At first he thought the monkey was speaking to him, but then he realized that his so-called partner was spilling the beans to their pigeon.

"You should be thanking me, Mud Boy," said Digence. "I came all the way from Chicago to save your life."

To save his life! Mo was working for the other side and the little idiot had forgotten about his microphone.

Loafers climbed out of the car, being careful to lock it. He would lose his deposit if the rental was stolen, and Miss Frazetti would take it out of his commission. There was a small pedestrian entrance in the wall beside the main gate. Mo Digence had left it open. Loafers slipped through and hurried down the avenue, careful to stay in the shadow of the trees.

In his ear, Mo kept chattering on. He laid out their entire plan to the Fowl kid without so much as the threat of torture. It was completely voluntary. Digence had somehow been working for the Irish kid all along. And what's more, Mo was not Mo, he was Mulch. What kind of a name was that? Mulch who was apparently a "Fairy Dwarf." This was getting weirder and weirder. Maybe the Fairy Dwarfs were some kind of gang. Although it wasn't much of a gang name. The *Fairy Dwarfs* were hardly going to strike terror into the hearts of the competition.

Loafers trotted up the avenue past a line of elegant silver birches and an honest-to-God croquet pitch. Two peacocks strutted around the edge of a water feature. Loafers snorted. Water feature! In the days before TV gardeners it would have been called a pond.

Loafers was wondering where the delivery entrance was when he saw the sign: DELIVERIES AT REAR. Thank you very much. He checked his silencer and load one more time, and tiptoed across the gravel driveway.

Artemis sniffed the air. "What's that smell?"

Mulch poked his head around the refrigerator door.

"Me, I'm afraid," he mumbled, an unfeasible amount of food revolving inside his mouth. "Sun block. Disgusting, I know, but I'd smell a whole lot worse without it. Think bacon strips on a flat rock in Death Valley."

"A charming image."

"Dwarfs are subterranean creatures," explained Mulch. "We lived underground, even during the Frond Dynasty."

Frond had been the first elfin king. During his reign, fairies and humans had shared the earth's surface.

"Being photosensitive makes it difficult to exist among humans. To be honest, I'm a bit fed up with this life."

"Your wish is my command," said a voice. It was Loafers. He was standing at the kitchen door, brandishing a very large gun.

In fairness to Mulch, he recovered well.

"I thought I told you to wait outside."

"It's true, you did. But I decided to come in anyway. And guess what. No septic tank, no effluent pipe. The back door is wide open."

Mulch tended to grind his teeth when he thought. It sounded like nails being scraped down a chalkboard.

"Ah . . . yes. A stroke of luck there. I took advantage of it, but unfortunately I was interrupted by the boy. I had just gained his confidence when you burst in."

"Don't bother," said Loafers. "Your microphone is on. I heard the whole thing, Mo. Or should I say Mulch, the Fairy Dwarf."

Mulch swallowed the half-chewed mass of food. Once again his big mouth had gotten him into trouble. Maybe it could get him out of trouble too. It was just possible that he could unhinge his jaw and swallow the little hit man. He'd eaten bigger. A quick burst of dwarf gas should be enough to propel him across the room. He'd just have to hope that the gun didn't go off before he could pass it.

Loafers caught the look in Mulch's eye.

"That's right, little man," he said, cocking his pistol. "You go for it. See how far you get."

Artemis was thinking too. He knew that he was safe for the moment. The newcomer would not harm him against orders. But Mulch's time was running out and there was no one to save him. Butler was too weak to intervene even if he had been there. Holly was away completing the Ritual. And

Artemis himself was not the best in physical situations. He would have to negotiate.

"I know what you're here for," he began. "The Cube's secrets. I'll tell you, but not if you harm my friend."

Loafers waved the gun barrel. "You'll do whatever I ask, when I ask. Possibly you'll cry like a girl, too. Sometimes that happens."

"Very well. I'll tell you what you want to know. Just don't shoot anyone."

Loafers swallowed a grin. "Sure. That's fine. You just come with me nice and quiet, and I won't hurt a soul. You have my word."

Butler entered the kitchen. His face was slick with perspiration, and his breath came in short gasps.

"I checked the monitor," he said. "The car is empty, the other man must be—"

"Here," said Loafers. "Old news to everyone except you, Grandpa. Now, no sudden moves and you might not have a heart attack."

Artemis saw Butler's eyes flitting around the room. He was searching for an angle. Some way to save them. Maybe yesterday's Butler could have done it, but today's Butler was fifteen years older and not yet fully recovered from magical surgery. The situation was desperate.

"You could tie the others up," ventured Artemis. "Then we could leave together."

Loafers smacked his own head. "What a great idea!

Then maybe I could agree to some other delaying tactic, on account of me being a complete amateur."

Loafers felt a shadow fall across his back. He spun around to see a girl standing in the doorway. Another witness. Carla Frazetti would be getting the bill for all these sundries. This whole job had been misrepresented from the start.

"Okay, miss," said Loafers. "Go join the others. And don't do anything stupid."

The girl at the door flicked her hair over one shoulder, blinking glittering green eyelids.

"I don't do stupid things," she said. Then her hand flicked out, brushing against Loafer's weapon. She grabbed the pistol's slide and deftly twisted it from the stock. The gun was now completely useless, except for hammering nails.

Loafers jerked backward. "Hey, hey. Watch it. I don't want to wound you by accident. This gun could go off."

That's what he thought.

Loafers continued brandishing his piece of harmless metal.

"Back off, little girl, I won't say it again."

Juliet dangled the slide under his nose. "Or what? You'll shoot me with this?"

Loafers stared cross-eyed at the piece of metal.

"Hey, that looks just like—"

Then Juliet hit him in the chest so hard he crashed through the breakfast bar.

Mulch stared over at the unconscious mobster, then at the girl in the doorway.

"Hey, Butler. Just a shot in the dark here, but I'd say that's your sister."

"You're right," said the manservant, hugging Juliet tightly. "How on earth did you guess?"

• ☆⨯⊡ • ⟨⚚⬡⊟⟊⟆⚘⨯ • ⯞⩚⟩⚱⟆ " ⤶◉

CHAPTER 7

THE BEST-LAID PLANS

Fowl Manor

It was time for consultation. That night, the group sat in the manor's conference room facing two monitors that Juliet had brought down from the security booth. Foaly had hijacked the monitors' frequency and was broadcasting live images of Commander Root and himself.

Much to his own annoyance, Mulch was still present. He had been attempting to weasel some kind of reward from Artemis when Holly returned and cuffed him to a chair.

Root's cigar smoke was hazing the screen. "Looks like the gang's all here," he said, using the fairy gift of tongues to speak English. "And guess what? I don't like gangs."

Holly had placed her headset in the center of the conference table, so all the room's occupants could be picked up.

"I can explain, Commander."

꣸ ⚬ ⟩⟨⚙ ⚘ ⚕ ⚴ ⟊ ⚬ ⚖ ⚶ ⟩⟨ ⟩⟨ ⚶ ⚲ ⟏

"Oh, I'll just bet you can. But strangely, I have a premonition that your explanation is going to cut no ice with me whatsoever, and I will have your badge in my drawer by the end of this shift."

Artemis tried to intervene. "Really, Commander. Holly—Captain Short is only here because I tricked her."

"Is that a fact? And then, pray tell, why is she still there? Doing lunch, are we?"

"This is no time for sarcasm, Commander. We have a serious situation here. Potentially disastrous."

Root exhaled a cloud of greenish smoke. "What you humans do to each other is your own affair. We are not your personal police force, Fowl."

Foaly cleared his throat. "We're involved whether we like it or not. Artemis was the one who pinged us. And that's not the worst of it, Julius."

Root glanced across at the centaur. Foaly had called him by his first name. Things must be serious.

"Very well, Captain," he said. "Continue with your briefing."

Holly opened a report on her handheld computer. "Yesterday I responded to a recording from the Sentinel warning system. The call was sent by Artemis Fowl, a Mud Man well known to the LEP for his part in suppressing the B'wa Kell uprising. Fowl's associate, Butler, had been mortally injured on the orders of another Mud Man, Jon Spiro, and he requested my assistance with a healing."

"Which you refused, and then requested technical backup to perform a mind wipe, as per regulations."

Holly could have sworn the screen was heating up.

"No. Taking into account Butler's considerable assistance during the goblin revolution, I performed the healing and transported Butler and Fowl back to their domicile."

"Tell me you didn't fly them."

"There was no alternative. They were wrapped in camfoil."

Root rubbed his temples. "One foot. If there was so much as one foot sticking out, we could be all over the Internet by tomorrow. Holly, why do you do this to me?"

Holly didn't reply. What could she say?

"There's more. We have detained one of Spiro's employees. A nasty piece of work."

"Did he see you?"

"No. But he heard Mulch say that he was a fairy dwarf."

"No problem," said Foaly. "Do a block mind wipe, and send him home."

"It's not that simple. The man is an assassin. He could be sent back to finish the job. I think we need to relocate him. Believe me. He won't be missed here."

"Okay," said Foaly. "Sedate him, do the wipe and get rid of anything that might trigger his memories. Then send him someplace where he can't do any harm."

The commander took several long puffs to calm himself. "Okay. Tell me about the probe. And if Fowl is responsible, is the alert over?"

"No. The human businessman, Jon Spiro, has stolen the fairy technology from Artemis."

"Which Artemis stole from us," noted Foaly.

"This Spiro character is determined to acquire the technology's secret and he's not particular how he gets it."

"And who knows the secret?"

"Artemis is the only one who can operate the C Cube."

"Do I want to know what a C Cube is?"

Foaly took up the narrative. "Artemis cobbled a microcomputer together from old LEP technology. Most of it is obsolete belowground, but by human standards it's approximately fifty years ahead of their developmental schedule."

"And therefore worth a fortune," concluded the commander.

"And therefore absolutely worth a fortune," agreed Foaly.

Suddenly Mulch was listening.

"A fortune? Exactly how much of a fortune?"

Root was relieved to have someone to shout at. "Shut your mouth, convict! This doesn't concern you. You just concentrate on enjoying your last few breaths of free air. This time tomorrow you'll be shaking hands with your cellmate, and I hope he's a troll."

Mulch was unbowed. "Give me a break, Julius. Every time there's a Fowl situation, I'm the one who saves your sorry hide. I have no doubt that whatever plan Artemis concocts will feature yours truly. Probably in some ridiculously dangerous capacity."

⁂ ⫛ ⵀ ⚇ ⵁ ⵜ · ⵍ ⵔ ⵟ ⵖ · ⵑ ⵟ ⵗ ⵢ ·

Root's complexion went from rosé to full-bodied red. "Well, Artemis? Do you plan on using the convict?"

"That depends."

"On what?"

"On whether or not you give me Holly."

Root's head disappeared behind a fog of cigar smoke. With the red tip glowing, he looked like a steam train coming out of a tunnel. Some of the smoke drifted across to Foaly's screen.

"It doesn't look good," commented the centaur.

Eventually, Root calmed down sufficiently to talk.

"Give you Holly? Gods give me patience. Have you any idea the amount of red tape I'm ignoring just for this conference?"

"Quite a lot, I'd imagine."

"A mountain of the stuff, Artemis. A mountain. I wouldn't be talking to you at all if it wasn't for the B'wa Kell thing. If this ever leaked out, I'd end up directing sewage-treatment subs in Atlantis."

Mulch winked at the screen. "I probably shouldn't have heard that."

The commander ignored him. "You have thirty seconds, Artemis. Sell me."

Artemis rose, standing directly before the screen. "Spiro has fairy technology. It is unlikely that he will be able to use it, but it will put his scientists onto ion technology. The man is a megalomaniac, with no respect for life or the environment. Who knows what ghastly machine he will construct from fairy technology. There is also the definite chance that his new technology will lead him to discover Haven itself, and if that happens, the life of every creature on the planet, and under it, is at risk."

Root wheeled his chair off camera, reappearing in Foaly's monitor. He leaned close to the centaur's ear, whispering in low tones.

"It doesn't look good," said Holly. "I could be on the next shuttle home."

Artemis drummed his fingers on the table. It was difficult to see how he could take on Spiro without fairy assistance. After several moments, the commander reappeared in his own screen.

"This is serious. We cannot afford to risk that this Spiro person will activate another probe. However small the possibility, there's still a chance. I have to put together an insertion team. The works, a fully tooled-up Retrieval team."

"A full team?" protested Holly. "In an urban area? Commander, you know what Retrieval are like. This could turn into a disaster. Let me take a crack at it."

Root considered. "It will take forty-eight hours to clear an operation, so that's what you have. I can cover for you for a couple of days. I can't let you have Foaly. He'll have enough to do putting this operation together. Diggums can help if he wants, it's his choice. I might drop a couple of the burglary charges, but he's still facing five to ten for the bullion robbery. That's all I can do. If you fail, then the Retrieval team is waiting in the wings."

Artemis thought about it. "Very well."

Root took a breath. "There is a condition." .

"I thought as much," said Artemis. "You want a mind wipe. Correct?"

"That's right, Artemis. You are becoming a severe liability to the People. If we are to assist you in this matter, then you and your staff will have to submit to mind wipes."

"And if we don't?"

"Then we go straight to plan B, and you get wiped anyway."

"No offense, Commander, but this is a technical matter. . . ."

Foaly stepped in. "There are two kinds of mind wipe. A block wipe, which takes out everything in the chosen period—Holly can do that with the equipment in her bag. And a fine-tune wipe, which only deletes certain memories. This is a more specialized procedure, but there is less danger of a drop in IQ. We do a fine-tune wipe on all of you. I detonate a data charge in your computer system that automatically deletes any fairy-related files. Also, I will need your permission to do a sweep of your house just in case there is any fairy memorabilia lying around. In practical terms, you will wake up the day after this operation with absolutely no record or memory of the fairy People."

"You're talking about nearly two years of memories."

"You won't miss them. Your brain will invent some new ones to fill the gaps."

It was a tough decision. On the one hand, his knowledge of the People was now a large part of Artemis's psychological makeup. On the other, he could no longer put people's lives at risk.

"Very well," said the teenager. "I accept your offer."

Root tossed the cigar into a nearby incinerator. "Okay, then. We have a deal. Captain Short, keep a channel open at all times."

"Yes, sir."

"Holly."

"Commander?"

"Be careful on this one. Your career won't survive another blow."

"Understood, sir," said Holly.

"Oh, and, convict?"

Mulch sighed. "You mean me, I suppose, Julius?"

Root scowled. "It's over, Mulch. You won't escape again, so get your brain ready for cold food and hard walls."

Mulch stood, presenting his back to the screen. Somehow the bum flap on his specially adapted tunneling trousers flopped open, presenting the commander with a lovely view of his rear end. In the dwarf world, presenting your behind was the ultimate insult, as it is in most cultures.

Commander Root terminated the link. After all, there was no comeback after an affront like that.

• ⚶ ☺ • ⸮ ⸟ ⸘ ⚎ • ⟩(⸮ ⸘ ⸘ • ⍕ ⚎ • ⟩(⚌⚌ • ⟩(

West of Wajir, Kenya

Loafers McGuire woke up with a debilitating headache. It was so painful that he felt obliged to come up with some imagery, in case he had to describe it later. His head felt, he decided, like there was an angry porcupine crawling around inside his cranium. Not bad, he thought. I should put that in the book.

Then he thought, What's a book?

His next thought was, Who am I? Shoes, something to do with shoes.

It was always this way when memory-implant subjects first regained consciousness. The old identity hangs around for a few moments trying to assert itself until outside stimuli wash it away.

Loafers sat up and the porcupine went crazy, jamming needles into every square inch of his soft brain tissue.

"Oh," groaned Loafers, cradling his aching skull. What did all this mean? Where was he? And how did he get here?

Loafers looked at his arms. For a second his brain projected tattoos onto the skin, but the images quickly disappeared. His skin was unblemished. Sunlight rolled across his forearms like white lightning.

All around him was scrubland. Terra-cotta earth stretched off to indigo hills in the distance. A golden disc of sun blasted cracks in the shimmering earth. Two figures ran through the heat waves, elegant as cheetahs.

The men were giants, easily seven feet tall. Each carried an oval, hide-covered shield, a thin spear, and a cell phone. Their hair, necks, and ears were decorated with multicolored beads.

Loafers jumped to his feet. Feet that, he noticed, were clad in leather sandals. The men were wearing Nikes.

"Help," he cried. "Help me!"

The men altered their course, jogging across to the confused mobster.

"*Jambo,* brother. Are you lost?" asked one.

"I'm sorry," said Loafers, in perfect Swahili. "I don't speak Swahili."

The man glanced at his partner. "I see. And what is your name?"

Loafers, said Loafers' brain. "Nuru," said his mouth.

"Well, Nuru. *Unatoka wapi?* Where are you from?"

The words were out before Loafers could do anything about it.

"I don't know where I'm from, but I want to go with you. To your village. That's where I should be."

The Kenyan warriors stared down at the little stranger. He was the wrong color, true, but he seemed sane enough.

The taller of the two unhooked a cell phone from his leopard-skin belt. He punched in the village chieftain's number.

"*Jambo,* Chief, this is Bobby. The earth spirits have left us another one."

Bobby laughed, looking Loafers up and down.

"Yes, he's tiny, but he looks strong and he's got a smile bigger than a peeled banana."

Loafers stretched his smile, just in case it was a factor. For some reason, all he wanted in this world was to go to the village and live a productive life.

"Okay, Chief, I'll bring him in. He can have the missionary's old hut."

Bobby clipped the cell phone onto his belt. "Very well, brother Nuru. You're in. Follow us, and try to keep up."

The warriors set off at a brisk run. Loafers, henceforth to be known as Nuru, raced after them, his leather sandals flapping beneath his feet. He really would have to see about getting a pair of Nikes.

Fifty meters over their heads, Captain Holly Short hovered, shielded from view, recording the entire incident.

"Relocation complete," she said into her helmet mike. "The subject has been adopted successfully. No apparent signs of original personality. But he will be monitored at monthly intervals, just in case."

Foaly was on the other end of the line. "Excellent, Captain. Return to shuttle port E77 immediately. If you open the throttle, you might just make the evening shuttle. We'll have you back in Ireland in a couple of hours."

Holly did not need to be told twice. It wasn't often you got clearance for a speed run. She activated her radar in case of buzzards and set the stopwatch on her visor.

"Now," he said. "Let's see if we can't break the airspeed record."

A record that had been set eighty years before by Julius Root.

PART 2

COUNTERATTACK

CHAPTER 8

HOOKS, LINES, AND SINKERS

Excerpt from Artemis Fowl's diary, disk 2 (encrypted)

Today Father was fitted for his prosthetic limb. He joked throughout the entire process, as though he were being measured for a new suit on Grafton Street. I must admit, his good humor was infectious, and I found myself making excuses just to sit in the corner of the hospital room and enjoy his presence.

It wasn't always this way. In the past, one needed valid grounds to visit my father. Of course he wasn't generally available, and even when he was, his time was limited. One did not burst into the Fowl study without good reason. But now, I feel welcome at his side. It is a nice feeling.

My father always liked to impart wisdom, but now it is more philosophical than financial. In the old days, he would direct my attention to the latest share prices in the Financial Times.

• ⚼ • ⏏ ⚌⚌ ⚌⚌ � • ⚡⚡⚡⚼ • ⚡♡ • ⚼ • ☾

"Look, Artemis," he would say. "Everything else falls, but gold stays steady. That is because there is not enough of it. And there never will be. Buy gold, boy, and keep it safe." I liked to listen to these pearls, but now they are harder to understand.

On the third day of his consciousness, I fell asleep on the hospital bed, while my father did his walking exercises. I woke to find him regarding me thoughtfully.

"Shall I tell you something, Arty?" he said.

I nodded, unsure what to expect.

"While I was a prisoner, I thought about my life, how I had wasted it gathering riches whatever the cost to my family and others around me. In a man's life, he gets few chances to make a difference. To do the right thing. To be a hero, if you will. I intend to become involved in that struggle."

This was not the kind of wisdom I was accustomed to hearing from my father. Was this his natural personality, or the fairy magic? Or a combination of both?

"I never got involved before. I always thought the world could not be changed."

Father's gaze was intense, burning with new passion.

"But things are different now. My priorities are different. I intend to seize the day. Be the hero that every father should be."

He sat on the bed beside me.

"And what about you, Arty? Will you make the journey with me? When the moment comes, will you take your chance to be a hero?"

I couldn't respond. I did not know the answer. I still do not.

Fowl Manor

For two hours Artemis locked himself in his study, sitting cross-legged in the meditative position taught to him by Butler. Occasionally, he would voice an idea aloud, to be picked up by a voice-activated digital recorder placed on the mat before him. Butler and Juliet knew better than to interrupt the planning process. This period was crucial to the success of their mission. Artemis had the ability to visualize a hypothetical situation and calculate the likely outcomes. It was almost a dream state, and any disturbance could send the thread of his ideas flying like vapors.

Eventually Artemis emerged, tired but satisfied. He handed the team members three writable CDs.

"I want you to study these files," he said. "They contain details of your assignments. When you have memorized the contents, destroy the disks."

Holly took the disks. "A CD. How quaint. We have these in museums."

"There are several computers in the study," continued Artemis. "Use any terminal you wish."

Butler was empty-handed. "Nothing for me, Artemis?"

Artemis waited until the others had gone. "I needed to give you your instructions verbally. I don't want to risk Foaly's picking them up from the computer."

Butler sighed deeply, sinking into a leather armchair by the fireplace.

162

"I'm not going with you. Am I?"

Artemis sat on the chair's arm. "No, old friend. But I have an important task for you."

"Really, Artemis," said Butler. "I've skipped right over my midlife crisis. You don't have to invent a job just to make me feel useful."

"No, Butler. This is of vital importance. It concerns the mind wipes. If my plan succeeds, we will have to submit to them. I see no way to sabotage the process itself, so I must ensure that something survives Foaly's search. Something that will trigger our memories of the People. Foaly once told me that a strong enough stimulus can result in total recall."

Butler shifted his position in the chair, wincing. His chest was still giving him trouble. Not surprising, really. He had been alive again less than two days.

"Any ideas?" Artemis asked.

"We need to lay a couple of false trails. Foaly will be expecting that."

"Of course. A hidden file on the server. I could send an e-mail to ourselves, but not pick it up. Then the first time we check our mail, all this information will come through."

Artemis handed the bodyguard a folded sheet of paper. "No doubt we will be *mesmerized* and questioned. In the past we have hidden from the *mesmer* behind mirrored sunglasses. We won't get away with that on this occasion. So, we need to come up with something else. Here are the instructions."

Butler studied the plans. "It's possible. I know someone

in Limerick. The best man in the country for this kind of specialized work."

"Excellent," said Artemis. "After that, you need to put everything we have on the People on a disk. All documents, video, schematics. Everything. And don't forget my diary. The whole story is there."

"And where do we hide this disk?" asked the ex-bodyguard.

Artemis untied the fairy pendant from around his neck.

"I'd say this was about the same size as a laser disk. Wouldn't you?"

Butler tucked the gold medallion into his jacket pocket.

"It soon will be," he said.

Butler prepared them a meal. Nothing fancy. Vegetarian spring rolls, followed by mushroom risotto with crème caramel to finish. Mulch opted for a bucket of diced worms and beetles, sautéed in a rainwater-and-moss vinaigrette.

"Has everybody studied their files?" Artemis asked, when the group had adjourned to the library.

"Yes," said Holly. "But I seem to be missing a few key pieces."

"Nobody has the entire plan. Just the parts concerning them. I think it's safer that way. Do we have the equipment I specified?"

Holly dumped the contents of her pack on the rug.

"A complete LEP surveillance kit, including camouflage foil, mikes and video clips, and a first-aid box."

"Plus we still have two intact LEP helmets and three laser handguns left over from the siege," added Butler. "And of course one of the prototype Cubes from the lab."

Artemis passed the cordless phone to Mulch.

"Very well, then. We may as well get started."

The Spiro Needle

Jon Spiro sat in his opulent office, staring glumly at the C Cube on his desk. People thought it was easy being him. How little they knew. The more money you had, the more pressure you were under. He had eight hundred employees in this building alone, all relying on him for a paycheck. They wanted yearly salary reviews, medical plans, daycare centers, regular coffee breaks, double pay for overtime, and even stock options, for heaven's sake. Sometimes, Spiro missed the times when a troublesome worker would be thrown out a high window and that was the end of him. These days, if you threw someone out of a window, they'd phone their lawyer on the way down.

But this Cube could be the answer to his prayers. A once-in-a-lifetime deal, the brass ring. If he could get this weird little gizmo working, the sky was the limit. Literally. The world's satellites would be his to command. He would have complete control over spy satellites, military lasers, communications networks, and most important of all, television stations. He could feasibly rule the world.

His secretary buzzed from reception.

"Mr. Blunt to see you, sir."

Spiro jabbed the intercom button.

"Okay, Marlene, send him in. And tell him he better look sorry."

Blunt did indeed look sorry when he pushed through the double doors. The doors themselves were imposing enough. Spiro had them stolen from the ballroom of the sunken *Titanic*. They were a perfect example of power gone mad.

Arno Blunt was not quite so cocky as he had been in London. Then again, it is difficult to look arrogant when your forehead is a mass of bruises and your mouth is full of gums and nothing else.

Spiro winced at the sight of his sunken cheeks.

"How many teeth did you lose?"

Blunt touched his jaw gingerly. "All ob 'em. Dentish shaid de roods were shaddered."

"It serves you right," said Spiro matter-of-factly. "What do I gotta do, Arno? I hand you Artemis Fowl on a platter, and you mess it up. Tell me what happened. And I don't want to hear about any earthquakes. I want the truth."

Blunt wiped a blob of drool from the corner of his mouth.

"I doh undershtan' ih. Shomeshin' explohduh. I dunno wha. Shome kinna shoun' grenay. Buh I tell you shomeshin'. Butlah ish dead. I sho' him in de har. No way he'sh geddin' uh affer da."

"Oh, shut up!" snapped Spiro. "You're giving me a head-ache. The sooner you get those new teeth, the better."

"My gumsh wi' be healed suffishently by thish afernoo'."

"I thought I told you to shut up!"

"Shorry, bosh."

"You've put me in a very difficult situation, Arno. Because of your incompetence I had to hire a team from the Antonellis. Carla is a smart girl. She could decide that they deserve a percentage. It could cost me millions."

Arno tried his best to look remorseful.

"And don't bother with the puppy-dog look, Blunt. It doesn't cut any ice with me. If this deal goes south, you'll be losing a lot more than a couple of teeth."

Arno decided to change the subject. "Sho, di' your shientishts geh de gube worging?"

"No," said Spiro, twisting his gold identity bracelet. "Fowl has it sealed up tight. An eternity code, or some such thing. That idiot, Pearson, couldn't get a peep out of it."

It was at that moment, dramatically enough, that a voice emanated from the C Cube's micro speaker mesh.

"Mr. Spiro?" said the voice. "This is Ireland calling. Do you read, Mr. Spiro?"

Jon Spiro was not a man who spooked easily. He hadn't seen a horror movie yet that could make him jump in his seat, but the voice coming out of that speaker almost knocked him off his chair. The quality was incredible. Close your eyes, and you'd swear that the person speaking was standing right in front of you.

"You wan' me to ansher da?"

"I told you to shut up! Anyway, I don't know how to answer this thing."

"I can hear you, Mr. Spiro," said the voice. "You don't need to do anything. Just talk. The box does the rest."

Spiro noticed that a digital wave meter had appeared on the Cube's screen. When he spoke, it registered.

"Okay, then. We got communication. Now, who the hell are you? And how did you get this box working?"

"The name is Mo Digence, Mr. Spiro. I'm the monkey from Carla Frazetti's team. I don't know what kind of box you have at your end, I just have a plain old telephone."

"Well, who dialed the number then?"

"A little kid I have here by the scruff of the neck. I impressed upon him how important it was that I talk to you."

"And how did you know to talk to me? Who gave you my name?"

"Again, the kid. He was very eager to tell me everything after he saw what I did to the metal man."

Spiro sighed. If the metal man was damaged, he would have to pay the Antonellis a fine.

"What did you do to the metal man?"

"Nothing permanent. But he won't be aiming any guns at kids for a while."

"Why did you feel it necessary to damage your own partner, Digence?"

There was a pause on the other end, while Mulch got the supposed sequence of events sorted out.

"It was like this, Mr. Spiro. Our instructions were to escort the kid across to the U.S. But Loafers goes crazy and starts waving a gun around. I figured this was the wrong way to go. So I stopped him. Forcibly. Anyway, the kid gets so scared that he tells me everything I want to know. And here I am now, having a conversation with you."

Spiro rubbed his hands together. "You did the right thing, Digence. There'll be a bonus in this for you. I'll see to it personally."

"Thanks, Mr. Spiro. Believe me, the pleasure was mine."

"Is the Fowl kid there?"

"Right beside me. A little pale, but not a scratch on him."

"Put him on," ordered Spiro, all traces of depression vanishing.

"Spiro, it's me." Artemis's voice was aloof, but with an unmistakable tremor.

Spiro squeezed the air, as though it were Artemis's neck.

"Not so cocky now, kid? It's like I told you, you don't have the guts for this job. Me on the other hand ... If I don't get what I want, then I'll have Mo put you out of my misery. Do we understand each other?"

"Yes. Loud and clear."

"Good," said Spiro, clamping a huge Cuban cigar between his teeth. It would be chewed to a pulp, but not lit. "Now, talk. What do I have to do to get this Cube working?"

Artemis's voice sounded even shakier than before. "It's not that simple, Mr. Spiro. The C Cube is encrypted. Something called an eternity code. I can remotely access certain basic functions; the phone, MP3 player, and so on, but to disable the code completely and unlock the Cube's potential, I need to have it here in front of me. If you could just bring the Cube here. . . ."

Spiro spat out the cigar. "Hold it right there, Fowl. Just how stupid do you think I am? I'm going to bring this priceless technology back to Europe? Forget it! If you're going to disable this thing, you're going to do it here. In the Spiro Needle!"

"But my tools, my lab?"

"I got tools here. And a lab. The best in the world. You do it here."

"Yes. Whatever you say."

"That's right, kid. Whatever I say. I want you to fuel up the Lear jet, which I happen to know you have, and do a quick hop across to O'Hare Airport. I'll have a chopper waiting for you."

"I don't suppose I have a choice."

"That's right, kid. You don't. But do this right and I might just let you go. Did you get all that, Digence?"

•)|�֍✷♋)(• ✷)(• ♨⫟(ᴋ✷⌂⫟ᴑ⍑• ⩎⫟⥾

"Loud and clear, Mr. Spiro."

"Good. I'm counting on you to get the kid here safely."

"Consider it done."

The line went dead.

Spiro chuckled. "I think I'm going to celebrate," he said, punching the intercom button. "Marlene, send in a pot of coffee, and no low-caffeine junk either, I want the real thing."

"But, Mr. Spiro, your doctor said . . ."

Spiro waited for his secretary to realize who she was arguing with.

"I'm sorry, sir. Right away, sir."

Spiro leaned back in his chair, lacing his fingers behind his head.

"You see, Blunt, this is going to turn out fine, in spite of your incompetence. I got that kid just where I want him."

"Yesh, shir. Masherfully done, shir."

Spiro laughed. "Shut up, you clown. You sound like some cartoon character."

"Yesh. Mosh amushing, shir."

Spiro licked his lips, anticipating his coffee. "For a supposed genius, that kid sure is gullible. Do this right and I might just let you go? He fell for that one, hook, line, and sinker."

Blunt tried to grin. It was not a pretty sight.

"Yesh, Mishuh Shpiro. Hoo, line, an' shinkuh."

༄ ⧈⬚⟩(• ⧓༄⟩⧈⬚⬚⧓♂⟩⟆ •)(⧈

Fowl Manor

Artemis hung up the phone, his face flushed with the thrill of the sting.

"What do you think?" he asked.

"I think he bought it," replied Butler.

"Hook, line, and sinker," added Mulch. "You have a jet? I presume there's a kitchen."

Butler drove them to Dublin Airport in the Bentley. It was to be his final act in this particular operation. Holly and Mulch huddled in the back, glad of the tinted glass.

The Butler siblings sat up front, dressed in corresponding black designer suits. Juliet had jazzed hers up with a pink cravat and glitter makeup. The family resemblance was clear, the same narrow nose and full lips. The same eyes, jumping in their sockets like roulette balls in the wheel. Watching, always watching.

"You don't need a traditional gun on this trip," said Butler. "Use an LEP blaster. They don't need reloading, they shoot in a straight line forever, and they're nonlethal. I gave Holly a couple from my stash."

"Got it, Dom."

Butler took the airport exit. "Dom. I haven't been called that in so long. Being a bodyguard becomes your world. You forget to have your own life. Are you sure that's what you want, Juliet?"

Juliet was twining her hair in a tight braid, at the end of which she attached an ornamental jade ring. Ornamental and dangerous.

"Where else would I get to body-slam people? Body-guarding fits the bill, for the moment."

Butler lowered his voice. "Of course, it's completely against protocol for you to have Artemis as your Principal. He already knows your first name, and truth be told I think he's a little fond of you."

Juliet slapped the jade ring against her palm. "This is just temporary. I'm not anybody's bodyguard just yet. Madam Ko doesn't like my style."

"I'm not surprised," said Butler, pointing to the jade ring. "Where did you get that?"

Juliet smiled. "My own idea. A nice little surprise for anyone who underestimates females."

Butler pulled into the set-down area.

"Listen to me, Juliet," he said, catching his sister's hand. "Spiro is dangerous. Look what happened to me, and in all modesty, I was the best. If this mission weren't so vital to humans and fairies, I wouldn't let you go at all."

Juliet touched her brother's face. "I'll be careful."

They climbed onto the walkway. Holly hovered, shielded, several feet above the throngs of business travelers and holiday makers. Mulch had applied a fresh layer of sun block, and the stink repelled every human who was unfortunate enough to get within ten feet of him.

Butler touched Artemis's shoulder.

"Are you going to be all right?"

Artemis shrugged. "I honestly don't know. Without you by my side, I feel as though one of my limbs is missing."

"Juliet will keep you safe. She has an unusual style, but she is a Butler, after all."

"It's one last mission, old friend. Then there will be no more need for bodyguards."

"It's a pity Holly couldn't have simply *mesmerized* Spiro through the Cube."

Artemis shook his head. "It wouldn't have worked. Even if we could have set up a link, a fairy needs eye-to-eye contact to *mesmerize* a strong mind like Spiro's. I don't want to take any chances with this man. He needs to be put away. Even if the fairies relocated him, he could do some damage."

"What about your plan?" Butler asked. "From what you told me, it's quite convoluted. Are you sure it's going to work?"

Artemis winked, a very unusual display of levity.

"I'm sure," he said. "Trust me. I'm a genius."

Juliet piloted the Lear jet across the Atlantic. Holly sat in the copilot's chair, admiring the hardware.

"Nice bird," she commented.

"Not bad, fairy girl," said Juliet, switching to autopilot. "Not a patch on fairy craft, I'd bet?"

"The LEP doesn't believe in comfort," said Holly.

"There's barely enough room in an LEP shuttle to swing a stink worm."

"If you wanted to swing a stink worm."

"True." Holly studied the pilot. "You've grown a lot in two years. The last time I saw you, you were a little girl."

Juliet smiled. "A lot can happen in two years. I spent most of that time wrestling big hairy men."

"You should see fairy wrestling. Two pumped-up gnomes going at it in a zero-G chamber. Not a pretty sight. I'll send you a video disk."

"No, you won't."

Holly remembered the mind wipes.

"You're right," she said. "I won't."

In the passenger section of the Lear jet, Mulch was reliving his glory days.

"Hey, Artemis," he said through a mouthful of caviar. "Remember the time I nearly blew Butler's head off with a blast of gas?"

Artemis did not smile. "I remember, Mulch. You were the wrench in an otherwise perfect works."

"To tell you the truth, it was an accident. I was just nervous. I didn't even realize the big guy was there."

"That makes me feel better. Done in by a bowel problem."

"And do you remember the time I saved your neck in Koboi Laboratories? If it hadn't been for me, you'd be locked up in Howler's Peak right now. Can't you do anything without me?"

Artemis sipped mineral water from a crystal flute. "Apparently not, though I live for the day."

Holly made her way back through the aisle.

"We better get you ready, Artemis. We land in thirty minutes."

"Good idea."

Holly emptied her kit onto the central table.

"Okay, what do we need for now? The throat mike and an iris camera."

The LEP captain selected what looked like a circular adhesive bandage from the pile. She peeled back the adhesive layer and stuck the material to Artemis's neck. It immediately turned the color of his skin.

"Memory latex," explained Holly. "It's almost invisible. Maybe an ant crawling up your neck might notice it, but apart from that . . . The material is also X-ray proof, so the mike is undetectable. It will pick up whatever is said in a ten-yard radius, and I record it on my helmet chip. Unfortunately, we can't risk an earpiece. Too visible, so we can hear you, but you won't be able to hear us."

Artemis swallowed, feeling the mike ride on his Adam's apple.

"And the camera?"

"Here we go."

Holly removed a contact lens from a jar of fluid.

⚌⚌ • ⅌⚍⚌⚌ • ⚌⚌⚌ • ⚌⚌⚌⚌ • ⚌⚌⚌

"This thing is a marvel. We've got high resolution, digital quality, recordable picture with several filter options, including magnification and thermal."

Mulch sucked a chicken bone dry. "You're starting to sound like Foaly."

Artemis stared at the lens. "A technological marvel it may be, but it's hazel."

"Of course it's hazel. My eyes are hazel."

"I'm glad to hear it, Holly. But my eyes are blue, as you well know. This iris-cam will not do."

"Don't look at me like that, Mud Boy. You're the genius."

"I can't go in there with one brown eye and one blue eye. Spiro will notice."

"Well, you should have thought of that while you were meditating. It's a little late now."

Artemis pinched the bridge of his nose. "You're right, of course. I am the mastermind here. Thinking is my responsibility, not yours."

Holly squinted suspiciously. "Was that an insult, Mud Boy?"

Mulch spat the chicken bone into a nearby bin. "I have to tell you, Arty, a screwup this early in the proceedings doesn't exactly fill me with confidence. I hope you're as clever as you keep telling everyone you are."

"I never tell anybody *exactly* how clever I am. They would be too scared. Very well, we will have to risk the hazel iris-cam. With any luck, Spiro might not notice. If he does, I can invent some excuse."

(K ⊃ • ⟨⟩ • ⟩⟩ ⟨⟨ ⟨⟨ ⟨⟩ ⟨ • ⟨⟨ ⟨⟩ ⟨ • ⟨⟨ ⟨ •

Holly placed the camera on the tip of her finger, sliding the lens under Artemis's lid.

"It's your decision, Artemis," she said. "I just hope you haven't met your match in Jon Spiro."

O'Hare International Airport

Spiro was waiting for them at O'Hare's private hangar. He wore a fur-collared greatcoat over his trademark white suit. Halogen lamps blasted the tarmac, and the downdraught from the chopper blades snagged his coattails. It was all very cinematic.

All we need now is background music, thought Artemis, as he descended the motorized steps.

As instructed, Mulch was putting on the gangster act.

"Move it, kid," he snarled, quite convincingly. "We don't want to keep Mr. Spiro waiting."

Artemis was about to respond, when he realized that he was supposed to be the "terrified kid." It wasn't going to be easy. Being humble was a real problem for Artemis Fowl.

"I said, move it!" repeated the dwarf, stressing the point with a firm shove.

Artemis stumbled the last few steps, almost colliding with a grinning Arno Blunt. This was no ordinary grin. Blunt's teeth had been replaced by a custom-crafted porcelain set. The tips had been filed to sharp points. The bodyguard looked for all the world like a human–shark hybrid.

Blunt caught Artemis's stare. "You like 'em? I got other sets, too. One is all flat. For crushing stuff."

A cynical sneer was forming on Artemis's mouth, before he remembered his role, replacing the sneer with a set of quivering lips. He was basing his performance on the effect Butler usually had on people.

Spiro was not impressed. "Nice acting, sonny. But pardon me if I doubt the great Artemis Fowl has fallen to pieces quite so easily. Arno, check the plane."

Blunt nodded curtly, ducking inside the private jet. Juliet was dressed in a flight attendant's uniform, straightening the headrest covers. For all her athletic ability, she was finding it difficult not to trip in her high heels.

"Where's the pilot?" growled Blunt, living up to his name.

"Master Artemis flies the plane," replied Juliet. "He's been flying it since he was eleven years old."

"Oh really? Is that legal?"

Juliet put on her best innocent face. "I don't know about legal, sir. I just serve the drinks."

Blunt grunted, charming as ever, and had a quick poke about the jet's interior. Eventually, he decided to accept the flight attendant's word. Lucky for him, because had he decided to argue, two things would have happened. First, Juliet would have clobbered him with the jade ring. And second, Holly, who was lying shielded in an overhead locker, would have blasted him into unconsciousness with her

Neutrino 2000. Of course, Holly could simply have *mesmerized* the bodyguard, but after what he had done to Butler, a blasting seemed more appropriate.

Blunt stuck his head through the hatch. "No one in there except some dumb attendant."

Spiro was not surprised. "I didn't think so. But they're here somewhere. Believe it or not, Digence, Artemis Fowl did not get suckered by a goon like you. He's here because he wants to be here."

Artemis was not surprised by this deduction. It was only natural that Spiro be suspicious.

"I don't know what you mean," he said. "I'm here because this odious little man threatened to crush my skull between his teeth. Why else would I come? The C Cube is useless to you, and I could easily construct another one."

Spiro was not even listening. "Yeah yeah, whatever you say, kid. But let me tell you something. You bit off more than you could chew when you agreed to come here. The Spiro Needle has the best security on the planet. We've got stuff in there that even the military don't have. Once those doors close behind you, you're on your own. Nobody is coming to save you. Nobody. Understand?"

Artemis nodded. He understood what Spiro was saying to him. That wasn't to say that he agreed with it. Jon Spiro might have "stuff" that the military didn't have, but Artemis Fowl had "stuff" that humans had never seen.

* * *

A Sikorsky executive helicopter whisked them downtown to the Spiro Needle. They landed on a helipad on the skyscraper's roof. Artemis was familiar with helicopter controls, and realized how difficult it must be to land in the bluster of the Windy City.

"The wind speed must be treacherous at this altitude," he said casually. Holly could record the information on her helmet chip.

"You're telling me," shouted the pilot over the rotors' din. "It gets to over sixty miles an hour on top of the Needle. The helipad can sway up to thirty feet in rough conditions."

Spiro groaned, giving Blunt a nod. Arno reached forward and whacked the pilot's helmet.

"Shut up, you moron!" snapped Spiro. "Why don't you give him the blueprints to the building while you're at it?" He turned to Artemis. "And in case you're wondering, Arty, there aren't any blueprints floating around. Anybody who goes looking in City Hall is going to find that file mysteriously missing. I have the only set, so don't bother getting one of your associates to do an Internet search."

No surprises there. Artemis had already run several searches himself, although he hadn't really expected Spiro to be so careless anyway.

They climbed down from the Sikorsky. Artemis was careful to point the iris-cam at any security feature that could be useful later. Butler had often told him that even a seemingly insignificant detail, like the number of steps in a stairwell, could be vital when planning an operation.

An elevator brought them down from the helipad to a key-coded door. Closed-circuit cameras were strategically placed to cover the entire rooftop. Spiro moved ahead to the keypad. Artemis felt a sharp sting in his eye, and suddenly the iris-cam magnified his vision by four. In spite of the distance and shadows, he could easily discern the entry code.

"I hope you got that," he muttered, feeling the mike vibrating on his throat.

Arno Blunt bent his knees, so his extraordinary teeth were an inch from Artemis's nose.

"Are you talking to someone?"

"Me?" said Artemis. "Who would I be talking to? We're eighty floors up, in case you hadn't noticed."

Blunt grabbed the teenager by the lapels, hoisting him off the tarmac. "Maybe you're wearing a wire. Maybe you have someone listening to us right now."

"How could I be wearing a wire, you big oaf? Your miniature hit man hasn't let me out of his sight for the entire journey. He even accompanied me to the bathroom."

Spiro cleared his throat noisily. "Hey there, Mr. I-Gotta-Make-My-Point, that kid slips over the side and you might as well throw yourself off, because that boy is worth more to me than an army of bodyguards."

Blunt set Artemis down.

"You're not going to be valuable forever, Fowl," he whispered ominously. "And when your stock falls, I'll be waiting."

* * *

They took a mirrored elevator to the eighty-fifth floor, where Dr. Pearson waited along with two more muscle-bound guards. Artemis could tell by the look in their eyes that these two weren't exactly brain surgeons. In fact, they were as close as you could get to being Rottweilers and still balance on two legs. It was probably handy to have these two around to break things and not ask questions.

Spiro called one of them over.

"Pex, do you know what the Antonellis charge if you lose their personnel?"

Pex had to consider it for a moment. His lips moved as he thought.

"Yeah, wait, I got it. Twenty grand for a metal man and fifteen for a monkey."

"That's dead, right?"

"Dead or incapati . . . incatacip . . . broken."

"Okay," said Spiro. "I want you and Chips to go over to Carla Frazetti's and tell her I owe her thirty-five grand for the team. I'll wire it to her Cayman Islands account in the morning."

Mulch was understandably curious, and not a little apprehensive.

"Excuse me? Thirty-five grand? But I'm still alive. You only owe twenty grand for Loafers, unless the extra fifteen K is my bonus?"

Spiro sighed with almost convincing regret.

"This is the way it is, Mo," he said, punching Mulch playfully on the shoulder. "This deal is huge. Mammoth. We're talking telephone numbers. I can't afford any loose ends. Maybe you know something, maybe you don't. But I'm not about to take the chance that you might tip off Phonetix or one of my other competitors. I'm sure you understand."

Mulch stretched his lips, revealing a row of tombstone teeth.

"I understand all right, Spiro. You're a backstabbing snake. You know, the kid offered me two million dollars to cut him loose."

"You should have taken the cash," said Arno Blunt, propelling Mulch into Pex's gigantic arms.

The dwarf kept talking, even as he was being dragged down the corridor.

"You better bury me deep, Spiro. You better bury me real deep."

Spiro's eyes narrowed to slits. "You heard the man, boys. Before you go to Frazetti's, bury him deep."

Dr. Pearson led the party through to the vault room. They had to pass through a small antechamber before entering the main security area.

"Please stand on the scanner pad," said Pearson. "We wouldn't want any bugs in here. Especially not the electronic kind."

Artemis stepped onto the mat. It sank like a sponge

beneath his feet, spurting jets of foam over his shoes.

"Anti-infection foam," explained Pearson. "Kills any virus you might have picked up. We're keeping some biotechnology experiments in the vault at the moment. Very susceptible to disease. The foam has the added advantage of shorting out any surveillance devices in your shoes."

Overhead, a mobile scanner bathed Artemis's shoes framed in purple light.

"One of my own inventions," said Pearson. "A combination scanner. I have incorporated thermal, X-ray, and metal-detector beams. The beam basically breaks your body down into its elements and displays them on this screen here."

Artemis saw a 3-D replica of himself being traced out on the small plasma screen. He held his breath, praying that Foaly's equipment was as clever as the centaur thought it was.

On screen, a red light pulsed on Artemis's jacket front.

"Aha," said Dr. Pearson, plucking off a button. "What have we here?" He cracked the button open, revealing a tiny chip, mike, and power source.

"Very clever. A micro bug. Our young friend was attempting to spy on us, Mr. Spiro."

Jon Spiro was not angry, in fact he was delighted to have the opportunity to gloat.

"You see, kid. You may be some kind of genius, but surveillance and espionage are my business. You can't slip anything past me. And the sooner you accept that, the sooner we can get this thing over with."

Artemis stepped off the pad. The decoy had worked, but the real bugs hadn't caused a blip in the system. Pearson was smart, but Foaly was smarter.

Artemis made sure to have a good look around the antechamber. There was more here. Every square inch of the metal surface contained a security or surveillance device. From what Artemis could see, an invisible ant would have trouble sneaking in here. Not to mention two humans, an elf, and a dwarf. Providing the dwarf had survived Pex and Chips.

The vault door itself was impressive. Most corporate vaults *looked* impressive, plenty of chrome and keypads, but that was just to make an impression on stockholders. In Spiro's vault there wasn't a tumbler out of place. Artemis spotted the very latest computer lock on the face of titanium double doors. Spiro keyed in another complicated series of numbers, and the meter-thick doors slid back to reveal another barrier. The secondary door.

"Imagine you were a thief," said Spiro, as if he were an actor introducing a play. "And you somehow get into the building, past the electronic eyes and the locked doors. Then, imagine you somehow cheat the sensor pad and open the first vault door, an impossible feat by the way. And while we're imagining all this, let's pretend you disable the half dozen cameras, and even then, even after all that, would you be able to do this?"

Spiro stood on a small red plate painted on the floor in front of the door. He placed a thumb on a gel-print scanner, held his left eyelid open, and enunciated clearly.

"Jon Spiro. I am the boss, so open up quick."

Four things happened. A retinal scanner filmed his left eye and fed the image into the computer. A print plate scanned his right thumb, and a vocal analyzer scrutinized Spiro's accent, timbre, and intonation. Once the computer had verified all this information, the alarms were deactivated and the secondary door slid open, revealing an expansive vault.

In the very center, in the middle of a custom-made steel column, rested the C Cube. It was encased in a Plexiglas box with at least six cameras focused on its various planes. Two burly guards stood back-to-back, forming a human barrier in front of the fairy technology.

Spiro could not resist a gibe. "Unlike you," he said, "I look after my technology. This is the only vault of its kind in the world."

"Live security in an airtight room. Interesting."

"These guys are trained at high altitude. Also, we change the guards on the hour, and they all carry oxygen cylinders to keep them going. What did you think? I was going to put air vents into a vault?"

Artemis scowled. "No need to show off, Spiro. I'm here, you win. So can we get on with it?"

Spiro punched a final number sequence into the column's keypad and the Plexiglas panes retracted. He took the Cube from its foam nest.

𝕬𝕵(𝕺)·𝕵(𝕺𝕫·𝕫𝕫𝕸𝕿𝕵(·𝕫𝕸𝕫𝕺𝕸𝕫𝕫

"Overkill, don't you think?" commented Artemis. "All of this is hardly necessary."

"You never know. Some crooked businessman could attempt to relieve me of my prize."

Artemis took a chance on some calculated sarcasm. "Really, Spiro. Did you think I would attempt a break-in? Perhaps you thought I would fly in here with my fairy friends and magic your box away?"

Spiro laughed. "You can bring all the fairy friends you like, Arty-boy. Short of a miracle that Cube is staying right where it is."

Juliet was an American citizen by birth, even though her brother had been born on the other side of the world. She was glad to be back in her home country. The discord of Chicago's traffic and the constant chorus of multicultural voices made her feel at home. She loved the skyscrapers and the steam vents and the affectionate sarcasm of the street vendors. If she ever got the chance to settle down, it would be in the U.S. On the West Coast though, somewhere with sun.

Juliet and Holly were circling the Spiro Needle in a blacked-out minivan. Holly sat in the back, watching video from Artemis's iris-cam on her helmet visor.

At one point she punched the air triumphantly.

Juliet stopped at a red light. "How are we doing?"

"Not bad," replied the fairy, raising her visor. "They're taking Mulch to bury him."

ᘔ • ⌒ ⚙ ♋ ☒ • ⫯ ⩚ ⟐ ⟐⚏ ⚞ ⩖ ᘔ # • ⫰ ⌒ ᘔ

"Cool. Just like Artemis said they would."

"And Spiro has just invited all of Artemis's fairy friends into the building."

This was a crucial development. The Book forbade fairies to enter human buildings without an invitation. Now Holly was free to break in and wreak havoc without violating fairy doctrine.

"Excellent," said Juliet. "We're in. I get to body-slam the guy who shot my brother."

"Not so fast. This building has the most sophisticated Mud Man security system I've ever seen. Spiro has a few tricks in there that I've never come across before."

Juliet finally found a space opposite the Needle's main revolving doors. "No problem for the little horsy guy, surely?"

"Yes, but Foaly's not supposed to help us."

Juliet focused a set of binoculars on the door. "I know, but it all depends on how you ask. A smart guy like Foaly, what he needs is a challenge."

Three figures emerged from the Needle. Two large men in black and a smaller, nervous-looking individual. Mulch's feet were treading air so fast that he seemed to be performing an Irish jig. Not that he had any hope of escaping. Pex and Chips had him tighter than two badgers fighting over a bone.

"Here comes Mulch now. We'd better give him backup. Just in case."

Holly strapped on her mechanical harness, extending the wings with the touch of a button.

"I'll follow them from the air. You keep an eye on Artemis."

Juliet ran a video lead from a spare helmet's handheld computer. Artemis's point of view sprang to life on the screen.

"Do you really think Mulch needs help?" she asked.

Holly buzzed into invisibility. "Help? I'm just going along to make sure he doesn't harm those two Mud Men."

Inside the vault, Spiro was finished playing the gracious host.

"Let me tell you a little story, Arty," he said, plucking the C Cube from its pressure pad. "There was this Irish kid who thought he was ready for the big time. So he messed with a very serious businessman."

Don't call me Arty, thought Artemis. My father calls me Arty.

"This businessman didn't appreciate being messed with, so he messed back. And this kid is dragged kicking and screaming into the real world. So, now this kid has to make a choice; does he tell the businessman what he needs to know, or does he put himself and his family in mortal danger? Well, Arty, which one is it?"

Spiro was making a serious mistake by toying with Artemis Fowl. It was difficult for adults to believe that this pale-faced thirteen-year-old could actually be a threat. Artemis had tried to take advantage of this by wearing casual clothes in place of his usual Armani suit. He had also been practicing an innocent, wide-eyed look on the jet, but wide-eyed was not how you wanted to look when one iris did not match the other.

Blunt prodded Artemis between the shoulder blades.

"Mr. Spiro asked you a question." His new teeth clicked as he talked.

"I'm here, am I not?" replied Artemis. "I'll do whatever you wish."

Spiro placed the Cube on a long steel table that ran down the center of the vault.

"What I wish is for you to disable your eternity code, and get this Cube working right now."

Artemis wished that he could make himself perspire, so his anxiety would seem more authentic.

"Right now? It's not that simple."

Spiro grabbed Artemis by the shoulders, staring him in the eye.

"And why wouldn't it be that simple? Just punch in the code word, and away we go."

Artemis averted his mismatched eyes, staring at the floor.

"There is no straightforward code word. An eternity code is built to be irreversible. I have to reconstruct an entire language. It could take days."

• ⚷🝓◒⧊)꙳ • ꙳🝓⧄🝓 • ◒🝓 • 🝓)⟩

"Don't you have any notes?"

"Yes. On disk. In Ireland. Your monkey wouldn't let me bring anything in case it was booby-trapped."

"Can we access your hard drive online?"

"Yes. But I only keep my notes on disk. We could fly back to Ireland. Eighteen hours, round-trip."

Spiro wouldn't even consider that option. "Forget it. As long as I have you here, I'm in control. Who knows what kind of reception is waiting for me in Ireland? We do it here. As long as it takes."

Artemis sighed. "Very well."

Spiro replaced the Cube in its Plexiglas case. "Get a good night's sleep, kid, because tomorrow you're going to peel this gizmo apart like an onion. And if you don't, what's about to happen to Mo Digence will happen to you."

Artemis wasn't unduly worried by that threat. He didn't believe Mulch to be in any danger. In fact if anyone was in trouble, it was those two musclemen, Pex and Chips.

CHAPTER 9
GHOSTS IN THE TIME MACHINE

Vacant lot, Malthouse Industrial Estate, South Chicago

Jon Spiro had not hired Pex and Chips for their debating skills. In the job interview, they had only been set one task. A hundred applicants were handed a walnut and asked to smash it however they could. Only two succeeded. Pex had shouted at the walnut for a few minutes, then flattened it between his giant palms. Chips had opted for a more controversial method. He placed the walnut on the table, grabbed his interviewer by the ponytail, and used the man's forehead to smash the nut. Both men were hired on the spot. They quickly established themselves as Arno Blunt's most reliable lieutenants for in-house work. They were not allowed outside Chicago, as this could involve map reading, something Pex and Chips were not very good at.

ꙩ ꙮ • ꙮ ꞇꞇ • ꙭ ꙡ • ꙭ ꙸ ꙷ ꙡ ꙓ • ꞇꞇ Ꙭ • ꙮ

At the moment Pex and Chips were bonding under a full moon, while Mulch dug a dwarf-size pit in the dry clay behind an abandoned cement factory.

"You wanna guess why they call me Pex?" asked Pex, flexing his chest muscles as a hint.

Chips opened a packet of the potato chips he was forever crunching.

"I dunno. Is it, like, short for something?"

"Like what?"

"I dunno," said Chips. He used that phrase a lot. "Francis?"

This sounded dumb, even to Pex. "Francis? How could Pex be short for Francis?"

Chips shrugged. "Hey. I had an Uncle Robert and everyone called him Bobby. That don't make no sense neither."

Pex rolled his eyes. "It's pec-tor-als, moron. Pex is short for pectorals, on account of me having big chest muscles."

In the pit, Mulch groaned. Listening to this mindless banter was almost as bad as having to dig a hole with a shovel. Mulch was tempted to deviate from the plan and launch himself into the flaky soil. But Artemis did not want any display of fairy powers at this stage of the proceedings. If he took off, and these goons escaped without being *mesmerized,* then Spiro's paranoia would be driven up another notch.

Up on the surface, Chips was eager to continue the game.

"Guess why they call me Chips," he said, hiding the bag of chips behind his back.

Pex kneaded his forehead. He knew this one.

"Don't tell me," he said. "I can work it out."

Mulch poked his head from the hole. "It's because he eats chips, you idiot. Chips eats chips. You two are the thickest Mud Men I have ever met. Why don't you just kill me? At least I won't have to listen to your drivel."

Pex and Chips were stunned. With all the mental exercise, they had almost forgotten about the little man in the hole. Plus, they were unaccustomed to prospective victims saying anything besides, "Oh no, please God, no."

Pex leaned over the grave's lip. "What do you mean drivel?"

"I mean that whole 'Chips Pex' thing."

Pex shook his head. "No, I mean what does the word *drivel* mean?"

Mulch was delighted to explain. "It means rubbish, garbage, claptrap, twaddle, baloney. Is that clear enough for you?"

Chips recognized the last one. "Baloney? Hey, that's an insult! Are you insulting us, little man?"

Mulch clasped his hands in mock prayer. "Finally, a breakthrough!"

The musclemen were uncertain how to react to actual abuse. There were only two people alive who insulted them regularly, Arno Blunt and Jon Spiro. But that was part of the job; you just ignored that by turning up the music in your head.

"Do we have to listen to his smart mouth?" Pex asked his partner.

"I don't think so. Maybe I should phone Mr. Blunt."

Mulch groaned. If stupidity were a crime, these two would be public enemies one and two.

"What you should do is kill me. That was the idea, wasn't it? Just kill me and get it over with."

"What do you think, Chips? Should we just kill him?"

Chips chewed on a handful of BBQ Blast Ruffles. "Yeah. Course. Orders is orders."

"But I wouldn't *just* kill me," interjected Mulch.

"You wouldn't?"

"Oh no. After the way I just insulted your intelligence? No, I deserve something special."

You could almost see the steam coming out of Pex's ears as his brain overheated.

"That's right, little man. We're gonna do something special to you. We don't take no insults from anybody!"

Mulch did not bother pointing out the double negative.

"You're right. I've got a smart mouth, and I deserve everything I've got coming to me."

There followed a short silence, as Pex and Chips tried to come up with something worse than the usual straight shooting. Mulch gave them a minute, then made a polite suggestion.

ย์วู • ฏฺ)(ว))วู๕ • ๕๕ ๕ • ๕ ๕ • ๕๕ •)(

"If it was me, I'd bury me alive."

Chips was horrified. "Bury you alive! That's terrible. You'd be screaming and clawing the dirt. I could get night-mares."

"I promise to lie still. Anyway, I deserve it. I did call you a pair of overdeveloped, single-cell Cro-Magnons."

"Did you?"

"Well, I have now."

Pex was the more impulsive of the duo. "Okay, Mr. Digence. You know what we're gonna do? We're going to bury you alive."

Mulch clapped two hands to his cheeks. "Oh, the horror!"

"You asked for it, buddy."

"I did, didn't I?"

Pex grabbed a spare shovel from the trunk. "Nobody calls me an overdeveloped, signal-bell crow magnet."

Mulch lay down obligingly in his grave. "No. I bet nobody does."

Pex shoveled furiously, his gym-sculpted muscles stretching his suit jacket. In minutes, Mulch's form was completely covered.

Chips was feeling a bit squeamish. "That was horrible. Horrible. That poor little guy."

Pex was unrepentant. "Yeah, well, he asked for it. Calling us . . . all those things."

"But—buried alive! That's like in that horror movie. Y'know—the one with all the horror."

𝄃 ⚘ ⟩⟩ • ⚛ ☺ ☻ • ⚘ ⚲ • ☾ ⚘ ⚭ 𝄃 ⚒ ⟩ •

"I think I saw that one. With all the words going up on the screen at the end?"

"Yeah, that was it. Tell you the truth, those words kinda ruined it for me."

Pex stamped on the loose earth. "Don't worry, buddy. There are no words in this movie."

They climbed back into their Chevrolet automobile. Chips was still a bit upset.

"You know, it's much more real than a movie when it's real."

Pex ignored a no-access sign, pulling onto the motorway. "It's the smell. You can't smell stuff in a movie."

Chips sniffed emotionally. "Digence musta been upset right there at the end."

"I'm not surprised."

"'Cause I could see him cryin'. His shoulders were shaking, like he was laughing. But he must have been crying. I mean what sort of crazy wacko would laugh when he's getting buried alive."

"He musta been crying."

Chips opened a bag of smoky bacon curls. "Yeah. He musta been crying."

Mulch was laughing so much that he nearly choked on the first mouthful of soil. What a pair of clowns. Then again, it was lucky for them that they had been clowns, otherwise they might have chosen their own method of execution.

Jaw unhinged, Mulch tunneled straight down for twenty feet and then veered north to the cover of some abandoned warehouses. His beard hair sent out sonar signals in all directions. You couldn't be too careful in built-up areas. There was always some wildlife, and Mud Men had a habit of burying things where you wouldn't expect them. Pipes, septic tanks, and barrels of industrial waste were all things he had taking an unwitting bite of in his day. And there is nothing worse than finding something in your mouth that you weren't expecting to be there, especially if it's wriggling.

It felt good to be tunneling again. This was what dwarfs were born to do. The earth felt right between his fingers, and he soon settled into his distance rhythm. Scooping muck between his grinding teeth, breathing through slitted nostrils, and pumping waste material out the other end.

Mulch's hair antennae informed him that there were no vibrations on the surface, so he kicked upward using the last vestiges of his dwarf gas to propel himself from his hole.

Holly caught him four feet above the ground. "Charming," she said.

"What can I tell you?" said Mulch unapologetically. "I'm a force of nature. You were up there all that time?"

"Yes, just in case things got out of hand. You put on quite a show."

Mulch slapped the clay from his clothes. "A couple of Neutrino blasts could have saved me a lot of digging."

Holly smiled in spooky imitation of Artemis. "That's not in *the plan*. And we must stick to *the plan*, now mustn't we?"

She draped a sheet of cam-foil around the dwarf's shoulders, and hooked him onto her Moonbelt.

"Take it easy now, won't you?" said Mulch anxiously. "Dwarfs are creatures of the soil. We don't like flying. We don't even like jumping too high."

Holly opened the throttle on her wings, heading downtown.

"I'll be just as considerate of your feelings as you are of the LEP's."

Mulch paled. Funny how this diminutive elf was much scarier than two six-foot hit men.

"Holly, if I ever did anything to offend you, I unreservedly—" He never finished that particular sentence, because their sudden acceleration forced the words back down his throat.

The Spiro Needle

Arno Blunt walked Artemis to his cell. It was comfortable enough, with its own bathroom and entertainment system. There were a couple of things missing: windows and a handle on the door.

Blunt patted Artemis on the head. "I don't know what happened in that London restaurant, but you try anything like that here, and I will turn you inside out and eat your organs." He gnashed his pointy teeth to make the point and leaned close, whispering into Artemis's ear. Artemis could hear the teeth click with every syllable.

"I don't care what the boss says, you're not going to be useful forever, so if I were you, I'd be very nice to me."

"If you were me," responded Artemis, "then I'd be you. And if I were you, then I'd hide somewhere far away."

"Oh, really. And why would you do that?"

Artemis looked him in the eyes, so Blunt could see the truth there.

"Because Butler is coming for you. And he's extremely annoyed."

Blunt backed off a few steps. "No way, kid. I saw him go down. I saw the blood."

Artemis grinned. "I didn't say he was alive, I just said he was coming."

"You're just messing with my mind. Mr. Spiro warned me about this."

Blunt edged out the door, never taking his eyes off Artemis.

"Don't worry, Blunt. I don't have him here in my pocket. You have hours, maybe days before the time comes."

Arno Blunt slammed the door so hard that the frame shook. Artemis's grin widened. Every cloud has a silver lining.

Artemis stepped into the shower, allowing the jet of hot water to pound him on the forehead. In truth, he felt a little anxious. It was one thing to formulate a plan in the safety of one's own home. It was quite another to execute that plan while trapped in the lion's den. And even though he would never admit it, his confidence had taken quite a pounding in the last few days. Spiro had outwitted him back in London, and without apparent effort. He had strolled into the entrepreneur's trap as naively as a tourist down a back alley.

Artemis was well aware of his talents. He was a plotter, a schemer, a planner of dastardly deeds. There was no thrill greater than the execution of a perfect plan. But lately his victories had been tainted by guilt, especially over what had happened to Butler. His old friend had been so close to death that it made Artemis queasy just to think about it.

Things had to change. His father would be watching soon, hoping that Artemis would make the right choices. And if he didn't, Artemis Senior would quite possibly take his choices away from him. He remembered his father's words. *And what about you, Arty? Will you make the journey with me? When the moment comes, will you take your chance to be a hero?*

Artemis still did not have the answer to that question.

Artemis wrapped himself in a robe monogrammed with his captor's initials. Not only was Spiro reminding him of his presence with the gold letters, but a motion-sensitive, closed-circuit camera was following Artemis around the room.

Artemis focused on the challenging task of breaking into Spiro's vault and stealing back the C Cube. He had anticipated many of Spiro's security measures and packed accordingly. However, some were unforeseen and quite ingenious. But Artemis had fairy technology on his side, and Foaly too, he hoped. The centaur had been ordered not to help, but if Holly presented the break-in as a test, Artemis felt sure that the centaur would be unable to resist.

Artemis sat on the bed, casually scratching his neck. The microphone's latex covering had survived the shower, as Holly had assured him it would. It was comforting to know that he was not alone in his prison.

Because the microphone operated on vibrations, Artemis did not have to speak aloud for his instructions to be transmitted.

"Good evening, friends," he whispered, his back to the camera. "Everything proceeds according to plan, taking it that Mulch made it back alive. I must warn you to expect a visit from Spiro's goons. I am certain his personnel have been monitoring the streets. It should lull him into a false sense of security if he believes my people to be wiped out. Mr. Spiro has kindly given me a tour of the facility, and I hope you have recorded everything we need to complete our mission. I believe the local term for this kind of operation is *heist*. This is what I want you to do."

Artemis whispered slowly, enunciating each point clearly. It was vital that his team members followed his instructions to the letter. If they did not, the entire plot could explode like an active volcano. And at the moment, he was sitting in the volcano's crater.

Pex and Chips were in a good mood. On their return to the Needle, not only had Mr. Blunt handed over their five-grand bonus for the Mo Digence job, but he had also given them another assignment. The Needle's external surveillance cameras had picked up a black van parked opposite the main door. It had been there for over three hours, and a review of the tapes showed the vehicle circling the building for over an hour looking for a space. Mr. Spiro had warned them to look out for suspicious vehicles. And this was certainly suspicious.

"Go down there," Blunt had ordered from his chair in the security office. "And if there's anything breathing inside, ask them why they're breathing outside my building."

This was the kind of instruction that Pex and Chips understood. No asking questions, no operating complex machinery. Just open the door, scare everything, close the door. Easy. They kidded around in the elevator, punching each other in the shoulder until their upper arms went numb.

"We could make big bucks tonight, partner," said Pex massaging his biceps to get the circulation going.

"We sure could," enthused Chips, thinking about all the Barney DVDs he could buy. "This must be worth another bonus. Five grand at least. Altogether that's . . ."

∛∛⅋ • ⏃⚇)(⟩⸞∞ ⏃⚄⚉ •)(∞ • ⒜⚄)(⒜⚄

There followed several moments' silence while both men counted on their fingers.

"That's a lot of cash," said Pex finally.

"A lot of cash," agreed Chips.

Juliet had her binoculars trained on the Needle's revolving door. It would have been easier to use the Optix on a fairy helmet, but unfortunately, her head had grown too large in the past couple of years. That wasn't the only thing to have changed. Juliet had transformed from gangly kid to toned athlete. She wasn't perfect bodyguard material though; there were still a few wrinkles to be ironed out. Personality wrinkles.

Juliet Butler was a fun-loving creature, she couldn't help it. She found the idea of standing poker-faced at the shoulder of some opinionated politician appalling. She'd go crazy from boredom. Unless Artemis asked her to stay on professionally. A person could never be bored at Artemis Fowl's side. But that was not likely to happen. Artemis had assured everyone that this was his last job. After Chicago he was going straight. If there was an after Chicago.

This stakeout business was boring too. Sitting quietly was not in Juliet's nature. Her hyperactive disposition had caused her to fail more than one class in Madam Ko's academy. *Be at peace with yourself, girl,* the Japanese instructor had said. *Find that quiet place at your core and inhabit it.*

Juliet generally had to stifle a yawn when Madam Ko

started on the kung fu wisdom stuff. Butler, on the other hand, had eaten it up. He was forever finding his *quiet place* and inhabiting it. In fact, he only came out of his *quiet place* to pulverize whoever was threatening Artemis at the time. Maybe that was why he had his blue diamond tattoo and Juliet didn't.

Two burly figures emerged from the Needle. They were grinning and punching each other on the shoulder.

"Captain Short, we're on," said Juliet into a walkie-talkie tuned to Holly's frequency.

"Understood," responded Holly from her position above the Spiro Needle. "How many hostiles?"

"Two. Big and dumb."

"You need backup?"

"Negative. I'll wrap these two. You can have a word on your return."

"Okay. I'll be down in five, as soon as I've had a talk with Foaly. And Juliet, don't mark them."

"Understood."

Juliet switched off the radio and climbed into the rear of the van. She swept a pile of surveillance equipment under a fold-up seat, just in case the two heavies actually managed to incapacitate her. It wasn't likely, but her brother would have hidden the incriminating equipment just in case. Juliet pulled off her suit jacket and placed a baseball cap backward on her head. She then popped the rear window and clambered out onto the road.

꒦ • ꒷ ꒰ ꒱ ꒤ ꒝ ꒨ ꒦ ꒧ • ꒦ ꒠ ꒪ ꒦ ꒦ ꒧ • ꒦ ꒣

* * *

Pex and Chips crossed State Street to the suspect van. It certainly looked suspicious, with its blacked-out windows, but the pair were not unduly concerned. Every testosterone-fueled college freshman had blacked-out windows these days.

"Whatcha think?" Pex asked his partner.

Chips curled his fingers into fists. "I think we don't bother knocking."

Pex nodded. This was the plan that they generally went with. Chips would have proceeded to wrench the door from its hinges had not a young lady appeared from around the hood.

"You guys looking for my dad?" said the girl in perfect MTV tones. "People are always, like, looking for him, and he's never around. Daddy is *so* not here. And I mean that literally *and* spiritually."

Pex and Chips blinked in unison. The blink being universal body language for *huh?* This girl was stunning, but she might as well have been talking Greek for all the comprehension that registered on the security men's faces. *Spiritually* had five syllables, for heaven's sake.

"You own this van?" asked Chips, taking the offensive.

The girl twisted her ponytail. "As much as any of us can, like, own anything. One world, one people, right, man? Ownership is like, you know, an illusion. Maybe we don't even own our own bodies. We could be, like, the daydreams of some greater spirit."

Pex cracked. "Do you own the van or not?" he shouted, wrapping thumb and forefinger around the girl's neck.

The girl nodded. There wasn't enough air in her windpipe for speech.

"That's better. Anyone inside?"

A shake of the head this time.

Pex relaxed his grip slightly.

"How many more in the family?"

The girl answered in a whisper, using as little air as possible.

"Seven. Dad, mom, two grandparents, and the triplets; Beau, Mo, and Joe. They went for sushi."

Pex cheered up considerably. Triplets and grandparents, that didn't sound like any problem.

"Okay. We wait. Open the door, kid."

"Sushi?" said Chips. "That's raw fish. You ever have that, buddy?"

Pex held the girl by the neck while she fiddled with the key.

"Yeah. I bought some in the supermarket once."

"Was it good?"

"Yeah. I threw it in the deep-fat fryer for ten minutes. Not bad."

The girl slid back the van door, climbing into the interior. Pex and Chips followed, ducking under the rim. Pex released the girl's neck momentarily to take the step. That was his mistake. A properly trained private enforcer would never allow an untethered prisoner to lead the way into an unsecured vehicle.

The girl stumbled accidentally, dropping to both knees on the interior's carpet.

"Sushi," said Pex. "It's good with french fries."

Then the girl's foot snapped back, catching him in the chest. The hired muscle collapsed gasping onto the floor.

"Oops," said the girl, straightening. "Accident."

Chips thought he must be having some kind of waking dream, because there was no way a little pop princess clone could have decked two hundred pounds of muscle and attitude.

"You . . . you just," he stuttered. "That's impossible. No way."

"Way," said Juliet, pirouetting like a ballerina. The jade ring in her ponytail swung around, loaded with centrifugal force. It struck Chips between the eyeballs like a stone from a sling. He staggered backward, landing in a heap on a leatherette sofa.

Behind her Pex's breath was returning. His eyeballs stopped rolling wildly, focusing on his assailant.

"Hi," said Juliet, bending over him. "Guess what?"

"What?" said Pex.

"You're not supposed to deep-fry sushi," said the girl, clapping the assassin on both temples with the palms of her hands. Unconsciousness was immediate.

Mulch emerged from the bathroom, buttoning the bum flap on his tunneling trousers.

"What did I miss?" he asked.

Holly hovered one hundred feet above Chicago's downtown district, known locally as the Loop, after the curve of elevated track that enclosed the area. She was up there for two reasons. First, they needed an X-ray scan of the Spiro Needle in order to construct 3-D blueprints. And second, she wanted to talk to Foaly alone.

She spotted a stone eagle perched on the roof of an early twentieth-century apartment block, and alighted on its head. She would have to move from her perch after a few minutes, or her shield vibration would begin to pulverize the rock.

Juliet's voice sounded in her earpiece.

"Captain Short, we're on."

"Understood," responded Holly. "How many hostiles?"

"Two. Big and dumb."

"You need backup?"

"Negative. I'll wrap these two. You can have a word on your return."

"Okay. I'll be down in five, as soon as I've had a talk with Foaly. And Juliet, don't mark them."

"Understood."

Holly smiled. Juliet was a piece of work. A chip off the Butler block. But she was a wild card, even on stakeout she couldn't stop chattering for more than ten seconds. None of her brother's discipline. She was a happy teenager. A kid. Artemis had no business dragging her into his crazy schemes. But there was something about the Irish boy that made you forget your reservations. In the past sixteen months, she had fought a troll for him, healed his entire family, and dived into the Arctic Ocean. Now she was preparing to disobey a direct order from Commander Root.

She opened a channel to LEP Operations.

"Foaly. Are you listening?

Nothing for several seconds, then the centaur's voice burst through the helmet's micro speaker.

"Holly. Hold on. You're a bit fuzzy, I'm just going to fine-tune the wavelength. Talk to me. Say something."

"Testing. One, two. One, two. Trolls in a tantrum cause terrible trouble."

"Okay. Gotcha. Crystal clear. How goes it in the land of mud?"

Holly gazed down at the city below her.

"No mud here. Just glass, steel, and computers. You'd like it."

"Oh no. Not me. Mud Men are Mud Men no matter if they're wearing suits or loincloths. The only good thing about humans is the television. All we get on PPTV is reruns. I'm almost sorry the goblin generals' trial is over. Guilty on all counts, thanks to you. Sentencing is next month."

Anxiety loosened its grip on Holly's stomach. "Guilty. Thank heaven. Things can finally go back to normal."

Foaly snickered. "Normal? You're in the wrong job for normal. You can kiss normal good-bye if we don't get Artemis's gizmo back from Spiro."

The centaur was right. Her life had not been *normal* since she'd been promoted to Recon from the vice squad. But did she really want a normal life? Wasn't that the reason why she had transferred from vice in the first place?

"So why the call?" asked Foaly. "Feeling a bit homesick, are you?"

"No," replied Holly. And it was true. She wasn't. The elf captain had barely thought of Haven since Artemis had embroiled her in his latest intrigue. "I need your advice."

"Advice? Oh really? That wouldn't be another way of asking for help now would it? I believe Commander Root's words were, 'You got what you got.' Rules are rules, Holly."

Holly sighed. "Yes, Foaly. Rules are rules. Julius knows best."

"That's right. Julius knows best," said Foaly, but he didn't sound convinced.

"You probably couldn't help anyway. Spiro's security is pretty advanced."

Foaly snorted, and a centaur snorting is something to hear.

"Yeah, sure. What has he got? A couple of tin cans and a dog? Ooh, scary."

⚭🝔 • ⚴ • 🝔 ⚘⚘ ⚘⚘ 🜚 • ☽⚴⚭🜚 ·· 🜹☽

"I wish. There's stuff in this building that I've never seen before. Smart stuff."

A small liquid crystal screen flickered into life in the corner of Holly's visor. Foaly was broadcasting a visual from Police Plaza. Technically, not something he should be doing for an unofficial operation. The centaur was curious.

"I know what you're doing by the way," said Foaly, wagging a finger.

"I have no idea what you mean," said Holly innocently.

"You probably couldn't help anyway. Spiro's security is pretty advanced," mimicked the centaur. "You're trying to light a fire under my ego. I'm not stupid, Holly."

"Okay. Maybe I am. Do you want the straight truth?"

"Oh, you're going to tell me the truth now. Interesting tactic for the LEP."

"The Spiro Needle is a fortress. There's no way in without you, even Artemis admits it. We're not looking for equipment or extra fairy power. Just advice over the airwaves, maybe a bit of camera work. Keep the lines open, that's all I'm asking."

Foaly scratched his chin. "No way in, eh? Even Artemis admits it."

"'We can't do it without Foaly.' His exact words."

The centaur struggled to keep the smugness from his features.

"Have you got any video?"

Holly took a handheld computer from her belt.

"Artemis shot some film inside the Needle, I'm mailing it to you now."

"I need a blueprint of the building."

Holly panned her visor left and right, so Foaly could see where she was.

"That's why I'm up here. To do an X-ray scan. It'll be in your mainframe in ten minutes."

Holly heard a bell chime in her speakers. It was a computer alert. Her mail had arrived in Police Plaza. Foaly opened the file.

"Key codes. Okay. Cameras. No problem. Wait until I show you what I've developed for CCTV cameras. I'm fast-forwarding through the corridors. Dum de dum de dum, ah, the vault. Pressure pads, antibiotic mats. Motion sensors. Temperature sensitive lasers. Thermal cameras. Voice recognition, retina and gel thumbprint scanners." He paused. "Impressive, for a Mud Man."

"You're telling me," agreed Holly. "A bit more than two tin cans and a dog."

"Fowl is right. Without me, you're sunk."

"So, will you help?"

Foaly had to milk the moment. "I'm not promising anything. . . ."

"Yes?"

"I'll keep a screen open for you. But if something comes up . . ."

"I understand."

"No guarantees."

"No guarantees. I owe you a carton of carrots."

"Two cartons. And a case of beetle juice."

"Done."

The centaur's face was flushed with the promise of a challenge.

"Will you miss him, Holly?" he asked suddenly.

Holly was caught off guard by the question.

"Miss who?" she said, though she already knew.

"The Fowl boy, of course. If everything goes according to plan, we'll be wiped from his memory. No more wild plots, or seat-of-the-pants adventures. It will be a quiet life."

Holly avoided Foaly's gaze, even though the centaur could not see her.

"No," she said. "I will not miss him."

But her eyes told the real story.

Holly circled the Needle several times at various altitudes, until the X-ray scanner had accumulated enough data for a 3-D model. She mailed a copy of the file to Foaly in Police Plaza and returned to the van.

"I thought I told you not to mark them," she said, bending over the fallen hit men.

Juliet shrugged. "Hey. No big deal, fairy-girl. I got carried away in the heat of battle. Just give him a shot of blue sparks and send him on his way."

Holly traced a finger around the perfectly circular bruise on Chips's forehead.

"You should have seen me," said Juliet. "Bang bang and they were down. Never had a chance."

Holly sent a solitary spark down her finger. It wiped away the bruise like damp cloth cleaning a coffee ring.

"You could have used the Neutrino to stun them, you know."

"The Neutrino? Where's the fun in that?"

Captain Short removed her helmet, glaring up at the teenage human.

"This is not supposed to be fun, Juliet. It's not a game. I thought you realized that, considering what happened to Butler."

Juliet's grin disappeared. "I know it's not a game, Captain. Maybe this is the way I deal with things."

Holly held her gaze. "Well then, maybe you're in the wrong line of work."

"Or maybe you've been in this line of work too long," argued Juliet. "According to Butler, you used to be a bit of a wild card yourself."

Mulch emerged from the bathroom. This time he had been applying a layer of sun block. It was the middle of the night, but the dwarf wasn't taking any chances. If this insertion went haywire, as it probably would, then he could very well be on the run by morning.

"What's the problem, ladies? If you're fighting over me,

don't bother. I make it a point never to date outside my species."

The tension deflated like a punctured balloon.

"Dream on, hairball," said Holly.

"Nightmare, more like," added Juliet. "*I* make it a point never to date anyone who lives in a dung heap."

Mulch was unperturbed. "You're both in denial. I have that effect on females."

"I don't doubt it," said Holly, grinning.

The LEP captain unfolded a stowaway table and placed her helmet on top. She switched her helmet-cam to PROJECT, and opened the 3-D plan of the Spiro Needle. It revolved in the air, a lattice of neon-green lines.

"Okay, everyone. Here's the plan. Team one, burn your way in through the wall of the eighty-fifth floor. Here. Team two, go in through the helipad door. Here."

Holly marked the entrances by tapping the corresponding spot on the screen of her handheld computer. An orange pulse appeared on the floating plan.

"Foaly has agreed to help, so he'll be with us over the airwaves. Juliet, you take this handheld computer. You can use it to conference with us on the move. Just ignore the Gnommish symbols, we'll send you any files you need to view. Wear an earpiece though, to cut out the speakers. The last thing we need is computers beeping at the wrong moment. That little indent below the screen is a microphone. Whisper-sensitive, so no need to shout."

Juliet strapped the credit card–sized computer onto her wrist.

"What are the teams, and what are their objectives?"

Holly stepped into the 3-D image. Her body was surrounded by strobes of light.

"Team one goes after the security and switches the vault guards' oxygen canisters. Team two goes after the box. Simple. We go in pairs. You and Mulch. Artemis and me."

"Oh no," said Juliet, shaking her head. "I have to go with Artemis. He's my Principal. My brother would stick to Artemis like glue, and so will I."

Holly stepped out of the hologram. "Won't work. You can't fly and you can't climb walls. There has to be one fairy per team. If you don't like it, take it up with Artemis next time you see him."

Juliet scowled. It made sense. Of course it did. Artemis's plans always made sense. It was only too clear now why Artemis had not revealed the entire plan in Ireland. He knew she would object. It was bad enough being separated for the past six hours. But the most difficult phase of the mission lay ahead, and Artemis would not have a Butler at his shoulder.

Holly stepped back into the hologram. "Team one, you and Mulch, climb the Needle and burn through on the eighty-fifth floor. From there you place this video clip on a CCTV cable." Holly held up what looked like a twist of wire. "Loaded fiber optic," she explained. "Allows for remote hijacking of any video system. With this in place, Foaly can send the signal from every camera in the building to our helmets. He can also send the humans any signal he wants them to see. You will also replace two oxygen cylinders with our own special mix."

Juliet placed the video clip in her jacket pocket.

"I will enter from the roof," continued Holly. "From there I proceed to Artemis's room. As soon as Team one gives us the all clear, we'll go after the C Cube."

"You make it sound so easy," said Juliet.

Mulch laughed. "She always does that," he said. "And it never is."

At the base of the Spiro Needle

Juliet Butler had been trained in seven martial arts disciplines. She had learned to ignore pain and sleep deprivation. She could resist torture both physical and psychological. But nothing had prepared her for what she would have to endure to get into this building.

The Needle had no blind sides. There was twenty-four-hour activity on each face, so they were forced to begin their ascent from the sidewalk. Juliet pulled the van around, double-parking it as close to the wall as she could.

They went out through the sunroof, draped in Holly's single sheet of camouflage foil. Juliet was clipped onto the Moonbelt on Mulch's waist.

She rapped on Mulch's helmet. "You stink."

Mulch's reply came through the cylindrical transmitter in Juliet's ear. "To you maybe, but to a dwarf female, I am the essence of a healthy male. You're the one that stinks, Mud Girl. To me, you smell worse than a skunk in two-month-old socks."

Holly stuck her head through the sunroof.

"Quiet!" she hissed. "Both of you! We're on a tight schedule, in case you've forgotten. Juliet, your precious Principal is stuck in a room up there waiting for me to show up. It's five minutes past four already. The guards are due to change in less than an hour, and I still have to finish *mesmerising* these goons. We have a fifty-five-minute window here. Let's not waste it arguing."

"Why can't you just fly us up to the ledge?"

"Basic military tactics. If we split up, then one team might make it. If we're together, then if one goes down, we all go down. Divide and conquer."

Her words sobered Juliet. The fairy girl was right, she should have known that. It was happening again, she was losing concentration at a vital moment.

"Okay. Let's go. I'll hold my breath."

Mulch stuck both palms in his mouth, sucking any vestiges of moisture from the pores.

"Hold on," he said, having removed his hands from his palate. "Here we go."

The dwarf flexed his powerful legs, leaping five feet to

the wall of the Spiro Needle. Juliet bobbed along behind, feeling for all the world as though she were under water. The problem with riding a Moonbelt was that along with weightlessness came loss of coordination and sometimes space nausea, too. Moonbelts were designed for carrying inanimate objects, not live fairies, and certainly not human beings.

Mulch had not had a drink for several hours, causing his dwarf pores to open to the size of pinholes. They sucked noisily, latching onto the smooth external surface of the Spiro Needle. The dwarf avoided the tinted windows, sticking to the metal girders. Though the pair was draped in a sheet of camouflage foil, there were still enough limbs sticking out for them to be recognized. Camouflage foil did not render the wearer completely invisible. Thousands of microsensors threaded through the material analyzed and reflected the surroundings, but one shower of rain could short out the whole thing.

Mulch climbed quickly, settling into a smooth rhythm. His double-jointed fingers and toes curled to grip the smallest groove. And where there were no grooves, the dwarf's pores adhered to the flat surface. His beard hair fanned out under the helmet's visor, probing the building's face.

Juliet had to ask.

"Your beard? That's a bit freaky. What's it doing? Searching for cracks?"

"Vibrations," grunted Mulch. "Sensors, current, maintenance men."

Obviously he wasn't going to devote any energy to full sentences.

"Motion sensor picks us up, we're finished. Foil or not."

Juliet didn't blame her partner for saving his breath. They had a long way to go. Straight up.

The wind picked up as they cleared the buffer provided by the adjacent buildings. Juliet's feet were plucked from beneath her, and she fluttered from the dwarf's neck like a scarf. Rarely had she felt so helpless. Events were utterly beyond her control. Training counted for absolutely nothing in this situation. Her life was in Mulch's hands completely.

The floors slid by in a blur of glass and steel. The wind pulled at them with grabby fingers, threatening to spin the pair into the night.

"There's a lot of moisture up here, from the wind," gasped the dwarf. "I can't hold on much longer."

Juliet reached in, running a finger along the outer wall. It was slick with tiny beads of dew. Sparks were popping along the sheet of camouflage foil as the moisture-laden wind shorted out its microsensors. Patches of the foil failed altogether. The effect was like patches of circuits apparently suspended in the night. The entire building was swaying too, maybe just enough to shake off a tired dwarf and his passenger.

Finally, the dwarf's fingers locked onto the ledge of the

eighty-fifth floor. Mulch climbed onto the narrow outcropping, directing his visor into the building.

"This room is no good," he said. "My visor is detecting two motion detectors and a laser sensor. We need to move along."

He scampered down the ledge, surefooted as a mountain goat. This was his business after all. Dwarfs did not fall off things. Not unless they were pushed. Juliet followed cautiously. Not even Madam Ko's academy could have prepared her for this.

Finally, Mulch arrived at a window that satisfied him.

"Okay," he said, his voice strained through Juliet's earpiece. "We got a sensor with a dead battery."

His beard hair latched on to the windowpane. "I don't feel any vibration, so nothing electrical running and no conversation. It seems safe."

Mulch trickled a few drops of dwarf rock polish onto the toughened pane. It liquefied the glass immediately, leaving a puddle of turgid liquid on the carpet. With any luck the hole would remain undiscovered over the weekend.

"Ooh," said Juliet. "That stinks nearly as much as you do."

Mulch did not bother returning the insult, preferring instead to tumble indoors to safety.

He checked the moonometer in his visor.

"Four-twenty. Human time. We're behind schedule. Let's go."

⨁⥁⬡ • ⥝⬧⥥⬡ • ⟨⥋⥊⬡ • ⥝⬔⥮⟨⟃ • ⟨

Juliet hopped through the hole in the window.

"Typical Mud Man," said Mulch. "Spiro spends millions on a security system, and it all falls apart because of one battery."

Juliet drew an LEP Neutrino 2000. She flicked aside the safety cap and pressed the power button. A button light changed from green to red.

"We're not in yet," she said, making for the door.

"Wait!" hissed Mulch, grabbing her arm. "The camera!"

Juliet froze. She'd forgotten the camera. They were barely a minute inside the building and she was already making mistakes. *Concentrate, girl, concentrate.*

Mulch aimed his visor at the recessed CCTV camera. The helmet's ion filter highlighted the camera's arc as a shimmering gold stream. There was no way past to the camera itself.

"There's no blind spot," he said. "And the camera cable is behind the box."

"We'll just have to huddle close together behind the camouflage foil," said Juliet, her lip curling at the idea.

Foaly's image popped onto the computer screen on her wrist. "You could do that. But unfortunately, cam foil doesn't work on screen."

"Why not?"

"Cameras have better eyes than humans. Did you ever see a TV picture on television? The camera breaks down the pixels. If we go down that corridor behind camouflage foil, we're going to look like two people behind a projector screen."

Juliet glared at the screen. "Anything else, Foaly? Maybe the floor is going to dissolve into a pool of acid?"

"Doubt it. Spiro is good, but he's not me."

"Can't you loop the video feed, pony boy?" said Juliet into the computer's microphone. "Just send them a false signal for a minute?"

Foaly gnashed his horsy teeth. "I am so unappreciated. No, I cannot set up a loop unless I am on site, as I was during the Fowl siege. That is what the video clip is for. I'm afraid you're on your own up there."

"I'll blast it, then."

"Negatory. A neutrino blast would certainly knock out one camera, and possibly chain-react along the entire network. You may as well dance a jig for Arno Blunt."

Juliet kicked the skirting board in frustration. She was stumbling at the first hurdle. Her brother would know what to do, but he was on the other side of the Atlantic. A mere twenty feet of corridor separated them from the camera, but it might as well have been a mile of broken glass.

She noticed that Mulch was unbuttoning his bum flap.

"Oh, great. Now the little man needs a potty break. This is hardly the time."

"I'm going to ignore your sarcasm," said Mulch, lying flat on the floor. "Because I know what Spiro can do to people he doesn't like."

Juliet knelt beside him. Not too close.

"I hope your next sentence is going to begin with, 'I have a plan.'"

The dwarf appeared to be aiming his rear end.

"Actually . . ."

"You're not serious."

"Deadly. I have quite a considerable force at my disposal here."

Juliet couldn't help smiling. The little guy was a dwarf after her own heart. Metaphorically. He was adapting to the situation, just as she would.

"All we have to do is swing the camera about twenty degrees on its stand, and we have a clear run to the cable."

"And you're going to do that with . . . wind power?"

"Precisely."

"What about the noise?"

Mulch winked. "Silent but deadly. I'm a professional. All you have to do is squeeze my little toe, when I give you the word."

In spite of arduous training in some of the world's toughest terrain, Juliet was not quite prepared to be involved in a wind offensive.

"Do I have to participate? It seems like a one-man operation to me."

Mulch squinted at the target, adjusting his posterior accordingly.

"This is a precision burst. I need a gunner to pull the

trigger, so I can concentrate on aiming. Reflexology is a proven science with dwarfs. Every part of the foot is connected to a part of the body. And it just so happens that the left little toe is connected to my—"

"Okay," said Juliet hurriedly. "I get the picture."

"Let's get on with it, then."

Juliet pulled Mulch's boot off. The socks were open-toed, and five hairy digits wiggled with a dexterity no human toes possessed.

"This is the only way?"

"Unless you have a better idea."

Juliet gingerly grasped the toe, its black curly hairs obligingly parting to allow her access to the joint.

"Now?"

"Wait." The dwarf licked his forefinger, testing the air. "No wind."

"Not yet," muttered Juliet.

Mulch fine tuned his aim. "Okay. Squeeze."

Juliet held her breath, and closed her fingers around the joint. The pressure sped up Mulch's leg in a series of jolts. The dwarf fought to keep his aim true in spite of his thrashings. Pressure built in his abdomen and exploded through his bum flap with a dull thump. Juliet could only relate the experience to crouching beside a mortar. A missile of compressed air shot across the room, heat blur surrounding it like waves of water.

"Too much topspin," groaned Mulch. "I loaded it."

The air ball spiraled toward the ceiling, shedding layers like an onion.

"Go right," urged Mulch. "Right, a bit."

The unlikely missile impacted against the wall a meter ahead of its target. Luckily, the ricochet clipped the camera box, sending it spinning like a plate on a stick. The intruders waited with bated breath for it to settle. The camera finally creaked to a halt after a dozen revolutions.

"Well?" asked Juliet.

Mulch sat up, checking the camera's ion stream through his visor.

"Lucky," he breathed. "Very lucky. We have a path straight through." He slapped his smoking bum flap. "It's been a while since I launched a torpedo."

Juliet took the video clip from her pocket, waving it in front of her visor, so Foaly could see it.

"So, I just wind this around any old cable? Is that it?"

"No, Mud Maid," sighed Foaly, comfortable in his familiar role as unappreciated genius. "That is a complex piece of nanotechnology, complete with micro filaments that act as receivers, broadcasters, and clamps. Naturally, it leeches its power from the Mud Men's own system."

"Naturally," said Mulch, trying to keep his eyes open.

"You need to ensure that it is firmly clamped to one of the video cables. Luckily its multi-sensor does not have to be in contact with all the wires, just one."

"And which ones are the video wires?"

"Well . . . all of them."

Juliet groaned. "So I just wind it around any old cable?"

"I suppose so," admitted the centaur. "But wind it tightly. All the filaments have to penetrate."

Juliet reached up, selected a wire at random, and wound the clip around it.

"Okay?"

There was a moment's pause while Foaly waited for reception. Below the earth, picture-in-picture screens began popping up on the centaur's plasma screen.

"Perfect. We have eyes and ears."

"Let's go then," said Juliet impatiently. "Start the loop."

Foaly wasted a minute delivering another lecture. "This is much more than a loop, young lady. I am about to completely wipe moving patterns from the surveillance footage. In other words, the pictures they see in the surveillance booth will be exactly as they should be, except you won't be in them. Just be careful never to stand still or you'll become visible. Keep something moving, even if it's only your little finger."

Juliet checked the digital clock on the computer face. "Four-thirty. We need to hurry."

"Okay. The security center is one corridor over. We take the shortest route."

Juliet projected the schematic into the air. "Down this corridor here, two rights, and there we are."

Mulch strode past her to the wall.

"I said the shortest route, Mud Girl. Think laterally."

The office was an executive suite, with a skyline view and floor-to-ceiling pine shelving. Mulch hauled back a section of the pine and knocked on the wall behind it.

"Plaster board," he said. "No problem."

Juliet closed the door behind them. "No debris, dwarf. Artemis said we weren't to leave any trace."

"Don't worry. I'm not a messy eater."

Mulch unhinged his jaw, expanding his oral cavity to basketball proportions. He opened his mouth to an incredible one hundred and seventy degrees, and took a whopping bite out of the wall. A ring of tombstone teeth soon reduced the Sheetrock to dust.

"A b' dry," he commented. "Har' to swallow."

Three bites later, they were through. Mulch climbed into the next office without a crumb dropping from his lips. Juliet followed, pulling the pine shelving across to cover the hole.

The next office was not quite so salubrious, the dark cubby of a vice president. No city view, and plain metal shelving. Juliet rearranged the shelving to cover the newly excavated entrance. Mulch knelt at the door, his beard hair latching on to the wood.

"Some vibration outside. That's probably the compressor. Nothing irregular, so no conversation. I'd say we were safe."

"You could just ask me," said Foaly, in his helmet earpiece. "I do have footage from every camera in the building.

That's over two thousand, in case you're interested."

"Thanks for the update. Well, are we clear?"

"Yes. Remarkably so. Nothing on this floor, except a guard on the lobby desk."

Juliet took two gray canisters from her backpack. "Okay. This is where I earn my keep. You stay here. This shouldn't take more than a minute."

Juliet cracked open the door, creeping along the corridor on rubber-soled boots. Airplane-style lighting strips were inlaid in the carpet; otherwise the only lighting came from exit boxes over the fire escape doors.

The schematic on her wrist computer told her that she had twenty yards to go before reaching the security office. After that, she could only hope that the oxygen rack was unlocked. And why shouldn't it be? Oxygen canisters were hardly high-risk objects. At least she would have ample warning if any personnel happened to be doing their rounds.

Juliet crept pantherlike down the corridor, her footfalls muffled by the carpet.

On reaching the final corner, she lay flat, inching her nose around the bend. She could see the floor's security station. Just as Pex had revealed under the *mesmer,* the vault guard's oxygen canisters were slotted in a rack in front of the desk.

There was only one guard on duty, and he was busy watching basketball on a portable television. Juliet inched forward on her stomach until she was directly below the rack. The guard had his back to her, concentrating on the game.

"What the hell?" exclaimed the security man, who was roughly the size of a refrigerator. He had noticed something in a security monitor.

"Move!" hissed Foaly in Juliet's earpiece.

"What?"

"Move! You're showing up on the monitors."

Juliet wiggled her toe. She had forgotten to keep moving. Butler would never have forgotten that.

Over her head, the guard employed the age-old method of rapid repair, slapping the monitor's plastic casing. The fuzzy figure disappeared.

"Interference," he muttered. "Stupid satellite TV."

Juliet felt a bead of sweat run along the bridge of her nose. The younger Butler reached up slowly and slipped two substitute oxygen canisters into the rack. *Oxygen canisters* was a bit of misnomer, because there was no oxygen in these canisters.

She checked her watch. It might already be too late.

Above the Spiro Needle

Holly hovered twenty feet above the Needle, waiting for the green light. She was not comfortable with this operation. There were too many variables. If this mission wasn't so vital to the future of the fairy civilization, she would have refused to participate in it altogether.

Her mood did not improve as the night progressed. Team one was proving extremely unprofessional, bickering like a pair of adolescents. Although, to be fair to Juliet, she was barely beyond adolescence. Mulch on the other hand couldn't have found his childhood with an encyclopedia.

Captain Short followed team one's progress on her helmet visor, wincing at each new development. Finally, and against all the odds, Juliet managed to switch the canisters.

"Go," said Mulch, doing his best to sound military. "I say again, we have a go situation on the black op' code-red thing."

Holly shut off Mulch's communication in the middle of the dwarf's giggling fit. Foaly could open a screen in her visor if there was a crisis.

Below her the Spiro Needle pointed spaceward like the world's biggest rocket. Low fog gathered around its base, adding to the illusion. Holly set her wings to descend, dropping gently toward the helipad. She called up the video file of Artemis's entry to the Needle on her visor and slowed it down at the point where Spiro keyed in the access code for the rooftop door.

"Thank you, Spiro," she grinned, punching in the key.

The door slid open silently. Automatic lights flickered into life along the stairwell. There was a camera every twenty feet. No blind spots. This didn't matter to Holly, as human cameras could not detect a shielded fairy, unless they were of the type with an extremely high frame-per-second rate. And even then, the frames had to be viewed as stills to catch a glimpse of the fairy folk. Only one human had ever managed to do this. An Irish one, who had been twelve years old at the time.

Holly floated down the stairwell, activating an argon-laser filter on her visor. This entire building could be criss-crossed with laser beams and she wouldn't know it until she set off an alarm. Even a shielded fairy had mass enough to stop a beam reaching its sensor, if only for a millisecond. The view before her turned a cloudy purple, but there were no beams. She was certain that wouldn't be the case when they came to the vault.

Holly continued her flight to the brushed-steel elevator doors.

"Artemis is on eighty-four," said Foaly. "The vault is on eighty-five, and Spiro's penthouse is on eighty-six, where we are now."

"How are the walls?"

"According to the spectrometer, mostly Sheetrock, steel studs, and wood paneling in the partition walls. Except around key rooms, which are reinforced steel."

"Let me guess; Artemis's room, the vault, and Spiro's penthouse."

"Dead on, Captain. But do not despair. I have plotted the shortest course. I am sending it to your helmet now."

• 🜨)(• 🜏)(• 🜏 🜍 • 🜹 ⸘ 🜼 🜲 • 🜏 ⊙)(⸰⸰ 🜳)(

Holly waited a moment until a quill icon flashed in the corner of her visor, informing her that she had mail.

"Open mail," she said into the helmet mike, enunciating clearly. A matrix of green lines superimposed themselves in front of her regular vision. Her trail was marked by a thick red line.

"Follow the laser, Holly. Foolproof. No offense."

"None taken, for now. But if this doesn't work, I'll be so offended, you won't believe it."

The red laser led straight into the belly of the elevator. Holly floated into the metal box and descended to the eighty-fifth floor. The guiding laser led her out of the elevator and down the corridor.

She tried the door to an office on her left. Locked. Hardly surprising.

"I'm going to have to unshield to pick this lock. Are you sure my pattern is wiped from the video?"

"Of course," said Foaly. Holly could imagine the childish pout on his lips.

Holly unshielded and took an omnitool from her belt. The omnitool's sensor would send an X-ray of the lock's workings to the chip and select the right bit. It even did the turning. Of course, the omnitool only worked on keyhole locks, which, in spite of their unreliability, the Mud Men still used.

In less than five seconds, the door lay open before her.

"Five seconds," said Holly. "This thing needs a new battery."

The red line in her visor ran to the office's center, and then took a right-angle turn downward through the floor.

"Let me guess. Artemis is down there."

"Yes. Asleep, judging by the pictures coming in on his iris-cam."

"You said the cell was lined with reinforced steel."

"True. But no motion sensors in the walls or roof. So all you have to do is burn through."

Holly drew her Neutrino 2000. "Oh, is that all?"

She chose a spot adjacent to a wall air conditioner and peeled back the carpet. Underneath the floor was dull and metallic.

"No trace, remember?" said Foaly in her earpiece. "That's vital."

"I'll worry about that later," said Holly, adjusting the AC to EXTRACT. "For now, I need to get him out of there. We're on a schedule."

Holly adjusted the Neutrino's output, concentrating the beam so it cut through the metal floor. Acrid smoke billowed from the molten gash, and was immediately siphoned off into the Chicago night by the AC.

"Artemis isn't the only one with brains around here," grunted Holly, sweat streaming down her face in spite of the helmet's climate control.

"The AC stops the fire alarm going off. Very good."

"Is he awake?" asked Holly, leaving the last inch of a two-foot square uncut.

𐌀𐌃𐌄𐌁𐌅𐌆𐌇𐌈 • 𐌉𐌊𐌋𐌌𐌍 • 𐌎𐌏𐌐𐌑𐌒 •

"Wide-eyed and bushy-tailed, to use centaurian imagery. A laser carving through the ceiling will do that to a person."

"Good," said Captain Short, cutting through the final section. The metal square twisted on a final strand of steel.

"Won't that make a lot of noise?" asked Foaly.

Holly watched the section fall.

"I doubt it," she said.

CHAPTER 10

FINGERS AND THUMBS

The Spiro Needle, Artemis Fowl's cell

Artemis was meditating when the first laser stroke cut through the ceiling. He rose from the lotus position, pulled a sweater over his pajamas and arranged some pillows on the floor. Moments later, a square of metal fell to the floor, its impact silenced by the cushions. Holly's face appeared in the hole.

Artemis pointed at the pillows. "You anticipated me."

The LEP captain nodded. "Only thirteen, and already predictable."

"I presume you used the air conditioner to vacuum the smoke?"

"Exactly. I think we're getting to know one another too well."

88 ⵌ • ⵂ ⳤⵕⵕ # • ⵊ ⵙⵕⵞⵟⵕⵕ • ⵂⵕⵙ ⵝⵝⵛ⯑

Holly reeled a piton line from her belt, lowering it into the room.

"Make a loop at the bottom with the clamp, and hop aboard. I'll reel you in."

Artemis did as he was told, and in seconds he was clambering through the hole.

"Do we have Mr. Foaly on our side?" he asked.

Holly handed Artemis a small cylindrical earpiece. "Ask him yourself."

Artemis inserted the miracle of nanotechnology.

"Well, Foaly. Astound me."

Below in Haven City, the centaur rubbed his hands together. Artemis was the only one who actually understood his lectures.

"You're going to love this, Mud Boy. Not only have I wiped you from the video, not only did I erase the ceiling falling in, but I have created a simulated Artemis."

Artemis was intrigued. "A sim? Really? How exactly did you do that?"

"Simple really," said Foaly modestly. "I have hundreds of human movies on file. I borrowed Steve McQueen's solitary-confinement scene from *The Great Escape* and altered his clothes."

"What about the face?"

"I had some digital interrogation footage from your last visit to Haven. I put the two together, and voilà. Our simulated Artemis can do whatever I tell him, whenever I say.

At the moment, the sim is asleep, but in half an hour I may just instruct him to go to the bathroom."

Holly reeled in her piton cord. "The miracle of modern science. The LEP pours millions into your department, Foaly, and all you can do is send Mud Boys to the toilet."

"You should be nice to me, Holly. I'm doing you a big favor. If Julius knew I was helping you, he'd be extremely angry."

"Which is exactly why you are doing it."

Holly moved quietly to the door, opening it a crack. The corridor was clear and silent, but for the drone of panning cameras and the hum of fluorescent lighting. One section of Holly's visor displayed miniature transparent feeds from Spiro's security cameras. There were eight guards doing the rounds on the floor.

Holly closed the door.

"Okay. Let's get going. We need to reach Spiro before the guards change."

Artemis arranged the carpet over the hole in the floor. "Have you located his apartment?"

"Directly above us. We need to get up there and scan his retina and thumb."

An expression flashed across Artemis's face. Just for a second.

"The scans. Yes. The sooner the better."

Holly had never seen that look on the human boy's features before. Was it guilt? Could it be?

· ꕮ ꖛ · ⸝⸝⸾⸟⸟ · ⟩⟨⸝⸟⸟ · ⩓⸟⸟ · ⟩⟨ ⸻⸻ · ⟩⟨

"Is there something you're not telling me?" she demanded.

The expression vanished, to be replaced by the customary lack of emotion.

"No, Captain Short. Nothing. And do you really think that now is the time for an interrogation?"

Holly wagged a threatening finger. "Artemis. If you mess with me now, in the middle of an operation, I won't forget it."

"Don't worry," said Artemis wryly. "I will."

Spiro's apartment was directly above Artemis's cell. It would have made sense to reinforce the same block. Unfortunately, Jon Spiro did not like the idea of anyone spying on him, so there were no cameras in his section of the building.

"Typical," muttered Foaly. "Power-crazed megalomaniacs never like anyone to see their own dirty secrets."

"I think someone's in denial," said Holly, focusing a tight beam from her Neutrino at the ceiling.

A section of floating ceiling melted like ice in a kettle, revealing the steel above. Molten beads of metal ate into the carpet as the laser sliced through the flooring. When the hole was of sufficient diameter, Holly shut down the beam and popped her helmet camera into the space.

Nothing appeared on the screen.

"Switching to infrared."

A rack of suits sprang into focus. They might have been white.

"The wardrobe. We're in the wardrobe."

"Perfect," said Foaly. "Put him to sleep."

"He *is* asleep. It's twenty-to-five in the morning."

"Well, make sure he doesn't wake up then."

Holly replaced the camera in its groove. She plucked a silver capsule from her belt and inserted it into the hole.

Foaly supplied the commentary for Artemis.

"The capsule is a Sleeper Deeper, in case you're wondering."

"Gaseous?"

"No. Brain waves."

Artemis was intrigued. "Go on."

"Basically it scans for brain-wave patterns, then replicates them. Anyone in the vicinity stays in the state they're in until the capsule dissolves."

"No trace?"

"None. And no aftereffects. Whatever they're paying me, it isn't enough."

Holly counted off a minute on her visor clock.

"Okay. He's out, providing he wasn't awake when the Sleeper Deeper went in. Let's go."

Spiro's bedroom was as white as his suits, except for the charred hole in the wardrobe. Holly and Artemis climbed through onto a white shag carpet. They stepped through the doors of the closet into a room that glowed in the dark. Futuristic furniture: white, of course. White spotlights and white drapes.

Holly took a moment to study a painting that dominated one wall.

"Oh, give me a break," she said.

The picture was in oils. Completely white. There was a brass plaque beneath. It read, *Snow Ghost*.

Spiro lay in the center of a huge futon, lost in the dunes of its silk sheets. Holly pulled back the covers, rolling Jon Spiro onto his back. Even in sleep the man's face was malevolent, as though his dreams were every bit as despicable as his waking thoughts.

"Nice guy," said Holly, using her thumb to raise Spiro's left eyelid. Her helmet camera scanned the eye, storing the information on its chip. It would be a simple matter to project the file onto the vault's scanner and fool the security computer.

The thumb scan would not be so simple. Because the device was a gel scanner, the tiny sensors would be searching for the actual ridges and whorls of Spiro's thumb. A projection would not do. It had to be 3-D. Artemis had come up with the idea of using a latex memory bandage, standard issue in any LEP first-aid kit—the same latex used to glue the microphone to his throat. All they had to do was wrap Spiro's thumb in a bandage for a moment and they would have a mold of the digit. Holly spooled a bandage from her belt, tearing off a six-inch strip.

"It won't work," said Artemis.

Holly's heart sank. This was it. The thing that Artemis hadn't told her.

⯎ • ⬡⬢⬙⬗⬔⯎⬚⬘⬕ • ⬙ • ⬛⬟⬞⬝⬜⯎⬛⬚⬙

"What won't work?"

"The memory latex. It won't fool the gel scanner."

Holly climbed off the futon. "I don't have time for this, Artemis. *We* don't have time for it. The memory latex will make a perfect copy, right down to the last molecule."

Artemis's eyes were downcast. "A perfect model, true, but in reverse. Like a photo negative. Ridges where there should be grooves."

"D'Arvit!" swore Holly. The Mud Boy was right. Of course he was. The scanner would read the latex as a completely different thumbprint. Her cheeks glowed red behind the visor.

"You knew this, Mud Boy. You knew it all along."

Artemis didn't bother denying it. "I'm amazed no one else spotted it."

"So why lie?"

Artemis walked around to the far side of the bed, grasping Spiro's right hand. "Because there is no way to fool the gel scanner. It has to see the real thumb."

Holly snorted. "What do you want me to do? Cut it off and take it with us?"

Artemis's silence was response enough.

"What? You want me to cut off his thumb? Are you insane?"

Artemis waited patiently for the outburst to pass.

"Listen to me, Captain. It's only a temporary measure. The thumb can be reattached. True?"

Holly raised her palms. "Just shut up, Artemis. Just close your mouth. And I thought you'd changed. The commander was right. There's no changing human nature."

"Four minutes," persisted Artemis. "We have four minutes to crack the vault and get back. Spiro won't feel a thing."

Holly felt as though her helmet were shrinking.

"Artemis, I'll stun you, so help me."

"Think, Holly. I had no choice but to lie about my plan. Would you have agreed if I had told you earlier?"

"No. And I'm not agreeing now."

Artemis's face glowed as pale as the walls. "You have to, Captain. There is no other way."

Holly waved Artemis away as though he were a persistent fly, and spoke into her helmet mike.

"Foaly, are you listening to this insanity?"

"It sounds insane, Holly, but if you don't get this technology back we could lose a whole lot more than a thumb."

"I can't believe it. Whose side are you on, Foaly? I don't even want to think about the legal ramifications of this."

The centaur snickered. "Legal ramifications? We're a tad beyond the court systems here, Captain. This is a secret operation. No records and no clearance. If this came out, we'd all be out of a job. A thumb here or there is not going to make any difference."

Holly turned on the climate control in her helmet, directing a blast of cold air at her forehead.

"Are you sure we can make it, Artemis?"

Artemis ran a few mental calculations. "Yes. I'm sure. And anyway, we have no option but to try."

Holly crossed to the other side of the futon.

"I can't believe I'm even considering this." She lifted Spiro's hand gently. He did not react, not so much as a sleep murmur. Behind his eyelids, Spiro's eyes jittered in REM sleep.

Holly drew her weapon. Of course, in theory it was perfectly feasible to remove a digit and then magically reattach it. There would be no harm done, and quite possibly the injection of magic would clear up a few of the liver spots on Spiro's hand. But that wasn't the point. This was not how magic was supposed to be used. Artemis was manipulating the People to his own ends, once again.

"Six-inch beam," said Foaly in her ear. "Very high frequency. We need a clean cut. And give him a shot of magic while you're doing it. It might buy you a couple of minutes."

For some reason, Artemis was checking behind Spiro's ears.

"Hmm," he said. "Clever."

"What?" hissed Holly. "What now?"

Artemis stepped back. "Nothing important. Continue."

Four minutes was the textbook healing deadline. After that there was no guarantee that the thumb would take. The skin would bind, but the muscles and nerve endings could reject.

A red glow reflected from her visor as a short burst of concentrated laser beam erupted from the nozzle of her Neutrino.

"One cut," said Artemis. "Clean."

Holly glared at him. "Don't, Mud Boy. Not a word. Especially not advice."

Artemis backed off. Certain battles were won by retreating.

Using her left thumb and forefinger, Holly made a circle around Spiro's thumb. She sent a gentle pulse of magic into the human's hand. In seconds the skin tightened, lines disappeared, and muscle tone returned.

"Filter," she said into her microphone. "X-ray."

The filter dropped, and suddenly everything was transparent, including Spiro's hand. The bones and joints were clearly visible below the skin. They only needed the print, so she would cut between the knuckles. It would be difficult enough reattaching under pressure without adding a complex joint into the equation.

Holly took a breath and held it. The Sleeper Deeper would act more effectively than any anesthetic. Spiro would not flinch or feel the smallest jolt of discomfort. She made the cut. A smooth cut that sealed as it went. Not a drop of blood was spilled.

Artemis wrapped the thumb in a handkerchief from Spiro's closet.

"Nice work," he said. "Let's go. The clock is ticking."

)(• ⚌ ⚇ ⚈)(⚗ ⚆ ⚒ •)(⚆ ⚄ ⚈ • ⟨ ⚌

* * *

Artemis and Holly climbed through the wardrobe to the eighty-fifth. There was almost a mile and a half of corridor on this floor, and six guards patrolling it in pairs at any time. Their routes were specially planned so that one pair would always have an eyeball sighting of the vault door. The vault corridor was a hundred yards long and took eighty seconds to travel. At the end of that eighty seconds, the next pair of guards stepped around the corner. Luckily, two of the guards were seeing things in a different light this particular morning.

Foaly gave them their cue.

"Okay. Our boys are approaching their corner."

"Are you sure it's them? These gorillas all look the same. Small heads, no necks."

"I'm sure. Their targets are showing up bright and clear."

Holly had painted Pex and Chips with a stamp generally used by customs and immigration for invisible visas. The stamps glowed orange when viewed through an infrared filter.

Holly pushed Artemis out the door in front of her. "Okay. Go. And no sarcastic comments."

There was no need for the warning. Even Artemis Fowl was not inclined to be sarcastic at such a dangerous stage of the plan.

He ran down the corridor straight toward the two mammoth security guards. Their jackets protruded angularly beneath their armpits. Guns no doubt. Big ones with lots of bullets.

"Are you sure they're *mesmerized*?" he asked Holly, who was hovering overhead.

"Of course. Their minds are so blank it was like writing with chalk on a board. But I could stun them, if you'd prefer."

"No," panted Artemis. "No trace. There must be no trace."

Pex and Chips were closer now, comparing the merits of various fictional characters.

"Captain Hook rocks," said Pex. "He would kick Barney's purple butt ten times out of ten."

Chips sighed. "You're missing the whole point of Barney. It's a values thing. Butt-kicking is not the issue."

They walked right past Artemis without seeing him. And why would they see him? Holly had *mesmerized* them not to notice anybody out of the ordinary on this floor, unless they were specifically pointed out to them.

The outer security booth lay before them. There were approximately forty seconds left before the next set of guards turned the corner. The *unmesmerized* set.

"Just over half a minute, Holly. You know what to do."

Holly turned up the thermo coils in her suit so they were exactly at room temperature. This would fool the lattice of lasers that crisscrossed the vault's entrance. Next, she set her wings to a gentle hover. Any more downdraught could activate the pressure pad underfoot. She pulled herself forward, finding purchase along the wall where her helmet told her no sensors were hidden. The pressure pad trembled from the air displacement, but not enough to activate the sensor.

Artemis watched her progress impatiently.

"Hurry, Holly. Twenty seconds."

Holly grunted something unprintable, dragging herself to within touching distance of the door.

"Video file Spiro three," she said, and her helmet computer ran the footage of Jon Spiro punching in the vault door code. She mimicked his actions, and inside the steel door six reinforced pistons retracted, allowing the counterweighted door to swing wide on its hinges. All external alarms were automatically shut off. The secondary door stood firm, three red lights burning on its panel. Only three barriers left now. The gel pad, the retina scan, and the voice activation.

This kind of operation was too complicated for voice command. Foaly's computers had been known to misinterpret orders, even though the centaur insisted it was fairy error. Holly ripped back the Velcro strap covering the helmet command pad on her wrist.

First, she projected a 3-D image of Spiro's eyeball to a height of five feet six. The retina scanner sent out a revolving beam to read the virtual eyeball. Apparently satisfied, it disabled the first lock. A red light switched to green.

The next step was to call up the appropriate sound-wave file to trick the voice check. The equipment was very sophisticated, and could not be fooled by a recording. A human recording, that is. Foaly's digital microphones made copies that were indistinguishable from the real thing. Even stink worms, whose entire bodies were covered with ears, could be attracted by a worm-mating hiss from Foaly's recording equipment. He was currently in negotiation with a fairy insect collection agency for the rights.

Holly played the file through her helmet speakers. "Jon Spiro. I am the boss, so open up quick."

Alarm number two disengaged. Another green light.

"Excuse me, Captain," said Artemis, an undercurrent of apprehension creeping into his voice. "We're almost out of time."

He unwrapped the thumb and stepped past Holly onto the red floor plate. Artemis pressed the thumb into the scanner. Green gel oozed into the severed digit's whorls. The alarm display flashed green. It had worked. Of course it had. The thumb was genuine, after all.

But nothing else happened. The door did not open.

Holly punched Artemis in the shoulder.

"Well? Are we in?"

"Apparently not. The punching is not helping my concentration, by the way."

Artemis glared at the console. What had he missed? *Think, boy, think.* Put those famed brain cells to work. He leaned closer to the secondary door, shifting his weight from his back leg. Beneath him, the red plate squeaked.

"Of course!" exclaimed Artemis. He grabbed Holly, hugging her close.

"It's not just a red marker," he explained hurriedly. "It's weight sensitive."

Artemis was right. Their combined mass was close enough to Spiro's own to hoodwink the scales. Obviously a mechanical device—a computer would never have been fooled. The secondary door slid into its groove below their feet.

Artemis handed Holly the thumb.

"Go," he said. "Spiro's time is running out. I'm right behind you."

Holly took the thumb. "And if you're not?"

"Then we go to plan B."

Holly nodded slowly. "Let's hope we don't have to."

"Let's hope."

Artemis strode into the vault. He ignored the fortune in jewels and bearer bonds, heading straight for the Cube's Plexiglas prison. There were two bullish security guards blocking the way. Both men had oxygen masks strapped over their faces and were unnaturally still.

"Excuse me, gentlemen. Would either of you mind if I borrowed Mr. Spiro's Cube?"

Neither man responded. Not so much as a flicker of an eyebrow. This was undoubtedly because of the paralytic gas in their oxygen tanks, concocted from the venom of a nest of Peruvian spiders. The gas was similar in chemical make-up to a salve used by South American natives as anesthetic.

Artemis keyed in the code, which Foaly was reciting in his ear, and the Plexiglas case slid open. The four sides of the Plexiglas box descended into the column on silent motors, leaving the C Cube unprotected. He reached out a hand for the box. . . .

Spiro's bedroom

Holly climbed through the wardrobe into Spiro's bedroom. The industrialist lay in the same position in which she had left him, his breath regular and normal. The stopwatch on Holly's visor read 3:57 and counting. Just in time.

Holly unwrapped the thumb gingerly, aligning it with the rest of the digit. Spiro's hand felt cold and unhealthy to her touch. She used the magnification filter in her visor to zoom in on the severed thumb. As close as she could figure, the two halves were lined up.

"Heal," she said, and the magical sparks erupted from the tips of her fingers, sinking into the two halves of Spiro's thumb. Threads of blue light stitched the dermis and epidermis together, fresh skin breaking through the old to conceal the cut. The thumb began to vibrate and bubble. Steam vented from the pores, forming a mist around Spiro's hand. His arm shook violently, the shock traveling across his bony chest. Spiro's back arched until Holly thought it would snap, then the industrialist collapsed onto the bed. Throughout the entire process, his heart never skipped a beat.

A few stray sparks skipped along Spiro's body like stones on a pond, targeting the areas behind both ears, exactly where Artemis had been looking earlier. Curious, Holly pulled back one ear to reveal a crescent-shaped scar, rapidly being erased by the magic. There was a matching scar behind the other ear.

Holly used her visor to zoom in on one of the scars. "Foaly. What do you make of these?"

"Surgery," replied the centaur. "Maybe our friend Spiro got himself a face lift. Or maybe . . ."

"Or maybe it's not Spiro," completed Holly, switching to Artemis's channel. "Artemis. It's not Spiro. It's a double. Do you hear me? Respond, Artemis."

Artemis didn't reply. Maybe because he wouldn't, maybe because he couldn't.

The vault

Artemis reached out a hand for the box, and a false wall hissed back pneumatically. Behind it stood Jon Spiro and Arno Blunt. Spiro's smile was so wide he could have swallowed a slice of watermelon.

He clapped his hands, jewelry jangling. "Bravo, Master

Fowl. Some of us didn't think you'd make it this far."

Blunt took a hundred-dollar bill from his wallet and handed it to Spiro.

"Thank you very much, Arno. I hope this teaches you not to bet against the house."

Artemis nodded thoughtfully. "In the bedroom. That was a double."

"Yes. Costa, my cousin. We've got the same-shaped head—one or two cuts and we could be peas in a pod."

"So you set the gel scanner to accept his print."

"For one night only. I wanted to see how far you'd get. You're an amazing kid, Arty. No one has ever made it into the vault before, and you'd be amazed how many professionals have tried. There are obviously a few glitches in my system, something the security people will have to look at. How did you get in here anyway? You don't appear to have Costa with you."

"Trade secret."

Spiro stepped down from a low platform. "No matter. We'll review the tapes. There are bound to be a couple of cameras you couldn't rig. One thing is for sure, you didn't do it without help. Check him for an earpiece, Arno."

It took Blunt less than five seconds to find the earpiece. He plucked it out triumphantly, crushing the tiny cylinder beneath his boot.

Spiro sighed. "I have no doubt, Arno, that that little electronic wonder was worth more than you will make in a lifetime. I don't know why I keep you around. I really don't."

Blunt grimaced. His teeth were Plexiglas and half filled with blue oil. A macabre wave machine.

"Sorry, Mr. Spiro."

"You will be sorrier still, my dentally challenged friend," said Artemis. "Because Butler is coming."

Blunt took an involuntary step backward.

"Don't think that mumbo jumbo is scaring me. Butler is dead. I saw him go down."

"Go down, perhaps. But did you see him die? If I remember the sequence of events correctly, after you shot Butler, he shot you."

Blunt touched the sutures on his temple. "A lucky shot."

"Lucky? Butler is a proud marksman. I wouldn't say that to his face."

Spiro laughed delightedly. "The kid is messing with your mind, Arno. Thirteen years old and he's playing you like a grand piano in Carnegie Hall. Get yourself a spine, man, you're supposed to be a professional."

Blunt tried to pull himself together, but the ghost of Butler haunted his features.

Spiro plucked the C Cube from its cushion. "This is fun, Arty. All this tough talk and repartee, but it doesn't mean anything. I win again, you've been outflanked. This has all been a game to me. Amusement. Your little operation has been most educational, if pathetic. But you gotta realize that it's over now. You're on your own, and I don't have time for any more games!"

Artemis sighed, the picture of defeat. "All of this has been a lesson, hasn't it? Just to show me who's boss."

"Exactly. It takes some people a while to learn. I find that the smarter the enemy, the bigger the ego. You had to realize that you were no match for me before you would do what I have asked." Spiro placed a bony hand on the Irish boy's shoulder. Artemis could feel the weight of his jewelry. "Now, listen carefully, kid. I want you to unlock this Cube. No more blarney. I never met a computer nerd yet who didn't leave himself a back door. You open this baby up now, or I'm gonna stop being amused, and believe me, you don't want that."

Artemis took the blue Cube in both hands, staring at its flat screen. This was the delicate phase of his plan. Spiro had to believe that once again he had outmaneuvered Artemis Fowl.

"Do it, Arty. Do it now."

Artemis ran a hand across his dry lips.

"Very well. I need a minute."

Spiro patted his shoulder. "I'm a generous man. Take two." He nodded at Blunt. "Stay close, Arno, I don't want our little friend setting any more booby traps."

Artemis sat at a stainless-steel table, exposing the Cube's inner workings. He quickly manipulated a complicated bunch of fiber optics, removing one strand altogether. The LEP blocker. After less than a minute, he resealed the Cube.

• ⟨𝄐 ⊰ ⟩ ⟨𝄐 ⟩ • ⟩⟨ ⟨𝄐 ⟨ ⟨𝄐 • ⟩𝄐 ⟨𝄐 " ⟨𝄐 ⟨𝄐 • ⟨𝄐 ⟩ •

Spiro's eyes were wide with anticipation, and dreams of unlimited wealth danced in his brain.

"Good news, Arty. I want good news only."

Artemis was more subdued now, as if the reality of his situation had finally eaten through his cockiness.

"I rebooted it. It's working. Except . . ."

Spiro waved his hands. Bracelets tinkled like cat bells. "Except! This better be an itty-bitty except kinda thing."

"It's nothing. Hardly worth mentioning. I had to revert to version 1.0. Version 1.2 was coded strictly to my voice patterns; 1.0 is less secure, if a bit more temperamental."

"Temperamental. You're a box, not my grandmother, Cube."

"I am not a box!" said Foaly, the Cube's new voice, thanks to the removed blocker. "I am a marvel of artificial intelligence. I live, therefore I learn."

"See what I mean?" said Artemis weakly. The centaur was going to blow it. Spiro's suspicions must not be aroused at this stage.

Spiro glared at the Cube as though it were an underling.

"Are you gonna give me attitude, Mister?"

The Cube did not reply.

"You have to address it by name," explained Artemis. "Otherwise it would answer every question within hearing distance of its sensors."

"And what is its name?"

Juliet often used the expression *duh*. Artemis never used

such colloquialisms himself, but it would have been apt at this particular moment.

"Its name is Cube."

"Okay, Cube. Are you going to give me attitude?"

"I will give you whatever it is in my processor's capacity to give."

Spiro rubbed his palms with childish glee, jewelry flashing like ripples in a sunset sea.

"Okay, let's try this baby out. Cube, can you tell me, are there any satellites monitoring the building?"

Foaly was silent for a moment. Artemis could imagine him calling up his sat-track information on a screen. "Just one at the moment, though judging from the ion trails, this building has been hit with more rays than the Millennium Falcon."

Spiro shot Artemis a glance.

"His personality chip is faulty," explained the boy. "That's why I discontinued him—it. We can fix that at any time."

Spiro nodded. He didn't want his very own technological genie growing the personality of a gorilla.

"What about that group, the LEP, Cube?" he asked. "They were monitoring me in London. Are they watching?"

"The LEP? That's a Lebanese satellite TV network," said Foaly, following Artemis's instructions. "Game shows mostly. Their footprint doesn't reach this far."

"Okay, forget about them, Cube. I need to know that satellite's serial number."

· 𐌄𐌋𐌉𐌆𐌂 · 𐌆 𐌀𐌄 𐌂𐌊𐌆 · 𐌅𐌊 · 𐌅𐌂𐌉𐌋 · 𐌀𐌄 · 𐌉𐌃 𐌆𐌆

Foaly consulted his screen.

"Ah . . . Let me see. U.S., registered to the Federal Government. Number ST1147W."

Spiro clenched both fists. "Yes! Correct. I happen to already have that information myself. Cube, you have passed my test."

The billionaire danced around the laboratory, reduced to childish displays by his greed.

"I'm telling you, Arty, this has taken years off me! I feel like putting on a tuxedo and going to the prom."

"Indeed."

"I don't know where to start. Should I make my own money? Or should I rip off somebody else's?"

Artemis forced a smile. "The world is your oyster."

Spiro patted the Cube gently. "Exactly. That's exactly what it is. And I'm going to take every pearl it has to offer."

Pex and Chips arrived at the vault door, guns drawn.

"Mr. Spiro!" stammered Pex. "Is this some kind of drill?"

Spiro laughed. "Oh, look. Here come the cavalry. An eternity too late. No, this is not a drill. And I would dearly love to know how little Artemis here got past you two!"

The hired muscle stared at Artemis as though he had just appeared from nowhere. Which for their *mesmerized* brains, he had.

"I don't know, Mr. Spiro. We never saw him. You want I should take him outside for a little accident?"

Spiro laughed, a short nasty bark. "I got a new word for

you two dumbbells. *Expendable.* You are and he isn't, just yet. Get it? So just stand there and look dangerous, otherwise I may replace you with two shaved gorillas."

Spiro gazed into the Cube's screen, as though there were nobody else in the room. "I reckon I've got twenty years left in me. After that the world can go to hell as far as I'm concerned. I have no family, no heirs. There's no need to build for the future. I'm going to suck this planet dry, and with this Cube I can do whatever I want to whoever I want."

"I know the first thing I'd do," said Pex. His eyes seemed surprised that the words were coming out of his mouth.

Spiro froze. He wasn't used to being interrupted in mid-rant.

"What would you do, dumbbell?" he said. "Buy yourself a booth at Merv's Rib 'n' Roast?"

"No," said Pex. "I'd stick it to those Phonetix guys. They've been rubbing Spiro Industries' nose in it for years."

It was an electric moment. Not only because Pex had actually had an idea, but because it was actually a good one.

The notion lit a thoughtful spark in Spiro's eyes.

"Phonetix. I hate those guys. Nothing would give me greater satisfaction than to destroy that bunch of second-rate phone freaks. But how?"

Now it was Chips's turn. "I hear they're working on a new top-secret communicator. Super-life battery, or something."

Spiro did a double take. First Pex, now Chips. Next

thing you knew, they'd be learning to read. Nevertheless . . .

"Cube," said Spiro. "I want you to access the Phonetix database. Copy the schematics for all their projects in development."

"No can do, bossman. Phonetix is operating on a closed system. No Internet connection whatsoever in their R and D Department. I have to be on site."

Spiro's euphoria disappeared. He rounded on Artemis.

"What is he talking about?"

Artemis coughed, clearing his throat. "The Cube cannot scan a closed system unless the omni-sensor is actually touching the computer, or at least close by. Phonetix is so paranoid about hackers that their research and development lab is completely contained. Buried under several floors of solid rock. They don't even have e-mail. I know because I've tried to hack it myself a few times."

"But the Cube scanned the satellite, didn't it?"

"The satellite is broadcasting. And if it's broadcasting, the Cube can trace it."

Spiro toyed with the links of his ID chain. "So, I'd have to go to Phonetix."

"I wouldn't recommend it," said Artemis. "It's a lot to risk for the sake of a personal vendetta."

Blunt stepped forward. "Let me go, Mr. Spiro. I'll get those plans."

Spiro chewed on a handful of vitamin supplements from a dispenser on his belt.

"It's a nice idea, Arno. Good work. But I am reluctant to hand control of the Cube over to anyone else. Who knows what temptation they might yield to? Cube, can you disable the Phonetix alarm system?"

"Can a dwarf blow a hole in his pants?"

"What was that?"

"Eh . . . nothing. Technical term. You wouldn't understand it. I have already disabled the Phonetix system."

"What about the guards, Cube? Can you disable them?"

"No *problemo*. I could remote activate the internal security measure."

"Which is?"

"Tanks of vapor inside the air vents. Sleeping gas. Illegal, by the way, according to Chicago State Law. But clever, no aftereffects, untraceable. The intruder comes to in lock-up two hours later."

Spiro cackled. "Those paranoid Phonetix boys. Go ahead, Cube, knock 'em out."

"Night night," said Foaly, with a glee that seemed all too real.

"Good. Now, Cube, all that stands between us and the Phonetix blueprints is an encrypted computer."

"Don't make me laugh. They haven't invented a unit of time short enough to measure how long it will take me to crack the Phonetix hard disk."

Spiro clipped the Cube onto his belt. "You know something? I'm starting to like this guy."

)(⏻⏚⏁ˑ ⏚⏃⏄⏅⏆⏇ ⏈ˑ)(⏚⏄⏚)(⏎⏚⏏⏐ˑ ⏚⏚

Artemis made one last sincere-sounding attempt to contain the situation. "Mr. Spiro, I really don't think that this is a good idea."

"Of course you don't," laughed Jon Spiro, jangling toward the door. "That's why I'm bringing you along."

Phonetix research and development laboratories, Chicago's industrial sector

Spiro selected a Lincoln Town Car from his extensive garage. It was a nineties model with fake registration. He often used it as a getaway vehicle. It was old enough to be unremarkable, and even if the police did get a shot of the plates, it wouldn't lead them anywhere.

Blunt parked opposite the Phonetix R & D lab's main entrance. A security guard was visible at his desk behind the glass revolving door. Arno pulled a pair of fold-up binoculars from the glove compartment. He focused on the guard.

"Sleeping like a baby," he announced.

Spiro clapped him on the shoulder.

"Good. We have less than two hours. Can we do it?"

"If this Cube is as good as he says he is, then we can be in and out in fifteen minutes."

"It's a machine," said Artemis coldly. "Not one of your steroid-munching associates."

Blunt glanced over his shoulder. Artemis sat in the backseat, squashed between Pex and Chips.

"You're very brave all of a sudden."

Artemis shrugged. "What have I got to lose? After all, things can hardly get worse."

There was a regular door beside the revolving one. The Cube remote activated the buzzer, admitting the band of intruders to the lobby. No alarms sounded, and no platoon of security guards came rushing to detain them.

Spiro strode down the corridor, emboldened by his newfound technological friend and the thought of finally putting Phonetix out of business. The security elevator put up no more resistance to the Cube than a picket fence would to a tank, and soon Spiro and Co. were riding the eight floors down to the sunken laboratory.

"We're going underground," chortled Pex. "Down where the dinosaur bones are. Did you know that after a million billion years, dinosaur dung turns into diamonds?"

Usually a comment like that would have been a shooting offense, but Spiro was in a good mood.

"No, I didn't know that, Pex. Maybe I should pay your wages in dung."

Pex decided that it would be better for his finances if he just kept his mouth shut from then on.

The lab itself was protected by a thumbprint scanner. Not even gel. It was a simple matter for the Cube to scan the fingerprint on the plate, then project it back onto the sensor. There wasn't even a key-code backup.

"Easy," crowed Spiro. "I should have done this years ago."

"A little credit would be nice," said Foaly, unable to hide his pique. "After all, I did get us in here and disable the guards."

Spiro held the box before him. "Not crushing you into scrap metal, Cube, is my way of saying thank you."

"You're welcome," grumbled Foaly.

Arno Blunt checked the security-monitor bank. Throughout the facility, guards lay unconscious, one with half a ham sandwich stuffed in his mouth.

"I gotta admit it, Mr. Spiro. This is beautiful. Phonetix is even gonna have to foot the bill for the sleeping gas."

Spiro glanced toward the ceiling. Several camera lights winked red in the shadows.

"Cube. Are we gonna have to raid the video room on our way out?"

"It ain't gonna happen," said Foaly, the method actor. "I wiped your patterns from the video."

Artemis was suspended by the armpits between Pex and Chips.

"Traitor," he muttered. "I gave you life, Cube. I am your creator."

"Yeah, well maybe you made me too much like you, Fowl. *Aurum Est Potestas.* Gold Is Power. I'm just doing what you taught me."

Spiro patted the cube fondly. "I love this guy. He's like the brother I never had."

ꤷ⬡ • ⬥⬚⧈ ⟩⟨ ⟩⟨ ⧈⬚ ⬗⬚⬚ • ⬠⟩ ⁞ • ⟩⟨ ⬡⬚⬚ •

"I thought you had a brother," said Chips, puzzled, which was not unusual for him.

"Okay," said Spiro. "He's like a brother I actually like."

The Phonetix server was located in the center of the lab, a monolithic hard drive with pythonlike cables rippling out to various workstations.

Spiro unclipped his new best friend from his belt.

"Where do you need to be, Cube?"

"Just pop me down on the lid of the server, and my omni-sensor will do the rest."

Spiro complied, and in seconds schematics were flickering across the C Cube's tiny screen.

"I have them," crowed Spiro, his hands two fists of triumph. "That's the last snide e-mail with stock prices I get from these guys."

"Download complete," said Foaly smugly. "We have every Phonetix project for the next decade."

Spiro cradled the Cube against his chest.

"Beautiful. I can launch our version of the Phonetix phone before they do, make myself a few extra million before I release the Cube."

Arno's attention was focused on the security monitors.

"Eh, Mr. Spiro. I think we have a situation here."

"A situation?" growled Spiro. "What does that mean? You're not a soldier anymore, Blunt. Speak English."

The New Zealander tapped a screen as if that would change what he was seeing.

"I mean we have a problem. A big problem."

Spiro grabbed Artemis by the shoulders.

"What have you done, Fowl? Is this some kind of . . ."

The accusation died before it could be completed. Spiro had noticed something.

"Your eyes. What's wrong with your eyes? They don't match."

Artemis treated him to his best vampire smile.

"All the better to see you with, Spiro."

In the Phonetix lobby, the sleeping security guard suddenly regained her senses. It was Juliet. She peeped out from under the brim of a borrowed cap to make sure Spiro had not left anyone in the corridor.

Following Artemis's capture in Spiro's vault, Holly had flown them both to Phonetix to initiate plan B.

Of course there had been no sleeping gas; for that matter there had only been two guards. One was taking a restroom break and the other was doing the rounds of the upper floors. Still, Spiro wasn't to know that. He was busy watching Foaly's family of sim security snoring all over the building, thanks to a video clip on the Phonetix system.

Juliet lifted the desk phone and dialed three numbers.

Nine . . . one . . . one . . .

Spiro reached two fingers delicately into Artemis's eye, plucking out the iris-cam. He studied it closely, noting the micro circuitry on the concave side.

⑥⇟⅄⑃ ∫ ⟨⟨ ⟩⟨ • ⚐⚐ ⟩(⟩〉 ⚐⚐ ⵣⵣ ⇟ ⟨⟨ ∫ • ⚐⚐ ⅌ • ⟩(

"This is electronic," he whispered. "Amazing. What is it?"

Artemis blinked a tear from his eye. "It's nothing. It was never here. Just as I was never here."

Spiro's face twisted in sheer hatred. "You were here all right, Fowl, and you'll never leave here."

Blunt tapped his employer on the shoulder. An act of unforgivable familiarity.

"Boss, Mr. Spiro. You really need to see this."

Juliet stripped off her Phonetix Security jacket. Underneath she wore a Chicago PD SWAT uniform. Things could get hairy in the R&D Lab, and it was her job to make sure that Artemis did not get hurt. She hid behind a pillar in the lobby and waited for the sirens.

Spiro stared at the lab's security monitors. The pictures had changed. There were no more guards slumbering around the facility. Instead, the screens played a tape of Spiro and his cronies breaking into Phonetix. With one crucial difference. There was no trace of Artemis on the screen.

"What's happening, Cube?" spluttered Spiro. "You said that we'd all be wiped from the tapes."

"I lied. It must be the criminal personality I'm developing."

Spiro smashed the Cube against the floor. It remained intact.

"Tough polymer," said Artemis, picking up the microcomputer. "Almost unbreakable."

꒐꒤•꒐꒪꒕꒬꒚꒚•꒭꒬꒒꒤•꒛꒚꒚°꒔꒜꒐

"Unlike you," retorted Spiro.

Artemis looked like a doll, between Pex and Chips. "Don't you understand yet? You're all on tape. The Cube was working for me."

"Big deal. So we're on tape. All I have to do is pay the security booth a visit and take the recordings."

"It's not going to be that simple."

Spiro still believed that there was a way out.

"And why not? Who's gonna stop me? Little old you?"

Artemis pointed to the screens. "No. Little old them."

The Chicago PD brought everything they had, and a few things they had to borrow. Phonetix was the city's biggest single employer, not to mention one of the top five subscribers to the Police Benevolent Fund. When the 911 call came in from their offices, the duty sergeant put out a citywide call.

In less than five minutes, there were twenty uniforms and a full SWAT team beating on the Phonetix doors. Two choppers hovered overhead and eight snipers lined the roofs of adjacent buildings. No one was leaving the area, unless they were invisible.

The Phonetix security guard had just returned from his rounds and noticed the intruders on the monitors. Shortly after that he noticed a group of Chicago PD tapping the door with their gun barrels.

He buzzed them in. "I was just about to call you guys," he

said. "There's a buncha intruders in the vault. They musta tunneled in or somethin', 'cause they didn't come past me."

The security guard on a restroom break was even more surprised. He was just finishing off the sports section of the *Herald Tribune* when two very serious-looking men in body armor burst into the cubicle.

"ID?" growled one, who apparently did not have the time for full sentences.

The security guard held up his laminated card with a shaking hand.

"Stay put, sir," advised the other police officer. He didn't have to say it twice.

Juliet slipped out from behind the pillar, joining the ranks of the SWAT team. She pointed her gun and roared with the best of them, and was instantly assimilated into the group. Their assault was cut short by a tiny problem. There was only one access point to the lab. The elevator shaft.

Two officers pried open the elevator door with crowbars.

"Here's our dilemma," said one. "We cut the power, then we can't get the elevator up here. If we call the elevator up here first, then we tip off our intruders."

Juliet shouldered herself to the front of the group.

"Excuse me, sir. Let me go down on the cables. I blow the doors and you cut the power."

The commander did not even consider it. "No. Too

dangerous. The intruders would have plenty of time to put a hundred rounds into the elevator. Who are you, anyway?"

Juliet took a small gripper from her belt. She clipped it onto the elevator cable and hopped into the shaft.

"I'm new," she said, disappearing into the blackness.

In the laboratory, Spiro and Co. were hypnotized by the monitors. Foaly had allowed the screens to show what was actually happening on the upper levels.

"SWAT," said Blunt. "Helicopters. Heavy armament. How did this happen?"

Spiro smacked his own forehead repeatedly.

"A setup. This entire thing. A setup. I suppose Mo Digence was working for you too."

"Yes. Pex and Chips too, even though they didn't know it. You would never have come here if I had suggested it."

"But how? How did you do this? It's not possible."

Artemis glanced at the monitors. "Obviously, it is. I knew you would be waiting for me in the Spiro Needle vault. After that, all I had to do was use your own hatred of Phonetix to lure you here, out of your environment."

"If I go down, so do you."

"Incorrect. I was never here, and the tapes will prove it."

"But you are here!" roared Spiro, his nerves shot. His whole body vibrated and spittle sprayed from his lips in a wide arc. "Your dead body will prove it. Give me the gun, Arno, I'm going to shoot him."

Blunt could not hide his disappointment, but he did as he was told. Spiro pointed the weapon with shaky hands. Pex and Chips stepped rapidly to one side. The boss was not known for his marksmanship.

"You have taken everything from me," he shouted. "Everything."

Artemis was strangely calm. "You don't understand, Jon. It's like I told you. I was never here." He paused for breath. "And one more thing. About my name, *Artemis*. You were right in London, it is generally a female name. After the Greek goddess of archery. But every now and then a male comes along with such a talent for hunting that he earns the right to use the name. I am that male. Artemis the hunter. I hunted you."

And just like that, he disappeared.

Holly had been hovering above Spiro and Co. all the way from the Spiro Needle to the Phonetix building. She had got permission to enter the facility minutes earlier, when Juliet had called to inquire about public tours.

Juliet had put on her best cutesy voice for the tour guide.

"Hey mister, is it okay if I bring my invisible friend?"

"Sure it is, honey," replied the guide. "Bring your security blanket too, if it makes you happy."

They were in.

Holly hovered at ceiling level, following Artemis's progress below. The Mud Boy's plan was fraught with risk. If

Spiro decided to shoot him in the Needle, then it was all over.

But no, just as Artemis had predicted, Spiro had opted to gloat for as long as possible, basking in the glow of his own demented genius. But of course it wasn't his own genius. It was Artemis's. Artemis had orchestrated this whole operation from beginning to end. It had even been his idea to *mesmerize* Pex and Chips. It was crucial that they plant the idea to invade Phonetix.

Holly was ready when the elevator door opened. She had her weapon charged and targets selected. But she couldn't go. Wait for the signal.

Artemis dragged it out. Melodramatic to the end. And then, just when Holly was about to disregard her orders and start blasting, he spoke.

"I am that male. Artemis the hunter. I hunted you."

Artemis the hunter. The signal.

Holly squeezed the manual throttle on her wing rig, descending to an altitude of three feet. She clipped Artemis onto a retractable cord on her Moonbelt, then dropped a sheet of cam foil in front of him. To everybody in the room, it would seem as though the boy had disappeared.

"Up we go," she said, though Artemis could not hear her, and opened the throttle wide. In less than a second they were nestled safely among the cables and ducts that ran along the ceiling.

Below them, Jon Spiro lost his mind.

* * *

Spiro blinked. The boy had gone. Just gone. It couldn't be. He was Jon Spiro! Nobody outsmarted Jon Spiro!

He turned to Pex and Chips, gesticulating wildly with the gun.

"Where is he?"

"Huh?" said the bodyguards in perfect unison. Unrehearsed.

"Where is Artemis Fowl? What did you do with him?"

"Nothing, Mr. Spiro. We were just standing here playing the shoulder game."

"Fowl said you were working for him. So hand him over."

Pex's brain was churning. This was an operation akin to a blender mixing concrete.

"Careful, Mr. Spiro, guns are dangerous. Especially the end with the hole."

"This isn't over, Artemis Fowl," Spiro roared at the ceiling. "I will find you. I will never give up. You've got Jon Spiro's word on it. My word!"

He began to fire random shots, blowing holes in monitors, vents, and conduits. One even came within three feet of Artemis.

Pex and Chips were not quite sure what was going on, but decided that it might be a good idea to join in the fun. They pulled out their weapons and began shooting up the lab.

Blunt did not get involved. He considered his contract

of employment terminated. There was no way out of this for Spiro; it was every man for himself. He crossed to the wall's metal paneling and began to dismantle it with a power screwdriver. A section dropped from its casing, behind it a two-inch cable space, then solid concrete. They were trapped.

Behind him, the elevator door *ding*ed.

Juliet was crouched in the lift shaft.

"We're clear," said Holly in her earpiece. "But Spiro is shooting up the lab."

Juliet frowned. Her Principal was in danger. "Knock them out with the Neutrino."

"I can't. If Spiro is unconscious when the police arrive, he could claim a frame-up."

"Okay. I'm going in."

"Negative. Wait for SWAT."

"No. You take out the weapons. I'll handle the rest."

Mulch had given Juliet a bottle of dwarf rock polish. She poured a little puddle on the elevator roof, and it dissolved like fat on a pan. Juliet hopped into the carriage, crouching low in case Blunt decided to put a few rounds into the elevator.

"On three."

"Juliet."

"I'm going on three."

"Okay."

𝖩𝖺𝖷⟩𝟤・⁹𝟣𝖢𝟪𝟪𝟙𝖢・𝖷𝖳・𝖳⟩𝟹𝖷⟩𝖢

Juliet reached up to the door open button. "One."

Holly drew her Neutrino, locking all four targets into her visor's targeting system.

"Two."

Holly unshielded for accuracy; the vibration would throw her aim right off. For a few seconds she would have to hide behind the foil with Artemis.

"Three."

Juliet pressed the button. Holly squeezed off four shots.

Artemis had less than a minute to make his move. Less than a minute while Holly targeted and disarmed Spiro and Co. The circumstances were hardly ideal; screaming, gunfire, and general mayhem. But then again, what better time to implement the final step in this stage of the plan? A very vital step.

The second Holly unshielded to fire, Artemis scrolled out a Plexiglas keyboard from the C Cube's base and began to type. In seconds he had hacked into Spiro's bank accounts. All thirty-seven of them, in institutions from the Isle of Man to the Caymans. The various account numbers locked into place. He had access to each secret fund.

The Cube quickly totted up the total funds: 2.8 billion U.S. dollars, not counting the contents of various safety-deposit boxes that could not be touched over the net. Two point eight billion. Plenty to restore the Fowls' status as one of the top-five richest Irish families.

Just as he was about to complete the transaction, Artemis remembered his father's words again. His father, returned to him by the fairy folk.

And what about you, Arty? Will you make the journey with me? When the moment comes, will you take your chance to be a hero?

Did he really need billions of dollars?

Of course he needed it. *Aurum Est Potestas.* Gold Is Power.

Really? *Will you take your chance to be a hero?* To make a difference.

Because he could not groan aloud, Artemis rolled his eyes and gritted his teeth. Well, if he was going to be a hero, he would be a well-paid one. He quickly deducted a ten-percent finder's fee from the 2.8 billion, then sent the rest to Amnesty International. He made the transaction irreversible, in case he weakened later on.

Artemis wasn't finished yet. There was one more good deed to be attended to. The success of this venture depended on Foaly's being too busy watching the show to notice Artemis hacking into his system.

He brought up the LEP site and set the code breaker working on a password. It took ten valuable seconds per minute, but he was soon flying around LEP micro sites. Artemis found what he needed on Perp Profiles. Mulch Diggums's complete arrest record. From there it was a simple matter to follow the electron trail back to the original search warrant for Mulch's dwelling. Artemis changed the date on the warrant to read the day *after* Mulch's arrest. This meant that all subsequent arrests and convictions were null and void. A good lawyer would have him out of prison in a heartbeat.

"I have not finished with you yet, Mulch Diggums," he whispered, logging out and clipping the Cube onto Holly's belt.

Juliet came through the door so fast her limbs were a blur. She had removed her helmet for better visibility, and the jade ring trailed behind her like a fishing lure on the end of a line.

Butler would never take chances like this, she knew. He would have some perfectly practical, safe plan. Which was why he had his blue diamond tattoo and she didn't. Well, maybe she didn't want a tattoo. Maybe she wanted a life of her own.

She quickly assessed the situation. Holly's aim was true. The two gorillas were rubbing their scorched hands and Spiro was stamping his feet like a spoiled child. Only Blunt was on the floor, going for his gun.

Even though the bodyguard was on his hands and knees, he was still almost at her eye level.

"Aren't you going to give me a chance to get up?" he asked.

"No," said Juliet, whipping the jade ring around like the

stone that felled Goliath. It struck the bridge of Blunt's nose, cracking it and effectively blinding him for a couple of minutes. Plenty of time for the Chicago Police to get down the shaft. Blunt was out of the game. Juliet had expected to feel some satisfaction. But all she felt was sadness. There was no joy in violence.

Pex and Chips felt they should do something. Perhaps disabling the girl would earn them a bonus from Mr. Spiro. They circled Juliet, fists raised.

Juliet wagged a finger at them. "Sorry, boys. You have to go to sleep."

The bodyguards ignored her, tightening the radius of their circle.

"I said go to sleep."

Still no response.

"You have to use the exact words that I *mesmerized* them to respond to," said Holly in her earpiece.

Juliet sighed. "If I must. Okay, gentlemen. Barney says, go to sleep."

Pex and Chips were snoring before they hit the ground.

That just left Spiro, and he was too busy gibbering to be any threat. He was still gibbering when the SWAT team put the cuffs on him.

"I'll talk to you back at base," said the captain sternly to Juliet. "You're a danger to your comrades and yourself."

"Yessir," said Juliet contritely. "I don't know what came over me, sir."

𝕒𝕤𝕘 • 𝕢 𝕩𝕩 ᶦᔐ • 𝕲𝕖 • 𝕲)(• ᒍᔐ𝕓ᔐ • ᗊ)(ᔐ

She glanced upward. A slight heat haze seemed to be drifting toward the elevator chute. The Principal was safe.

Holly holstered her weapon, buzzing up her shield.

"Time to go," she said, the volume on her P.A. turned to minimum.

Holly wrapped the cam foil tightly around Artemis, making certain no limbs were peeking out. It was imperative they leave while the elevator was empty. Once forensics and the press got here, even a slight shimmer in the air might be caught on film.

As they flew across the room, Spiro was being led from the lab. He had finally managed to calm down.

"This is a setup," he proclaimed in his best innocent voice. "My lawyers are gonna rip you guys apart."

Artemis could not resist speaking as they floated past his ear.

"Farewell, Jon," he whispered. "Never mess with a boy genius."

Spiro howled at the ceiling like a demented wolf.

Mulch was waiting across the street from the Phonetix lab, revving the van like a Grand Prix driver. He sat behind the wheel on an orange crate, with a short plank taped to his foot. The other end of the plank was taped to the accelerator.

Juliet studied the system nervously. "Shouldn't you untie that foot? In case you need to use the brake?"

))≷⑥ • 88♋ • ⚖♉ • ⚹⚹ •)(⟨ ⟩88⟩⟩ • ⚹⚹

"Brake?" Mulch laughed. "Why would I use the brake? I'm not doing my driving test here."

In the back of the van, Artemis and Holly simultaneously reached for their seat belts.

CHAPTER 11

THE INVISIBLE MAN

Fowl Manor

They reached Ireland without major incident, though Mulch did attempt to escape Holly's custody fifteen times. Including once on the Lear jet, where he was discovered in the washroom with a parachute and a bottle of dwarf rock polish. Holly did not let him out of her sight after that.

Butler was waiting for them at Fowl Manor's front door.

"Welcome back. Glad to see everyone's alive. Now I need to go."

Artemis put a hand on his arm.

"Old friend. You're in no condition to go anywhere."

Butler was determined. "One last mission, Artemis. I have no choice. Anyway, I've been doing Pilates. I feel much more limber."

⬠🜍 · 𝌆🜍𝌆 · 𝌆🜍𝌆 · 🜍🜍 ·

"Blunt?"

"Yes."

"But he's in prison," protested Juliet.

Butler shook his head. "Not anymore."

Artemis could see that his bodyguard was not about to be turned from his path.

"At least take Holly. She can be of some help."

Butler winked at the elf. "I was counting on it."

The Chicago Police had put Arno Blunt in a wagon with a couple of officers. Two would be sufficient, they reasoned, since the perp was handcuffed and manacled. They revised this opinion when the van was discovered six miles south of Chicago with the officers manacled and no sign of the suspect. To quote Sergeant Iggy Lebowski's report: "The guy ripped those handcuffs apart as though they were links in a paper chain. He came at us like a steam train. We never had a chance."

But Arno Blunt did not escape clean. His pride had taken a severe beating in the Spiro Needle. He knew that word of his humiliation would soon spread through the bodyguard network. As Pork Belly LaRue later put it on the Soldiers for Hire Web site: "Arno done got hisself outsmarted by some snot-nosed kid." Blunt was painfully aware that he would have to suffer chortles every time he walked into a room full of tough guys. Unless he avenged the insult paid to him by Artemis Fowl.

⏃⚙⟨⧖• ⚼⟨⌇⊑• ⚘⚙⟨⧖·⟐⚯⌇⊑

The bodyguard knew that he had minutes before Spiro gave up his address to the Chicago PD, so he packed a few spare sets of teeth and took the shuttle to O'Hare.

Blunt was delighted to find that the authorities had not yet frozen his Spiro corporate credit card, and used it to purchase a first-class British Airways Concorde ticket to Heathrow, London. From there he would enter Ireland on the Rosslare ferry. Just another one of five hundred tourists visiting the land of the leprechaun. It wasn't a terribly complicated plan, and it would have worked if it hadn't been for one thing. The passport official in Heathrow just happened to be Sid Commons, the ex–Green Beret who had served with Butler on bodyguard duty in Monte Carlo. The second Blunt opened his mouth, alarm bells went off in Commons's head. The gentleman before him fit the description Butler had faxed to him perfectly. Right down to the strange teeth. Blue oil and water, if you don't mind. Commons pressed a button under his desk, and in seconds a squad of security men relieved Blunt of his passport and took him into custody.

The chief security official took out his mobile phone as soon as the detainee was under lock and key. He dialed an international number. It rang twice.

"The Fowl residence."

"Butler? It's Sid Commons, in Heathrow. A man came through here you might be interested in. Funny teeth, neck tattoos, New Zealand accent. Detective Justin Barre faxed out the description from Scotland Yard a few days ago, he said you might be able to ID him."

"Do you still have him?" asked the manservant.

"Yes. He's in one of our holding cells. They're running a check right now."

"How long will that take?"

"A couple of hours. Max. But if he's the professional you say he is, a computer check won't turn up anything. We need a confession to turn him over to Scotland Yard."

"I will meet you in the arrival hall under the departure board in thirty minutes," said Butler, severing the connection.

Sid Commons stared at his cell phone. How could Butler possibly get here in thirty minutes from Ireland? It wasn't important. All Sid knew was that Butler had saved his life a dozen times in Monte Carlo all those years ago, and now the debt was about to be repaid.

Thirty-two minutes later, Butler showed up in the arrival hall.

Sid Commons studied him as they shook hands.

"You seem different. Older."

"The battles are catching up with me," said Butler, a palm pressing his heaving chest. "Time to retire, I think."

"Is there any point asking how you got here?"

Butler straightened his tie. "Not really. You're better off not knowing."

)⊱ • (ᛦⴲⴲⴲⵊⵑⵕⵑ • ⵊ • ⵟⴲ ꒡ ⵜⵑⵕ)ⵑⵟⴲ • ⵊ

"I see."

"Where's our man?"

Commons led the way toward the rear of the building, past hordes of tourists and card-bearing taxi drivers.

"Through here. You're not armed, are you? I know we're friends, but I can't allow firearms in here."

Butler spread his jacket wide. "Trust me. I know the rules."

They took a security elevator up two floors and followed a dimly lit corridor for what seemed like miles.

"Here we are," said Sid eventually, pointing at a glass rectangle. "In there."

The glass was actually a two-way mirror. Butler could see Arno Blunt seated at a small table, drumming his fingers impatiently on the Formica surface.

"Is that him? Is that the man who shot you in Knightsbridge?"

Butler nodded. It was him all right. The same indolent expression. The same hands that pulled the trigger.

"A positive ID is something, but it's still your word against his, and to be honest, you don't look too shot."

Butler laid a hand on his friend's shoulder. "I don't suppose . . ."

Commons didn't even let him finish. "No. You cannot go in there. Absolutely not. I'd be out of a job for sure, and anyway even if you did pry a confession out of him it would never hold up in court."

Butler nodded. "I understand. Do you mind if I stay? I want to see how this turns out."

Commons agreed eagerly, relieved that Butler hadn't pressured him.

"No problem. Stick around as long as you like. But I have to get you a visitor's badge." He strode down the corridor, then turned.

"Don't go in there, Butler. If you do, we lose him forever. And anyway, there are cameras all over this place."

Butler smiled reassuringly. Something he didn't do very often.

"Don't worry, Sid. You won't see me in that room."

Commons sighed. "Good. Great. It's just that sometimes, when you get that look in your eye . . ."

"I'm a different man now. More mature."

Commons laughed. "That'll be the day."

He rounded the corner, his chuckles lingering in the air. He was no sooner gone than Holly unshielded beside Butler's leg.

"Cameras?" hissed the bodyguard from the corner of his mouth.

"I checked the ion beams. I'm clear right here." She pulled a sheet of camouflage foil from her backpack, laying it on the floor. She then twisted a video clip around a cable tacked to the cell's outer wall.

"Okay," she said, listening to Foaly's voice in her ear. "We're in. Foaly has wiped our patterns from the video. We are camera- and mike-proof now. Do you know what to do?"

Butler nodded. They had been through this before, but Holly had a soldier's need to double check.

"I'm going to shield again. Give me a second to move, then put the foil on and do your thing. I give you two minutes tops before your friend returns. After that you're on your own."

"Understood."

"Good luck," said Holly, shimmering out of the visible spectrum.

Butler waited a beat, then took two steps to the left. He picked up the foil and draped it over his head and shoulders. To the casual passerby, he was now invisible. But if anyone paused on their way down the corridor, something of the manservant's bulk was bound to be poking out from under the foil. Best to move quickly. He slid the latch on the cell door, and stepped inside.

Arno Blunt was not unduly worried. This was a bum rap. How long could you be held without charge, for heaven's sake? Not much longer, that was for sure. Maybe he would sue the British government for trauma, and retire home to New Zealand.

The door swung open a foot, then closed again. Blunt sighed. It was an old interrogator's trick. Let the prisoner sweat for a few hours, then open the door to make him think help was on the way. When no one entered, the prisoner would be plunged into even deeper despair. Ever closer to the breaking point.

"Arno Blunt," sighed a voice, from nowhere. Blunt stopped drumming his fingers and sat up straight.

"What is this?" he sneered. "Are there speakers in here? That's lame, guys. Really lame."

"I've come for you, said the voice. "I've come to even the score."

Arno Blunt knew that voice. He'd been dreaming about it since Chicago. Ever since the Irish kid had warned him Butler would return. Okay, it was ridiculous, there were no such things as ghosts. But there was something about Artemis Fowl's stare that made you believe everything he told you.

"Butler? Is that you?"

"Ah," said the voice. "You remember me."

Arno took a deep shuddering breath. Composing himself.

"I don't know what's going on here, but I'm not falling for it. What? I'm supposed to cry like a baby now, because you found somebody who sounds like one of my . . . Somebody I knew?"

"This is no trick, Arno. I'm right here."

"Sure. If you're right there, why can't I see you?"

"Are you sure you can't see me, Arno? Look closely."

Blunt's stare hopped wildly around the room. There was no one else in here. No one. He was certain of it. But there was a patch of air in the corner of the room. It seemed to be bending light, like a floating mirror.

"Ah, you've spotted me."

"I've spotted nothing," said Blunt shakily. "All I see is a heat blur. Maybe from a vent or something."

"Oh, really?" said Butler, throwing off the camouflage foil. To Blunt it seemed as though he had stepped from the air. The bodyguard stood up abruptly, catapulting his chair against the wall.

"Oh God! What are you?"

Butler bent his knees slightly. Ready for action. He was older now, true. And slower. But the fairy magic had bolstered his reaction time, and he had so much more experience than Blunt. Juliet would have liked to handle this job for him, but there were some things you had to finish personally.

"I am your guide, Arno. I've come to take you home. There are a lot of people waiting to see you."

"H-h-home?" stammered Blunt. "What do you mean home?"

Butler took a step forward. "You know what I mean, Arno. Home. The place you've always been headed. The place you've sent so many others. Including me."

Blunt pointed a shaky finger. "You stay away from me. I killed you once, I can do it again."

Butler laughed. It was not a pleasant sound. "That's where you're wrong, Arno. I can't be killed again. Anyway,

ᘔᘓᗺ • ⏾ᘓᘗᘔᗺᘓᗺ • ⏾⟨ᘓᘓ • ⟨ᘔᘓᘔᘗ • ⏾⟨ᘔᘓᘔ

death is no big deal, not compared to what comes after."

"What comes after . . ."

"There is a hell, Arno," said Butler. "I've seen it, and believe me, so will you."

Blunt was utterly convinced. After all, Butler had appeared from nowhere.

"I didn't know," he sobbed. "I didn't believe it. I never would have shot you, Butler. I was just following Spiro's orders. You heard him give the order. I was just the metal man, that's all I've ever been."

Butler laid a hand on his shoulder. "I believe you, Arno. You were just following orders."

"That's right."

"But that's not enough. You need to clear your conscience. If you don't, I have to take you with me."

Blunt's eyes were red with tears. "How?" he pleaded. "How do I do that?"

"Confess your sins to the authorities. Leave nothing out, or I will be back."

Blunt nodded eagerly. Prison was better than the alternative.

"Remember, I will be watching. This is your one chance to save yourself. If you don't take it, I will be back."

Blunt's teeth popped from his open mouth, rolling across the floor.

"Don' worry. I'll confeth. I promith."

𝔸 • 🜍 ⬡)(⬡ 𝔸 ⚏ • ⩎ ♗ 🜂 • ♗ ⬡ ⚎ •

Butler lifted the camouflage foil, concealing himself completely.

"See that you do, or there'll be hell to pay."

Butler stepped into the corridor, stuffing the cam foil inside his jacket. Seconds later Sid Commons reappeared with a security badge.

He caught sight of Arno Blunt standing stunned in his cell.

"What did you do, Butler?" he said.

"Hey, it wasn't me. Check your tapes. He just went crazy, talking to thin air. Yelling how he wanted to confess."

"He wants to confess? Just like that?"

"I know how it sounds, but that's what happened. If I were you, I'd give Justin Barre a call over at Scotland Yard. I have a feeling that Blunt's statement could clear up a lot of outstanding cases."

Commons squinted at him suspiciously. "Why do I have a feeling that you know more than you're telling?"

"Search me," said Butler. "But feelings aren't evidence, and your own surveillance tapes will prove that I never set foot in that room."

"Are you sure that's what they'll show?"

Butler glanced at the patch of air shimmering above Sid Commons's shoulder.

"I am positive," he said.

CHAPTER 12

MIND WIPE

Fowl Manor

The return trip from Heathrow took more than an hour thanks to some particularly strong turbulence and an easterly wind over the Welsh hills. When Holly and Butler finally touched down on the grounds of Fowl Manor, the LEP were busy hauling their mind-wiping gear up the avenue under cover of night.

Butler unclipped himself from the Moonbelt, leaning against the trunk of a silver birch.

"You okay?" asked Holly.

"Fine," replied the bodyguard, massaging his chest. "It's this Kevlar tissue. Handy if I get shot with a small caliber weapon, but it's playing havoc with my breathing."

Holly sheathed her mechanical wings. "It's the quiet life for you, from now on."

Butler noticed an LEP pilot attempting to park his shuttle in the double garage, nudging the Fowl Bentley's bumper.

"Quiet life," he muttered, heading for the garage. "I wish."

Once Butler had finished terrorizing the pixie pilot, he made for the study. Artemis and Juliet were waiting for him. Juliet hugged her brother so tightly that the air was squeezed from his lungs.

"I'm okay, little sister. The fairies have fixed it that I will live to well over a hundred. I'll still be around to keep an eye on you."

Artemis was all business. "How did you fare, Butler?"

Butler opened a wall safe behind an air conditioning vent. "Pretty well. I got everything on the list."

"What about the custom job?"

Butler laid out six small vials on the baize-covered desk.

"My man in Limerick followed your instructions to the letter. In all his years in the trade, he's never done anything like this. They're in a special solution to stop corrosion. The layers are so fine that once they come into contact with the air, they begin to oxidize right away, so I suggest we don't insert them until the last possible moment."

"Excellent. In all probability, I am the only one who will need these, but just in case, we should all put them in."

Butler held the gold coin up by its leather cord. "I copied

your diary and fairy files onto a laser minidisk, then brushed on a layer of gold leaf. It won't stand up to close examination I'm afraid, but molten gold would have destroyed the information on the disk."

Artemis tied the cord around his neck. "It will have to do. Did you plant the false trails?"

"Yes. I sent an e-mail that has yet to be picked up, and I hired a few megabytes on an Internet storage site. I also took the liberty of burying a time capsule in the maze."

Artemis nodded. "Good. I hadn't thought of that."

Butler accepted the compliment, but he didn't believe it. Artemis thought of everything.

Juliet spoke for the first time. "You know, Artemis. Maybe it would be better to let these memories go. Give the fairies some peace of mind."

"These memories are part of who I am," responded Artemis.

He examined the vials on the table, selecting two.

"Now, everybody, it's time to put these in. I'm sure the People are eager to wipe our minds."

Foaly's technical crew set up shop in the conference room, laying out a complex assembly of electrodes and fiber-optic cable. Each cable was connected to a plasma screen that converted brain waves to actual binary information. In layman's terms, Foaly would be able to read the humans' memories like a book and edit out what shouldn't be there.

Possibly the most incredible part of the entire procedure was that the human brain itself would supply alternative memories to fill the blank spots.

"We could do the mind wipes with a field kit," explained Foaly, once the patients were assembled. "But field kits are just for blanket wipes. It would erase everything that's happened over the past sixteen months. That could have serious implications for your emotional development, not to mention your IQ. So it's better that we use the lab kit and simply erase the memories that pertain to the People. Obviously we will have to erase completely the days you spent in fairy company. We can't take any chances there."

Artemis, Butler, and Juliet were seated around the table. Technical gnomes swabbed their temples with disinfectant.

"I've thought of something," said Butler.

"Don't tell me," interrupted the centaur. "The age thing, right?"

Butler nodded. "A lot of people know me as a forty-year-old man. You can't wipe them all."

"Way ahead of you, Butler. We're going to give your face a laser peel while you're unconscious. Get rid of some of that dead skin. We even brought a cosmetic surgeon to give your forehead a Dewer injection, to smooth out the wrinkles."

"Dewer?"

"Fat," explained the centaur. "We take it from one area, and inject it into another."

Butler was not enthused at the idea. "This fat. It doesn't come from my behind, does it?"

Foaly shuffled uncomfortably. "Well, it doesn't come from *your* behind."

"Explain."

"Research has shown that of all the fairy races, dwarfs have the greatest longevity. There's a miner in Poll Dyne who is allegedly over two thousand years old. Haven't you ever heard the expression, 'smooth as a dwarf's bottom'?"

Butler slapped away a technician who was attempting to attach an electrode patch to his head.

"Are you telling me that fat from a dwarf's backside is going to be injected into my head?"

Foaly shrugged. "The price of youth. There are pixies on the west bank paying a fortune for Dewer treatments."

Butler spoke through gritted teeth. "I am not a pixie."

"We've also brought some gel to color any hair you may decide to grow in the future, and some dye to cover the cell corruption on your chest," continued the centaur hurriedly. "By the time you wake up, your exterior will look young again, even if your interior is old."

"Clever," said Artemis. "I expected as much."

Holly entered with Mulch in tow. The dwarf was wearing cuffs, and looking extremely sorry for himself.

"Is this really necessary?" he whined. "After all we've been through?"

"My badge is on the line," retorted Holly. "The

commander said to come back with you, or not at all."

"What do I have to do? I donated the fat, didn't I?"

Butler rolled his eyes. "Please—no."

Juliet giggled. "Don't worry, Dom. You won't remember a thing about it."

"Knock me out," said Butler. "Quickly."

"Don't mention it," grumbled Mulch, attempting to rub his behind.

Holly uncuffed the dwarf, but stayed within grabbing distance.

"He wanted to say good-bye. So here we are." She nudged Mulch with her shoulder. "So say good-bye."

Juliet winked. "Bye, Smelly."

"So long, Stinker."

"Don't go chewing through any concrete walls."

"I don't find that kind of thing funny," said Mulch, with a pained expression.

"Who knows? Maybe we'll see each other again."

Mulch nodded at the technicians, busy firing up their hard drives.

"If we do, thanks to these people, it'll be the first time."

Butler knelt to the dwarf's level.

"You look after yourself, little friend. Stay clear of goblins."

Mulch shuddered. "You don't have to tell me that."

Commander Root's face appeared on a roll-down screen erected by an LEP officer.

"Maybe you two would like to get married?" he barked. "I don't know what all the emotion is about. In ten minutes you people won't even remember this convict's name!"

"We have the commander online," said a technician, a tad unnecessarily.

Mulch stared at the button camera mounted on the screen. "Julius, please. Do you realize that all of these humans owe me their lives? This is an emotional moment for them."

Root's rosy complexion was exaggerated by poor reception.

"I couldn't care less about your touchy-feely moment, I'm here to make sure this wipe goes smoothly. If I know our friend, Fowl, he's got a few tricks up his sleeve."

"Really, Commander," said Artemis. "Such suspicion is wounding."

But the Irish teenager couldn't suppress a grin. Everybody knew that he would have hidden items to spark residual memories; it was up to the LEP to find them. Their final contest.

Artemis stood and approached Mulch Diggums.

"Mulch. Of all the fairy people, I will miss your services the most. We could have had such a future together."

Mulch looked a touch teary. "True. With your brains and my special talents."

"Not to mention your mutual lack of morals," interjected Holly.

"No bank on the planet would have been safe," said the dwarf. "A missed opportunity."

Artemis tried his best to look sincere. It was vital for the next step in the plan.

"Mulch, I know you risked your life betraying the Antonelli family, so I'd like to give you something."

Mulch's imagination churned with visions of trust funds and offshore accounts.

"There's no need. Really. Although it was incredibly brave, and I was in mortal danger."

"Exactly," said Artemis, untying the gold medallion from around his neck. "I know this isn't much, but it means a lot to me. I was going to keep it, but I realized that in a few minutes it will mean absolutely nothing. I would like you to have it. I think Holly would, too. A little memento of our adventures."

"Gee," said Mulch, hefting the medallion. "Half an ounce of gold. Great. You really broke the bank there, Artemis."

Artemis gripped the dwarf's hand. "It's not always about money, Mulch."

Root was craning his neck, trying to see more. "What's that? What has he given to the convict?"

Holly snatched the medallion, holding it up for the camera.

"Just a gold coin, Commander. I gave it to Artemis myself."

Foaly glanced at the small medal. "Actually, this kills two stink worms with one skewer. The medallion could have triggered some residual memories. Highly unlikely, but possible."

"And the other stink worm?"

"Mulch gets something to look at in prison."

Root mulled it over for several moments.

"Okay. He can keep it. Now get that convict into the shuttle, and let's get on with this. I've got a Council meeting in ten minutes."

Holly led Mulch out, and Artemis realized that he really was sorry to see the dwarf go. But more than that, he was sorry that the memory of their friendship could soon be gone forever.

The technicians descended like flies on a carcass. In seconds every human in the room had electrodes attached to temples and wrists. Each set of electrodes ran through a neural transformer and onto a plasma screen. Memories flickered on the screens.

Foaly studied the images. "Way too early," he announced. "Calibrate them to sixteen months ago. Actually, make that about three years. I don't want Artemis planning his initial kidnap all over again."

"Bravo, Foaly," said Artemis bitterly. "I was hoping you might miss that."

The centaur winked. "That's not all I didn't miss."

On the pull-down screen, Root's pixelated mouth stretched into a smile. "Tell him, Foaly. I can't wait to see the human's face."

Foaly consulted a file on his handheld computer. "We checked your e-mail, and guess what?"

"Do tell."

"We found a fairy file, just waiting to be delivered. We also ran a search on the Internet in general. And lo and behold, someone with your e-mail address had rented some storage megabytes. More fairy files."

Artemis was unrepentant. "I had to try. I'm sure you understand."

"Nothing else you want to tell us about?"

Artemis opened his eyes wide, the epitome of innocence. "Nothing. You're too clever for me."

Foaly took a small laser disk from a toolbox, sliding it into the drive of a networked computer on the table. "Well, just in case, I'm going to detonate a data charge in your computer system. The virus will leave your files unharmed, unless they pertain to the People. Not only that, but the virus will monitor your system for a further six months, just in case you have outwitted us somehow."

"And you're telling me all this because I won't remember it anyway."

Foaly did a little four-step, clapping his hands together. "Exactly."

Holly pushed through the door, dragging a metallic capsule behind her.

"Look what they found buried in the grounds." She flipped the lid, pouring the capsule's contents on the

Tunisian carpet. Several computer disks and hard copies of Artemis's diary fanned across the carpet.

Foaly examined a disk. "Something else you forgot to mention."

Artemis was not quite so cocky now. His lifelines to the past were being cut one by one.

"It slipped my mind."

"That's it, I suppose. There's nothing else."

Artemis returned to his chair, folding his arms. "And if I say yes, you'll believe me, I suppose."

Root laughed so hard that it seemed the screen was shaking.

"Oh yes, Artemis. We trust you completely. How could we not after all you've put the People through? If you don't mind we'd like to ask you a few questions under the *mesmer,* and this time you won't be wearing sunglasses."

Sixteen months previously, Artemis had successfully deflected Holly's hypnotic gaze with mirrored sunglasses. It was the first time he had outwitted the fairies. It was not to be the last.

"Well, then, let's get on with it."

"Captain Short," barked Root. "You know what to do."

Holly removed her helmet, massaging the tips of her ears to get the circulation going.

"I'm going to *mesmerize* you and ask a few questions. It's not the first time you've been under, so you know that the procedure is not painful. I advise you to relax. If you try to resist, it could cause memory loss or even brain damage."

Artemis held up his palm. "Wait a moment. Am I right in thinking that when I wake up again, this will all be over?"

Holly smiled. "Yes, Artemis. This is good-bye, for the last time."

Artemis's face was composed, in spite of the emotions churning inside him.

"Well, then, I have a few things to say."

Root was curious in spite of himself. "One minute, Fowl. Then nighty-night."

"Very well. First, thank you. I have my family and friends around me thanks to the People. I wish I didn't have to forget that."

Holly laid a hand on his shoulder. "It's better this way, Artemis. Believe me."

"And second, I want you all to think back to the first time you met me. Remember that night?"

Holly shuddered. She remembered the cold individual who had attacked her by a magical hotspot in Southern Ireland. Commander Root would never forget escaping an exploding tanker by the skin of his wings, and Foaly's first encounter with Artemis had been via a recording of the negotiations for Holly's release. He had been a despicable creature.

"If you take away the memories and influences of the People," continued Artemis, "I might become that person again. Is that what you really want?"

· ꗉꞮꞬ)Ƀꗇ)ꗇ · ꗇꙄꙴꙶ · ꗇ · ꙅꙡꙂꗇ · ꙭ ·

It was a chilling thought. Were the People responsible for Artemis's transformation? And were they to be responsible for changing him back?

Holly turned to the screen. "Is it possible? Artemis has come a long way. Do we have the right to destroy all that progress?"

"He's right," added Foaly. "I never thought I would say this, but I kinda like the new model."

Root opened another computer window on the screen. "The Psych Brotherhood did this probability report for us. They say the chances of a reversion are slim. Fowl will still have strong positive influences from his family and the Butlers."

"The Psych Brotherhood?" objected Holly. "Argon and his cronies? And when exactly did we start trusting those witch doctors?"

Root opened his mouth to yell, but thought better of it—not something that happened every day.

"Holly," he said, almost gently. "The future of our culture is at stake here. The bottom line is that Artemis's future is not our problem."

Holly's mouth was a grim slash. "If that's true, then we're as bad as the Mud Men."

The commander decided to revert to his usual mode of communication.

"Listen to me, Captain," he roared. "Being in command means making tough decisions. Not being in command means shutting up and doing what you're told. Now *mesmerize* those humans before we lose the link."

"Yes, sir. Whatever you say, sir."

Holly stood directly in front of Artemis, careful to make eye contact.

"Good-bye, Holly. I won't see you again, though I'm sure you will see me."

"Just relax, Artemis. Deep breaths."

When Holly spoke again, her voice was layered with bass and alto. The hypnotic layers of the *mesmer*.

"That was some job we did on Spiro, eh?"

Artemis smiled sleepily. "Yes. The last adventure. No more hurting people."

"How do you come up with these plans?"

Artemis's lids drooped. "Natural ability, I suppose. Handed down by generations of Fowls."

"I bet you would do anything to hang onto your fairy memories."

"Almost anything."

"So what *did* you do?"

Artemis smiled. "I played a few little tricks."

"What kind of tricks?" pressed Holly.

"It's a secret. I can't tell you."

Holly added a few more layers to her voice.

"Tell me, Artemis. It will be our secret."

A vein pulsed in Artemis's temple. "You won't tell? You won't tell the fairies?"

Holly glanced guiltily at the screen. Root gestured at her to continue.

"I won't tell. It will be just between us."

"Butler hid a capsule in the maze."

"And?"

"I sent myself an e-mail. But I expect Foaly to find that. It's to throw him off guard."

"Very clever. Is there anything you don't expect him to find?"

Artemis smiled craftily. "Butler buried a capsule in the grounds, and I hid a file on an Internet storage site. Foaly's data charge won't affect it. The provider will mail me a reminder in six months. When I retrieve the data, it should trigger residual memories and possibly total recall."

"Anything else?"

"No. The storage site is our last hope. If the centaur finds that, then the fairy world is lost to me forever."

Root's image crackled on the screen. "Okay. The uplink is breaking up. Knock them out and wipe them. Tape the whole process. I won't believe Artemis is out of the game until I see the footage."

"Commander. Maybe I should ask the others a few questions."

"Negative, Captain. Fowl said it himself. The storage site was their last hope. Hook them up and run the program."

The Commander's image disappeared in waves of static.

"Yes, sir." Holly turned to the technical crew. "You heard

the fairy. Let's go. Sunup is in a couple of hours. I want us belowground before that."

The techies checked that the electrodes had strong contacts, then unwrapped three sets of sleep goggles.

"I'll do that," said Holly, taking the masks.

She hooked the elastic over Juliet's ponytail. "You know something?" she said. "Personal protection is a cold business. You have too much heart for it."

Juliet nodded slowly. "I'll try to hold on to that thought."

Holly settled the eyepieces gently.

"I'll keep an eye on you."

Juliet smiled. "See you in my dreams."

Holly pressed a small button on the sleep mask, and a combination of hypno-lights in the eyepieces and a sedative administered through the seals knocked Juliet out in less than five seconds.

Butler was next. The technical crew had added a length of elastic to the mask's strap, so that it could encircle his shaven crown.

"Make sure Foaly doesn't go crazy with that mind wiper," said the bodyguard. "I don't want to wake up with four decades of nothing in my head."

"Don't worry," said Holly reassuringly. "Foaly generally knows what he's doing."

"Good. Remember, if the People ever do need help. I'm available."

Holly pressed the button.

⦁ ⵌ♋Ϙ Ⱦ)(つ♋♋ⴸ ⦁)(つ϶⸴ ⦁ つ♋♋϶Ϡ♏⍑

"I'll remember that," she whispered.

Artemis was last in the line. In his *mesmerized* state, he seemed almost peaceful. For once there were no thought lines wrinkling his brow, and if Holly hadn't known him, he could almost seem like a normal thirteen-year-old human.

Holly turned to Foaly. "Are you sure about this?"

The centaur shrugged. "What choice do we have? Orders are orders."

Holly placed the mask over Artemis's eyes and pushed the button. Seconds later the teenager slumped in his chair. Immediately, lines of Gnommish text began to flash across the screen behind him. In the days of Frond, Gnommish had been written in spirals. But reading in spirals gave most fairies migraines.

"Commence deleting," ordered Foaly. "But keep a copy. Sometime when I have a few weeks off I'm going to find out what makes this guy tick."

Holly watched Artemis's life being written in green symbols on the screen.

"This doesn't feel right," she commented. "If he found us once, he could find us again. Especially if he goes back to being the monster he was."

Foaly tapped commands into an ergodynamic keyboard. "Maybe. But next time we'll be ready."

Holly sighed. "It's a pity, because we were almost friends."

The centaur snorted. "Sure. Like you can be friends with a viper."

Holly suddenly shut her helmet visor, hiding her eyes.

"You're right, of course. We could never have been friends. It was circumstance that pushed us together, nothing more."

Foaly patted her shoulder. "That's the girl. Keep your ears up. Where are you going?"

"Tara," replied Holly. "I'm going to fly. I need the fresh air."

"You don't have clearance for a flight," objected Foaly. "Root will have your badge."

"For what?" said Holly, firing up her wings. "I'm not supposed to be here, remember?"

And she was gone, flying in a lazy loop through the entrance hall. She cleared the main door with inches to spare, climbing quickly into the night sky. For a second her slim frame was backlit by the full moon, and then she disappeared, vibrating out of the visible spectrum.

Foaly watched her go. Emotional creatures, elves. In some respects they made the worst Recon operatives. All decisions were made from the heart. But Root would never fire Holly, because policing was what she was born to do. And anyway, who else would save the People if Artemis Fowl ever found them again?

Mulch sat in the shuttle's holding booth feeling extremely sorry for himself. He tried to sit on the bench without actually touching it with his tender behind. Not an easy task.

Things did not look good, it had to be said. Even after all he'd done for the LEP, they were going to lock him up for at least a decade. Just for stealing a few measly bars of gold. And it didn't seem likely that he'd get an opportunity to escape. He was surrounded by steel and laser bars, and would remain so until the shuttle docked in Haven. After that, it was a quick jaunt to Police Plaza, a summary hearing and off to a secure facility until his beard turned gray. Which it would, if he was forced to spend more than five years out of the tunnels.

But there was hope. A tiny glimmer. Mulch forced himself to wait until all the technical staff had cleared their equipment from the shuttle, then he casually opened his right hand, rubbing his temples with thumb and forefinger. What he was actually doing was reading the tiny note concealed in his palm. The one slipped to him by Artemis Fowl when they shook hands.

> *I have not finished with you yet, Mulch Diggums.*
> *On your return, tell your lawyer to check the date on the original search warrant for your cave. When you are released keep your nose clean for a couple of years. Then bring the medallion to me. Together we will be unstoppable.*
>
> *Your friend and benefactor,*
> *Artemis Fowl II*

(K °1 �🝆 • ⨝ ☺)(⚏ •)(⨳ 1⨝ ☺ ⊐ • ⨳ • 1)

Mulch crumpled the note. He made a cylinder of his fingers, and sucked the paper into his mouth. His dwarf molars quickly destroyed the evidence.

Mulch breathed deeply through his nose. It wasn't time to pop the Skaylian rock-worm wine cork just yet. A review of his case could take months, possibly years. But there was hope.

The dwarf wrapped his fingers around Artemis's medallion. Together they would be unstoppable.

𝕬𝕹𝕯 · 𝕾𝕺 · 𝕴𝕿 · 𝕰𝕹𝕯𝕾

Artemis Fowl's diary, disk 1 (encrypted)

I have decided to keep a diary. In fact, I am surprised that the idea has never occurred to me before. An intellect such as mine should be documented, so that future generations of Fowls can take advantage of my brilliant ideas.

Of course, I must be careful with such a document. As valuable as it would be to my descendants, it would be more valuable to the law enforcement agents who are forever trying to gather evidence against me.

It is even more important that I keep this journal a secret from my father. He is not himself since his escape from Russia. He has become obsessed with nobility and heroism. Abstract concepts at best. As far as I know, nobility and heroism are not accepted by any of the world's major banks. The family's fortune is in my hands, and I will preserve it in the way I always have, through ingenious plots. Most of these plots will be illegal. The best always are. Real profit lies in the shadowy areas beyond the law.

I have decided however, out of respect for my parents' values, to change my criteria for victim selection. It would seem better for the world's ecology if several global corporations went bankrupt, and so I have resolved to help them on their way. Not victimless crimes, but ones where few tears will be shed for the injured parties. This does not mean that I have become a weak, latter-day Robin Hood—far from it. I intend to reap substantial benefits from my crimes.

My father is not the only one to have changed. Butler has grown old almost overnight. His appearance is the same as ever, but he has slowed down considerably, no matter how he tries to hide it. But I will not replace him. He has been a loyal employee and his expertise in matters of intelligence will be invaluable. Perhaps Juliet will accompany me when actual protection is needed, though she now claims that a life in personal protection is not for her. Next week she travels to the United States to try out for a wrestling team. Apparently she has chosen Jade Princess as her stage name. I can only hope that she fails the audition. Though I doubt it. She is a Butler, after all.

Of course I have some ongoing ventures which I can work on without the aid of a bodyguard. In recent years I have developed software to divert funds from various bank accounts to my own. This software will have to be upgraded to stay ahead of the computer-crime squads. Version 2.0 should be online within six months. Then there is my talent for art forgery. In the past I have favored the Impressionists, but now for some reason I am drawn to more fantastical subject matter, such as the fairy creatures depicted by Arthur Rackham. But these projects must be suspended temporarily, for today I discovered that I am the victim of a conspiracy.

The day began strangely. When I awoke, I experienced an instant of weakness. For a single moment before I opened my eyes I felt content, my drive to accumulate wealth forgotten. This has never happened before. Perhaps the mood was left over from some magical dream, or perhaps my father's newfound positive attitude is contagious. Whatever the cause, I must be careful to avoid such lapses in the future. With my father in his current frame of mind, this is no time to lose my resolve. I must remain as driven as always. Crime is the way forward for the Fowls. Aurum Est Potestas.

Minutes later, a greater mystery presented itself. As I washed my face at the basin, two tiny objects fell from my eyes. Close examination in the lab revealed them to be semi-corroded tinted contact lenses. Not only that, but a mirrored layer had been added behind the tinted lens. Ingenious. Undoubtedly the work of a master craftsman. But to what purpose? It is strange, but even though I have no knowledge of these lenses or how they came to be in my eyes, I feel the answer is somewhere in my own brain. Hidden in the shadows.

Imagine my surprise when Juliet and Butler discovered mirrored lenses in their own eyes. These lenses are so clever they could have been my own invention, so obviously this unknown adversary must not be underestimated.

I will track the culprit down, make no mistake. No clue will be left uninvestigated. Butler has a contact in Limerick. An expert in the field of lenses and scopes. He may recognize our intruder's handiwork. Butler is on his way there, as I write.

And so, a new chapter begins in the life of Artemis Fowl II. In a matter of days my father returns with his newfound conscience. I will shortly be shipped off to boarding school, where I will have access only to a pathetic computer center and an even more pathetic laboratory. My bodyguard seems to be too old for physical tasks and there is an unknown adversary planting strange objects on my very person.

Overwhelming difficulties, you may think. An ordinary person would draw the shutters and hide from the world. But I am no ordinary person. I am Artemis Fowl, the latest in the Fowl crime dynasty, and I will not be turned from my path. I will find whoever planted those lenses and they will pay for their presumption. And once I am rid of this nuisance, my plans will proceed unhindered. I shall unleash a crime wave the likes of which has never been seen. The world will remember the name of Artemis Fowl.

Key to the Gnommish Alphabet

TOTALLY OBSESSED

**The J. Argon Clinic, Haven City,
the Lower Elements; Three Months Earlier**

The J. Argon Clinic was not a state hospital. Nobody stayed there for free. Argon and his staff of psychologists only treated fairies who could afford it. Of all the clinic's wealthy patients, Opal Koboi was unique. She had set up an emergency fund for herself more than a year before she was committed, *just in case* she ever went insane and needed to pay for treatment. It was a smart move. If Opal hadn't set up the fund, her family would undoubtedly have moved her to a cheaper facility. Not that the facility itself made much difference to Koboi, who had spent the past year drooling and having her reflexes tested. Dr. Argon doubted if Opal would have noticed a bull troll beating its chest before her.

The fund was not the only reason why Opal was unique.

Koboi was the Argon Clinic's celebrity patient. Following the attempt by the B'wa Kell goblin triad to seize power, Opal Koboi's name had become the most infamous four syllables under the world. After all, the pixie billionairess had formed an alliance with disgruntled LEP officer Briar Cudgeon, and funded the triad's war on Haven. Koboi had betrayed her own kind, and now her own mind was betraying her.

For the first six months of Koboi's incarceration, the clinic had been besieged by media filming the pixie's every twitch. The LEP guarded her cell door in shifts, and every staff member in the facility was treated to background checks and stern glares. Nobody was exempt. Even Dr. Argon himself was subjected to random DNA swabs to ensure that he was who he said he was. The LEP wasn't taking any chances with Koboi. If she escaped from Argon Clinic, not only would they be the laughingstock of the fairy world, but a highly dangerous criminal would be unleashed on Haven City.

But as time went by, fewer camera crews turned up at the gates each morning. After all, how many hours of drooling can an audience be expected to sit through? Gradually, the LEP crews were downsized from a dozen to six and finally to a single officer per shift. Where could Opal Koboi go? the authorities reasoned. There were a dozen cameras focused on her, twenty-four hours a day. There was a sub-cutaneous seeker-sleeper under the skin of her upper arm, and she was DNA swabbed four times daily. And even if someone did get Opal out, what could they do with her? The pixie couldn't even stand without help, and the sensors said her brain waves were little more than flat lines.

That said, Dr. Argon was very proud of his prize patient, and mentioned her name often at dinner parties. Since Opal Koboi had been admitted to the clinic, it had become almost fashionable to have a relative in therapy. Almost every family on the rich list had a crazy uncle in the attic. Now that crazy uncle could receive the best of care in the lap of luxury.

If only every fairy in the facility was as docile as Opal Koboi. All she needed was a few intravenous tubes and a monitor, which had been more than paid for by her first six months' medical fees. Dr. Argon fervently hoped that little Opal never woke up. Because once she did, the LEP would haul her off to court. And when she had been convicted of treason her assets would be frozen, including the clinic's fund. No, the longer Opal's nap lasted, the better for everyone, especially her. Because of their thin skulls and large brain volume, pixies were susceptible to various maladies, such as catatonia, amnesia, and narcolepsy. So it was quite possible that her coma would last for several years. And even if Opal did wake up, it was quite possible that her memory would stay locked up in some drawer in her huge pixie brain.

Dr. J. Argon did his rounds every night. He didn't

perform much hands-on therapy anymore, but he felt that it was good for the staff to feel his presence. If the other doctors knew that Jerbal Argon kept his finger on the pulse, then they were more likely to keep their own fingers on that pulse, too.

Argon always saved Opal for last. It calmed him somehow to see the small pixie asleep in her harness. Often at the end of a stressful day, he even envied Opal her untroubled existence. When it had all become too much for the pixie, her brain had simply shut down, all except for the most vital functions. She still breathed, and occasionally the monitors registered a dream spike in her brain waves. But other than that, for all intents and purposes, Opal Koboi was no more.

On one fateful night, Jerbal Argon was feeling more stressed than usual. His wife was suing for divorce on the grounds that he hadn't said more than six consecutive words to her in over two years. The Council was threatening to pull his government grant because of all the money he was making from his new celebrity clients, and he had a pain in his hip that no amount of magic could seem to cure. The warlocks said it was probably all in his head. They seemed to think it was funny.

Argon limped down the clinic's eastern wing, checking the plasma chart of each patient as he passed their room. He winced each time his left foot touched the floor.

The two janitor pixies, Mervall and Descant Brill, were outside Opal's room, picking up dust with static brushes.

Pixies made wonderful employees. They were methodical, patient, and determined. When a pixie was instructed to do something, you could rest assured that that thing would be done. Plus, they were cute, with their baby faces and disproportionately large heads. Just looking at a pixie cheered most people up. They were walking therapy.

"Evening, boys," said Argon. "How's our favorite patient?"

Merv, the elder twin, glanced up from his brush. "Same old, same old, Jerry," he said. "I thought she moved a toe earlier, but it was just a trick of the light."

Argon laughed, but it was forced. He did not like to be called Jerry. It was his clinic after all; he deserved some respect. But good janitors were like gold dust, and the Brill brothers had been keeping the building spotless and ship-shape for nearly two years now. The Brills were almost celebrities themselves. Twins were very rare among the People. Mervall and Descant were the only pixie pair currently residing in Haven. They had been featured on several TV programs, including *Canto*, PPTV's highest-rated chat show.

LEP's Corporal Grub Kelp was on sentry duty. When Argon reached Opal's room, the corporal was engrossed in a movie on his video goggles. Argon didn't blame him. Guarding Opal Koboi was about as exciting as watching toenails grow.

"Good film?" inquired the doctor pleasantly.

Grub raised the lenses. "Not bad. It's a human Western. Plenty of shooting and squinting."

"Maybe I'll borrow it when you're finished?"

"No problem, doctor. But handle it carefully. Human disks are very expensive. I'll give you a special cloth."

Argon nodded. He remembered Grub Kelp now. The LEP officer was very particular about his possessions. He had already written two letters of complaint to the clinic board about a protruding floor rivet that had scratched his boots.

Argon consulted Koboi's chart. The plasma screen on the wall displayed a constantly updated feed from the sensors attached to her temples. There was no change, nor did he expect there to be. Her vitals were all normal, and her brain activity was minimal. She'd had a dream earlier in the evening but now her mind had settled. And finally, as if he needed telling, the seeker-sleeper implanted in her arm informed him that Opal Koboi was indeed where she was supposed to be. Generally, the seeker-sleepers were implanted in the head, but pixie skulls were too fragile for any local surgery.

Jerbal punched in his personal code on the reinforced door's keypad. The heavy door slid back to reveal a spacious room with gently pulsing floor mood lights. The walls were soft plastic, and gentle sounds of nature spilled from recessed speakers. At the moment a brook was splashing over flat rocks.

In the middle of the room, Opal Koboi hung suspended in a full body harness. The straps were gel padded and they adjusted automatically to any body movement. If Opal did happen to wake, the harness could be remotely triggered to seal like a net, preventing her from harming herself or escaping.

Argon checked the monitor pads, making sure they had good contact on Koboi's forehead. He lifted one of the pixie's eyelids, shining a pencil light at the pupil. It contracted slightly, but Opal did not avert her eyes.

"Well, anything to tell me today, Opal?" asked the doctor softly. "An opening chapter for my book?"

Argon liked to talk to Koboi, just in case she could hear. When she woke up, he reasoned, he would have already established rapport.

"Nothing? Not a single insight?"

Opal did not react. As she hadn't for almost a year.

"Ah well," said Argon, swabbing the inside of Koboi's mouth with the last cotton ball in his pocket. "Maybe tomorrow, eh?"

He rolled the cotton ball across a sponge pad on his clipboard. Seconds later, Opal's name flashed up on a tiny screen.

"DNA never lies," muttered Argon, tossing the ball into a recycling bin.

With one last look at his patient, Jerbal Argon turned toward the door.

"Sleep well, Opal," he said almost fondly.

He felt calm again, the pain in his hip almost forgotten.

Koboi was as far under as she had ever been. She wasn't going to wake up any time soon. The Koboi fund was safe.

It's amazing just how wrong one gnome can be.

Opal Koboi was not catatonic, but neither was she awake. She was somewhere in between, floating in a liquid world of meditation, where every memory was a bubble of multi-colored light popping gently in her consciousness.

Since her early teens Opal had been a disciple of Gola Schweem, the cleansing coma guru. Schweem's theory was that there was a deeper level of sleep than experienced by most fairies. The cleansing coma state could usually only be reached after decades of discipline and practice. Opal had reached her first cleansing coma at the age of fourteen.

The benefits of the cleansing coma were that a fairy could spend the sleep time thinking, or in this case, plotting, and also awake feeling completely refreshed. Opal's coma was so complete that her mind was almost entirely separated from her body. She could fool the sensors, and felt no embarrassment at the indignities of intravenous feeding and assisted bathings. The longest recorded consciously self-induced coma was forty-seven days. Opal had been under for eleven months and counting, though she wasn't planning to be counting much longer.

When Opal Koboi had joined forces with Briar Cudgeon and his goblins, she had realized that she would need a backup plan. Their scheme to overthrow the LEP had been ingenious, but there had always been a chance that something could go wrong. In the event that it did, Opal had had no intention of spending the rest of her life in prison. The only way she could make a clean getaway was if everybody thought she was still locked up. So Opal had begun to make preparations.

The first had been to set up the emergency fund for the Argon Clinic. This would ensure that she would be sent to the right place if she had to induce a cleansing coma. The second step had been to get two of her most trusted personnel installed in the clinic, to help with her eventual escape. Then she began siphoning huge amounts of gold from her businesses. Opal did not wish to become an impoverished exile.

The final step had been to donate some of her own DNA, and green-light the creation of a clone that would take her place in the padded cell. Cloning was completely illegal, and had been banned by fairy law for more than five hundred years, since the first experiments in Atlantis. Cloning was by no means a perfect science. Doctors had never been able to create an exact fairy clone. The clones looked fine, but they were basically shells with only enough brain power to run the body's basic functions. They were missing the spark of true life. A fully grown clone resembled nothing more than the original person in a coma. Perfect.

Opal had had a greenhouse lab constructed far from Koboi Industries, and had diverted enough funds to keep the project active for two years: the exact time it would take to grow a clone of herself to adulthood. Then, when she wanted to escape from the Argon Clinic, a perfect replica of herself would be left in her place. The LEP would never know she was gone.

As things had turned out, she had been right to plan ahead. Briar had proved treacherous, and a small group of fairies and humans had ensured that his betrayal would lead to her own downfall. Now Opal had a goal to bolster her willpower. She would maintain this coma for as long as it took, because there was a score to be settled. Foaly, Root, Holly Short, and the human Artemis Fowl. They were the ones responsible for her defeat. Soon she would be free of this clinic, and then she would visit those who had caused her such despair and give them a little despair of their own. Once her enemies were defeated she could proceed with the second phase of her plan: introducing the Mud Men to the People in a way that could not be covered up by a few mind wipes. The secret life of fairies was almost at an end.

Opal Koboi's brain released a few happy endorphins. The thought of revenge always gave her a warm fuzzy feeling.

The Brill brothers watched Dr. Argon limp up the corridor.

"Moron," muttered Merv, using his telescopic vacuum pole to chase some dust out of a corner.

"You said it," agreed Scant. "Old Jerry couldn't analyze a bowl of vole curry. No wonder his wife is leaving him. If he was any good as a shrink, he would've seen that coming."

Merv collapsed the vacuum. "How are we doing?"

Scant checked his moonometer. "Ten past eight."

"Good. How's Corporal Kelp?"

"Still watching the movie. This guy is perfect. We have to go tonight. The LEP could send someone smart for the next shift. And if we wait any longer, the clone will grow another inch."

"You're right. Check the spy cameras."

Scant lifted the lid on what appeared to be a janitor's trolley, festooned as it was with mops, rags, and sprays. Hidden beneath a tray of vacuum nozzles was a color monitor split into several screens.

"Well?" hissed Merv.

Scant did not answer immediately, taking time to check all the screens. The video feed was from various micro-cameras that Opal had installed around the clinic before her incarceration. The spy cameras were actually genetically engineered organic material. So the pictures they sent were literally a live feed. The world's first living machines. Totally undetectable by bug sweepers.

"Night crew only," he said at last. "Nobody in this sector except Corporal Idiot over there."

"What about the parking lot?"

"Clear."

Merv held out his hand. "Okay, brother. This is it. No turning back. Are we in? Do we want Opal Koboi back?"

Scant blew a lock of black hair from one round pixie eye.

"Yes, because if she comes back on her own, Opal will find a way to make us suffer," he said, shaking his brother's hand. "So yes, we're in."

Merv took a remote control from his pocket. The device was tuned to a sonix receiver planted in the clinic's gable wall. This in turn was connected to a balloon of acid that lay gently on the clinic's main power cube in the parking lot junction box. A second balloon sat atop the backup cube in the maintenance basement. As the clinic's janitors, it had been a simple matter for Merv and Scant to plant the acid balloons the previous evening. Of course, the Argon Clinic was also connected to the main grid, but if the cubes did go down, there would be a two-minute interval before the main power kicked in. There was no need for more elaborate arrangements; after all, this was a medical facility, not a prison.

Merv took a deep breath, flicked the safety cover, and pressed the red button. The remote control emitted an infrared command activating two sonix charges. The charges sent out sound waves that burst the balloons, and the balloons dumped their acidic contents on the clinic's power cubes. Twenty seconds later the cubes were completely eaten away and the whole building was plunged into darkness. Merv and Scant quickly put on night-vision goggles.

As soon as the power failed, green strip lights began

pulsing gently on the floor, guiding the way to the exits. Merv and Scant moved quickly and purposefully. Scant steered the trolley, and Merv made straight for Corporal Kelp.

Grub was pulling the video glasses from over his eyes.

"Hey," he said, disoriented by the sudden darkness. "What's going on here?"

"Power failure," said Merv, bumping into him with calculated clumsiness. "Those lines are a nightmare. I've been telling Dr. Argon, but nobody wants to spend money on maintenance when there are fancy company cars to be bought."

Merv was not chatting for the fun of it; he was waiting for the soluble sedative pad he had pressed onto Grub's wrist to take effect.

"Tell me about it," said Grub, suddenly blinking a lot more than he generally did. "I've been lobbying for new lockers at Police Plaza. I'm really thirsty. Is anyone else thirsty?" Grub stiffened, frozen by the serum that was spreading through his system. The LEP officer would snap out of it in under two minutes and be instantly alert. He would have no memory of his unconsciousness, and with luck, he would not notice the time lapse.

"Go," said Scant tersely.

Merv was already gone. With ease, he punched Dr. Argon's code into Opal's door. He completed this action faster than Argon ever could, due to hours spent practicing on a stolen pad in his apartment. Argon's code changed every week, but the Brill brothers made certain that they were cleaning outside the room when Argon was on his rounds. The pixies generally had the complete code by midweek.

The battery-powered pad light winked green, and the door slid back. Opal Koboi swung gently before him, suspended in her harness like a bug in an exotic cocoon.

Merv winched her down onto the trolley. Moving briskly, and with practiced precision, he rolled up Opal's sleeve and located the scar in her upper arm where the seeker-sleeper had been inserted. He gripped the hard lump between his thumb and forefinger.

"Scalpel," he said, holding out his free hand. Scant passed him the instrument. Merv took a breath, held it, and made a one-inch incision in Opal's flesh. He wiggled his index finger into the hole and rolled out the electronic capsule. It was encased in silicone and roughly the size of a pain-killer.

"Seal it up," he ordered.

Scant bent close to the wound and placed a thumb at each end.

"Heal," he whispered, and blue sparks of fairy magic ran rings around his fingers, sinking into the wound. In seconds the folds of skin had zipped themselves together, with only a pale pink scar to show that a cut had been made—a scar almost identical to the one that already existed. Opal's own magic had dried up months ago, as she was in no position to complete a power-restoring ritual.

"Miss Koboi," said Merv briskly. "Time to get up. Wakey-wakey."

He unstrapped Opal completely from the harness. The unconscious pixie collapsed onto the lid of the cleaning trolley. Merv slapped her across the cheek, bringing a blush to her face. Opal's breathing rate increased slightly, but her eyes remained closed.

"Jolt her," said Scant.

Merv pulled an LEP-issue buzz baton from inside his jacket. He powered it up and touched Opal on the elbow. The pixie's body jerked spasmodically, and Opal Koboi shot into consciousness, a sleeper waking from a nightmare.

"Cudgeon," she screamed. "You betrayed me!"

Merv grabbed her shoulders. "Miss Koboi. It's us, Mervall and Descant. It's time."

Opal glared at him, wild eyed.

"Brill?" she said after several deep breaths.

"That's right. Merv and Scant. We need to go."

"Go? What do you mean?"

"Leave," said Merv urgently. "We have about a minute."

Opal shook her head, dislodging the after-trance daze. "Merv and Scant. We need to go."

Merv helped her from the trolley's lid. "That's right. The clone is ready."

Scant peeled back a sealed foil false bottom in the

trolley. Inside lay a cloned replica of Opal Koboi wearing an Argon Clinic coma suit. The clone was identical, down to the last follicle. Scant removed an oxygen mask from the clone's face, hauled it from its resting place, and began cinching her into the harness.

"Remarkable," said Opal, brushing the clone's skin with her knuckle. "Am I that beautiful?"

"Oh yes," said Merv. "That and more."

Suddenly, Opal screeched. "Idiots. Its eyes are open. It can see me!"

Scant closed the clone's lids hurriedly. "Don't worry, Miss Koboi, it can't tell anyone, even if its brain could decipher what it sees."

Opal climbed groggily into the trolley. "But its eyes can register images. Foaly may think to check. That infernal centaur."

"Don't fret, Miss," said Scant, folding the trolley's false bottom over his mistress. "Very soon now, that will be the least of Foaly's worries."

Opal strapped the oxygen mask across her face. "Later," she said, her voice muffled by the plastic. "Talk, later."

Koboi drifted into a natural sleep, exhausted by even this small exertion. It could be hours before the pixie regained consciousness. After a coma of that length, there was even the risk that Opal would never be quite as smart as she once was.

"Time?" said Merv.

Scant glanced at his moonometer. "Thirty seconds left."

Merv finished cinching the straps exactly as they had been. Pausing only to dab sweat from his brow, he made a second incision with his scalpel, this time in the clone's arm, and inserted the seeker-sleeper. While Scant sealed the cut with a blast of magical sparks, Merv rearranged the cleaning paraphernalia over the trolley's false section.

Scant bobbed impatiently. "Eight seconds, seven. By the gods, this is the last time I break the boss out of a clinic and replace her with a clone."

Merv spun the trolley on its castors, pushing it through the open doorway. "Five . . . four . . ."

Scant did one last check around, running his eyeballs across everything they had touched.

"Three . . . two . . ."

They were out, pulling the door behind them.

"One . . ."

Corporal Grub slumped slightly, then jerked to attention.

"Hey . . . what the? I'm really thirsty. Is anyone else thirsty?"

Merv stuffed the night-vision goggles into the trolley, blinking a bead of sweat from his eyelid. "It's the air in here. I get dehydrated all the time. Terrible headaches."

Grub pinched the bridge of his nose. "Me too. I'm going to write a letter, as soon as the lights come back."

Just then the lights did come back, flickering on one after another down the length of the corridor.

"There we go." Scant grinned. "Panic over. Maybe now they'll buy us some new circuits, eh, brother?"

Dr. Argon came barreling down the passageway, almost keeping pace with the flickering lights.

"Your hip is better, then, Jerry?" said Merv.

Argon ignored the pixies, his eyes wide, his breath ragged.

"Corporal Kelp," he panted. "Koboi, is she? Has she . . ."

Grub rolled his eyes. "Calm yourself, doctor. Miss Koboi is still suspended where you left her. Take a look."

Argon flattened his palms against the wall, first checking the vitals.

"Okay, no change. No change. A two-minute lapse, but that's okay."

"I told you," said Grub. "And while you're here, I need to talk to you about these headaches I've been having."

Argon brushed him aside. "I need a cotton ball. Scant, do you have any?"

Scant slapped his pockets. "Sorry, Jerry. Not on me."

"Don't call me Jerry!" howled Jerbal Argon, ripping the lid from the cleaning trolley. "There must be cotton balls in here somewhere," he said, sweat pasting thin hair across his wide gnome's forehead. "It's a janitor's box, for heaven's sake." His blunt fingers scrabbled through the trolley's contents, scraping across the false bottom.

Merv elbowed him out of the way before he could discover the secret compartment or spy screens. "Here we are, doctor," he said, grabbing a tub of cotton balls. "A month's supply. Knock yourself out."

Argon fumbled a single ball from the pack, discarding the rest.

"DNA never lies," he muttered, punching his code into the keypad. "DNA never lies."

He rushed into the room and roughly swabbed the inside of the clone's mouth. The Brill brothers held their breath. They had expected to be out of the clinic before this happened. Argon rolled the cotton ball's head across the sponge pad on his clipboard. A moment later, Opal Koboi's name flashed onto the board's miniplasma screen.

Argon heaved a massive sigh, resting his hands on both knees. He threw the observers a shamefaced grin. "Sorry. I panicked. If we lost Koboi, the clinic would never live it down. I'm just a little paranoid, I suppose. Faces can be altered, but . . ."

"DNA never lies," said Merv and Scant simultaneously.

Grub reset his video goggles. "I think Dr. Argon needs a little vacation."

"You're telling me." Merv snickered, rolling the trolley toward the maintenance elevator. "Anyway, we'd better get going, brother. We need to isolate the cause of the power failure."

Scant followed him down the corridor. "Any idea where the problem could be?"

"I have a hunch. Let's try the parking lot, or maybe the basement."

"Whatever you say. After all, you are the older brother."

"And wiser," added Merv. "Don't forget that."

The pixies continued down the corridor, their brisk banter masking the fact that their knees were shaking and their hearts were battering their rib cages. It wasn't until they had removed the evidence of their acid bombs, and were well on their way home in the van, that they began to breathe normally again.

Back in the apartment he shared with Scant, Merv unzipped Koboi from her sealed hiding place. Any worries they'd had about Opal's IQ taking a dip immediately vanished. Their employer's eyes were bright and aware.

"Bring me up to speed," she said, climbing shakily from the trolley. Even though her mind was fully functioning, it would take a couple of days in an electromassager to get her muscles back to normal.

Merv helped her onto a low sofa. "Everything is in place. The funds, the surgeon, everything."

Opal drank greedily straight from a jug of core water on the coffee table. "Good, good. And what of my enemies?"

Scant stood beside his brother. They were almost identical except for a slight wideness in Merv's brow. Merv had always been the smart one.

"We have kept tabs on them, as you asked," said Scant.

Opal stopped drinking. "Asked?"

"Instructed," stammered Scant. "Instructed, of course. That's what I meant."

Koboi's eyes narrowed. "I do hope the Brill brothers haven't developed any independent notions since I've been asleep."

Scant stooped slightly, almost bowing. "No, no, Miss Koboi. We live to serve. Only to serve."

"Yes," agreed Opal. "And you live only as long as you do serve. Now, my enemies. They are well and happy, I trust."

"Oh yes. Julius Root goes from strength to strength as LEP Commander. He has been nominated for the Council."

Opal smiled a vicious wolverine's smile. "The Council. Such a long way to fall. And Holly Short?"

"Back on full active duty. Six successful reconnaissance missions since you induced your coma. Her name has been put on the list for promotion to major."

"Major, indeed. Well, the least we can do is to make sure that promotion never comes through. I plan to wreck Holly Short's career, so she dies in disgrace."

"The centaur Foaly is as obnoxious as ever," continued Scant Brill. "I suggest a particularly nasty . . ."

Opal raised a delicate finger, cutting him off. "No. Nothing happens to Foaly just yet. He will be defeated by intellect alone. Twice in my life, someone has outsmarted me. Both times it was Foaly. Just killing him requires no ingenuity. I want him beaten, humiliated, and alone." She clapped her hands in delighted anticipation. "And then I will kill him."

"We have been monitoring Artemis Fowl's communications. Apparently the human youth has spent most of the past year trying to find a certain painting. We have traced the painting to Munich."

"A painting? Really?" Cogwheels turned in Opal's brain. "Well, let's make sure we get to it before he does. Maybe we can add a little something to his work of art."

Scant nodded. "Yes. That's not a problem. I'll go tonight."

Opal stretched out on the sofa like a cat in the sunlight. "Good. This is turning out to be a lovely day. Now, send for the surgeon."

The Brill brothers glanced at each other.

"Miss Koboi?" said Mervall nervously.

"Yes, what is it?"

"The surgeon. This kind of operation cannot be reversed, even by magic. Are you sure you wouldn't like to think . . ."

Opal leaped from the sofa. Her cheeks were crimson with rage. "Think! You'd like me to think about it! What do you imagine I have been doing for the past year? Thinking! Twenty-four hours a day. I don't care about magic. Magic did not help me to escape, science did. Science will be my magic. Now, no more advice, Merv, or your brother will be an only child. Is that clear?"

Merv was stunned. He had never seen Opal in such a rage. The coma had changed her.

"Yes, Miss Koboi."

"Now, summon the surgeon."

"At once, Miss Koboi."

Opal lay back on the sofa. Soon everything would be right in the world. Her enemies would shortly be dead or discredited. Once those loose ends were tied up, she could get on with her new life. Koboi rubbed the tips of her pointed ears. What would she look like, she wondered, as a human?

The first book in a new series about
Artemis Fowl's younger brothers,
by internationally best-selling author Eoin Colfer

There are things to know about the world.

Surely you realize that what you know is not everything there is to know. In spite of humankind's ingenuity, there are shadows too dark for your kind to fully illuminate. The very mantle of our planet is one example; the ocean floor is another. And in these shadows we live. The Hidden Ones. The magical creatures who have removed ourselves from the destructive human orbit. Once, we fairies ruled the surface as humans do now, as bacteria will in the future, but for now, we are content for the most part to exist in our underground civilization. For ten thousand years, fairies have used our magic and technology to shield ourselves from prying eyes, and to heal the beleaguered Earth mother, Danu. We fairies have a saying that is writ large in golden tiles on the altar mosaic of the Hey Hey Temple, and the saying is this: WE DIG DEEP AND WE ENDURE.

But there is always one maverick who does not care a fig for fairy mosaics and is hell-bent on reaching the surface. Usually this maverick is a troll. And specifically in this case, the maverick is a troll who will shortly and for a ridiculous reason be named Whistle Blower.

For here begins the second documented cycle of Fowl adventures.

MEET THE ANTAGONISTS

The Baddie: Lord Teddy Bleedham-Drye.
The Duke of Scilly.

If a person wants to murder the head of a family, then it is very important that the entire family also be done away with, or the distraught survivors might very well decide to take bloody revenge, or at least make a detailed report at the local police station. There is, in fact, an entire chapter on this exact subject in *The Criminal Mastermind's Almanac*, an infamous guidebook for aspiring ruthless criminals by Professor Wulf Bane, which was turned down by every reputable publisher but is available on demand from the author. The actual chapter name is "Kill Them All. Even the Pets." A gruesome title that would put most normal people off from reading it, but Lord Teddy Bleedham-Drye, Duke of Scilly, was not a normal person, and the juiciest phrases in his copy of *The Criminal Mastermind's Almanac* were marked in pink highlighter, and the book itself was dedicated as follows:

> To Teddy
> From one criminal mastermind to another
> Don't be a stranger
> Wulfy

Lord Bleedham-Drye had dedicated most of his one hundred and fifty years on this green earth to staying *on* this green earth as long as possible—as opposed to being buried beneath it. In television interviews he credited his youthful appearance to yoga and fish oil, but in actual fact, Lord Teddy had spent much of his inherited fortune traveling the globe in search of any potions and pills, legal or not, that would extend his life span. As a roving ambassador for the Crown, Lord Teddy could easily find an excuse to visit the most far-flung corners of the planet in the name of culture, when in fact he was keeping his eyes open for anything that grew, swam, waddled, or crawled that would help him stay alive for even a minute longer than his allotted four score and ten.

So far in his quest, Lord Teddy had tried every so-called *eternal youth therapy* for which there was even the flimsiest of supporting evidence. He had, among other things, ingested tons of willow-bark extract, swallowed millions of antioxidant tablets, slurped gallons of therapeutic arsenic, injected the cerebrospinal fluid of the endangered Madagascan lemur, devoured countless helpings of

Southeast Asian liver-fluke spaghetti, and spent almost a month suspended over an active volcanic rift in Iceland, funneling the restorative volcanic gas up the leg holes of his linen shorts. These and other extreme practices—never ever to be tried at home—had indeed kept Bleedham-Drye breathing and vital thus far, but there had been side effects. The lemur fluid had caused his forearms to elongate so that his hands dangled below his knees. The arsenic had paralyzed the left corner of his mouth so that it was forever curled in a sardonic-looking sneer, and the volcanic embers had scalded his bottom, forcing Teddy to walk in a slightly bowlegged manner as though trying to keep his balance in rough seas. Bleedham-Drye considered these secondary effects a small price to pay for his wrinkle-free complexion, luxuriant mane of hair, and spade of black beard, and of course the vigor that helped him endure lengthy treks and safaris in the hunt for any more rumored life-extenders.

But Lord Teddy was all too aware that he had yet to hit the jackpot, therapeutically speaking, in regards to his quest for an unreasonably extended life. It was true that he had eked out a few extra decades, but what was that in the face of eternity? There were jellyfish that, as a matter of course, lived longer than he had. Jellyfish! They didn't even have brains, for heaven's sake.

Teddy found himself frustrated, which he hated, because stress gave a fellow wrinkles.

A new direction was called for.

No more penny-ante half measures, cribbing a year here and a season there.

I must find the fountain of youth, he resolved one evening while lying in his brass tub full of electric eels, which he had heard did wonders for a chap's circulation.

As it turned out, Lord Bleedham-Drye did find the fountain of youth, but it was not a fountain in the traditional sense of the word, as the life-giving liquid was contained in the venom of a mythological creature. And the family he would possibly have to murder to access it was none other than the Fowls of Dublin, Ireland, who were not overly fond of being murdered.

This is how the entire regrettable episode kicked off.

Lord Teddy Bleedham-Drye reasoned that the time-honored way of doing a thing was to ask the fellows who had already done the thing how they had managed to do it, and so he set out to interview the oldest people on earth. This was not as easy as it might sound, even in the era of worldwide-webbery and marvelous miniature communication devices, for many aged folks do not advertise the fact that they have passed the century mark lest they be plagued by health-magazine journalists or telegrams from various queens. But nevertheless, over the course of five years, Lord Teddy managed to track down several of these elusive oldsters, finding them all to be either tediously virtuous, which was of little use to him, or lucky, which could neither be counted on nor stolen. And such was the way of it until he located an Irish monk who was working in an elephant sanctuary in California, of all places, having long since given up on helping humans. Brother Colman looked not a day over fifty, and was, in fact, in remarkable shape for a man who claimed to be almost five hundred years old.

Once Lord Teddy had slipped a liberal dose of sodium pentothal into the Irishman's tea, Brother Colman told a very interesting story of how the holy well on Dalkey Island had come by its healing waters when he was a monk there in the fifteenth century.

Teddy did not believe a word of it, but the name *Dalkey* did sound an alarm bell somewhere in the back of his mind. A bell he muted for the present.

The fool is raving, he thought. *I gave him too much truth serum.*

With the so-called monk in a chemical daze, Bleedham-Drye performed a couple of simple verification checks, not really expecting anything exciting.

First he unbuttoned the man's shirt, and found to his surprise that Brother Colman's chest was latticed with ugly scars, which would be consistent with the man's story but was not exactly proof.

The idiot might have been gored by one of his own elephants, Teddy realized. But Lord Bleedham-Drye had seen many wounds in his time and never anything this dreadful on a living body.

There ain't no fooling my second test, thought Teddy, and with a flash of his pruning shears he snipped off Brother Colman's left pinky. After all, radiocarbon dating never lied.

It would be several weeks before the results came back from the Advanced Accelerator Mass Spectrometer Laboratory, and by that time Teddy was back in England once again, lounging dejectedly in his bath of electric eels in the family seat: Childerblaine House, on the island of St. George in the Scilly Isles. Interestingly enough, the island had been so named because in one of the various versions of the St. George legend, the beheaded dragon's body had been dumped into Cornish waters and drifted out to the Scilly Isles, where it settled on a submerged rock and fossilized, which provided a romantic explanation for the small island's curved spine of ridges.

When Lord Teddy came upon the envelope from AAMSL in his pile of mail, he sliced it open listlessly, fully expecting that the Brother Colman excursion had been a big waste of precious time and shrinking fortune.

But the results on that single page made Teddy sit up so quickly that several eels were slopped from the tub.

"Good heavens!" he exclaimed, his halo of dark hair curled and vibrating from the eel charge. "I'm off to Dalkey Island, begorra."

The laboratory report was brief and cursory in the way of scientific reports:

The supplied specimen, it read, *is in the four-hundred- to five-hundred-year-old age range.*

Lord Teddy outfitted himself in his standard apparel of high boots, riding breeches, and a tweed hunting jacket, all topped off with his old commando beret. And he loaded up his wooden speedboat for what the police these days like to call a stakeout. It was only when he was halfway across the Irish Sea in the Juventas that Lord Teddy realized why the name *Dalkey* sounded so familiar. The Fowl fellow hung his hat there.

Artemis Fowl.

A force to be reckoned with. Teddy had heard a few stories about Artemis Fowl, and even more about his son Artemis II.

Rumors, he told himself. *Rumors, hearsay, and balderdash.*

And even if the stories were true, the Duke of Scilly's determination never wavered.

I shall have that troll's venom, he thought, opening the V-12 throttles wide. *And I shall live forever.*

The Goodies (relatively speaking)
Dalkey Island, Dublin, Ireland.
Three Weeks Later.

Behold Myles and Beckett Fowl, passing a late summer evening on the family's private beach. If you look past the superficial differences—wardrobe, spectacles, hairstyles, and so on—you notice that the boys' facial features are very similar but not absolutely identical. This is because they are dizygotic twins, and were, in fact, the first recorded nonidentical twins to be born conjoined, albeit only from wrist to little finger. The attending surgeon separated them with a flash of her scalpel, and neither twin suffered any ill effects, apart from matching pink scars that ran along the outside of their palms. Myles and Beckett often touched scars to comfort each other. It was their version of a high five, which they called a wrist bump. This habit was both touching and slightly gross.

Apart from their features, the fraternal twins were, as one tutor noted, "very different animals." Myles had an IQ of 170 and was fanatically neat, while Beckett's IQ was a mystery, because he chewed the test into pulpy blobs from which he made a sculpture of a hamster in a bad mood, which he titled *Angry Hamster*.

Also, Beckett was far from neat. In fact, his parents were forced to take up Mindfulness just to calm themselves down whenever they attempted to put some order on his catastrophically untidy side of the bedroom.

It was obvious from their early days in a double cradle that the twins did not share similar personalities. When they were teething, Beckett would chew pacifiers ragged, while Myles chose to nibble thoughtfully on the eraser end of a pencil. As a toddler, Myles liked to emulate his big brother, Artemis, by wearing tiny black suits that had to be custom-made. Beckett preferred to run free as nature intended, and when he finally did agree to wear something, it was plastic training pants, which he used to store his pet goldfish, Gloop (named for the sound it made—or at least the sound the goldfish was blamed for).

As the brothers grew older, the differences between them became more obvious. Myles became ever more fastidious, 3-D–printing a fresh suit every day and taming his wild jet-black Fowl hair with a seaweed-based gel that both moisturized the scalp and nourished the brain, while Beckett made zero attempt to tame the wild blond curls that he had inherited from his mother's side of the family, and continued to sulk when he was forced to wear any clothes, with the exception of the only article he never removed—a golden necktie that had once been Gloop. Myles had cured and laminated the goldfish when it passed away, and Beckett wore it always as a keepsake. This habit was both touching and extremely gross.

Perhaps you have heard of the Fowl family of Ireland? They are quite notorious in certain shadowy circles. The twins' father was once the world's preeminent crime lord, but he had a change of heart and reinvented himself as a champion of the environment. Myles and Beckett's older brother, Artemis II, had also been quite the criminal virtuoso, hatching schemes involving massive amounts of gold bullion, fairy police forces, and time travel, to name but a few. Fortunately for more or less everyone except aliens,

Artemis had recently turned his attention to outer space, and was currently six months into a five-year mission to Mars in a revolutionary self-winding rocket ship that he had built in the family barn. By the time the world's various authorities, including NASA, ASCO, ALR, CSNA, and UKSA, had caught wind of the project and begun to marshal their objections, Artemis had already passed the moon.

The twins themselves were to have many adventures, some of which would kill them (though not permanently), but this particular episode began a week after their eleventh birthday. Myles and Beckett were walking along the stony beach of Dalkey Island, where the Fowl family had recently moved to Villa Éco, a newly built, state-of-the art, environmentally friendly house attached to a renovated Martello tower. The twins' father had donated Fowl Manor, their rambling ancestral home, to a cooperative of organic farmers, declaring, "It is time for the Fowls to embrace planet Earth."

On this summer evening, the twins' mother was delivering a lecture in Dublin's National Library with her husband in attendance. Some years previously, Angeline had suffered from what Shakespeare called "the grief that does not speak," and, in an effort to understand her depression, had completed a mental health doctorate at Trinity College and now spoke at conferences around the world. The twins were being watched over by the house itself, which had an Artemis-designed Nano Artificial Neural Network

Intelligence system, or NANNI, to keep an electronic eye on them.

Myles was collecting seaweed for his homemade hair gel, and Beckett was trying to learn seal language from a dolphin just off-shore.

"We must be away, brother," Myles said. "Bedtime. Our young bodies require ten hours of sleep to ensure proper brain development."

Beckett lay on a rock and clapped his hands. "*Arf*," he said. "*Arf.*"

Myles tugged at his suit jacket and frowned behind the frames of his thick-rimmed glasses. "Beck, are you attempting to speak in seal language?"

"*Arf*," said Beckett, who was wearing knee-length cargo shorts and his gold necktie.

"That is not even a seal. That is a dolphin."

"Dolphins are smart," said Beckett. "They know things."

"That is true, brother, but a dolphin's vocal cords make it impossible for it to speak in the language of a seal. Why don't you simply learn the dolphin's language?"

Beckett beamed. "Yes! You are a genius, brother. Step one, swap barks for whistles."

Myles sighed. Now his twin was whistling at a dolphin, and they would once again fail to get to bed on time.

Myles stuffed a handful of seaweed into his bucket. "Please, brother. My brain will never reach optimum productivity if we don't leave now." He tapped an earpiece in his right ear. "NANNI, help me out. Please send a drobot to carry my brother home."

"Negative," said the house system in a strangely accented female voice, which Beckett instinctively trusted for some reason. "No flying Beckett home. Mother's orders."

Myles could not understand why his mother refused to authorize short-range flights for Beckett. In tests, the drone/robots had only dropped the dummy Becketts twice, but his mother insisted the drobots were for emergencies only.

"Beckett!" he called. "If you agree to come back to the house, I will tell you a story before bed."

Beckett flipped over on the rock. "Which story?" he asked.

"How about the thrilling discovery of the Schwarzschild radius, which led directly to the identification of black holes?" suggested Myles.

Beckett was not impressed. "How about the adventures of Gloop and Angry Hamster in the Dimension of Fire?"

Now it was Myles's turn to be unimpressed. "Beck, that's preposterous. Fish and hamsters do not even share the same environment. And neither could survive in a dimension of fire."

"You're preposterous," said Beckett and went back to his whistling.

The crown of Beck's head will be burned by the evening UV rays, thought Myles.

"Very well," he said. "Gloop and Angry Hamster it is."

"And Dolphin," said Beckett. "He wants to be in the story, too."

Myles sighed. "Dolphin, too."

"Hooray!" said Beckett, skipping across the rocks. "Story time. Wrist bump?"

Myles raised his palm for a bump and wondered, *If I'm the smart one, why do we always do exactly what Beck wants us to?*

Myles asked himself this question a lot.

"Now, brother," he said, "please say good night to your friend, and let us be off."

Beckett turned to do as he was told, but only because it suited him.

If Beckett had not turned to bid the dolphin farewell, then perhaps the entire series of increasingly bizarre events that followed might have been avoided. There would have been no nefarious villain, no ridiculously named trolls, no shadowy organizations, no interrogations by a nun (which are known in the intelligence community as *nunterrogations*, believe it or not), and a definite lack of imaginary head lice. But Myles did turn, precisely two seconds after a troll had surged upward through the loose shale at the water's edge and collapsed onto the beach.

Fairies are defined as being "small, humanoid, supernatural creatures possessed of magical powers," a description that applies neatly to elves, gnomes, sprites, and pixies. It is, however, a human definition, and therefore as incomplete as human knowledge on the subject. The fairies' definition of themselves is more concise and can be found in the Fairy Book, which is their constitution, so to speak, the original of which is behind crystal in the Hey Hey Temple in Haven City, the subterranean fairy capital. It states:

```
Fairy, faerie, or faery: A creature of
the earth. Often magical. Never will-
fully destructive.
```

No mention of *small* or *humanoid*. It may surprise humans to know that they themselves were once considered fairies and did indeed possess some magic, until many of them stepped off the path and became extremely willfully destructive, and so magic was bred out of humans over the centuries, until there was nothing left but an empath here and there, and the occasional telekinetic.

Trolls are classed as fairies by fairies themselves, but would not be so categorized according to the human definition, as they are not magical—unless their longevity can be considered supernatural. They are, however, quite feral and only slightly more sentient than the average hound. Fairy scientists have discovered that trolls are highly susceptible to chemical-induced psychosis while also tending to nest in chemically polluted sites, in much the same way as humans are attracted to the sugar that poisons them.

The toxins ingested by trolls often result in uncharacteristically aggressive behavior and uncontrollable rage. Again, similar to how humans behave when experiencing sugar deprivation.

But this particular troll was not sick, sluggish, or aggressive—in fact, he was in remarkable physical health, all pumping limbs and scything tusks, as he followed his second most powerful instinct:

REACH THE SURFACE.

Trolls' most powerful instinct being *EAT, GOBBLE, DEVOUR.*

This troll's bloodstream was clear because he had never swum across a chromium-saturated lake and he had never carved out his burrow in mercury-rich soil. Nevertheless, healthy or not, this specimen would never have made it to the surface had the Earth's crust under Dalkey Island not been exceptionally thin, a mere mile and a quarter, in fact. This troll was able to squeeze himself into fissures that would have made a claustrophobe faint, and he wriggled his way to the open air. It took the creature four sun cycles of agonizingly slow progress to break through, and you might think the cosmos would have granted the fellow a little good fortune after such Herculean efforts, but no, he had to pop out right between the Fowl twins and Lord Teddy Bleedham-Drye, who was lurking on a mainland balcony and spying on Dalkey Island through a telescopic monocular, thus providing the third leg of a teetering tripod of fate, which, considering the personalities and intellects involved, could not result in anything but skulduggery.

So, the troll emerged, joint by joint, reborn to the atmosphere, gnashing and clawing. And in spite of his almost utter exhaustion, some spark of triumph drove him to his feet for a celebratory howl, which was when Lord Teddy, for diabolical reasons that shall presently be explored, shot him.

Once the shot had been fired, the entire troll-related rigmarole really got rigmarolling, because the microsecond that NANNI's sensors detected the bullet's sonic boom, she upgraded her alert status from beige to red, sounded the alarm Klaxon, and set the security system to Siege mode. Two armored drobots were dispatched from their charging plates to extract the twins, and forty decoy flares were launched from mini mortar ports in the roof as countermeasures to any infrared-guided missiles that may or may not be inbound.

This left the twins with approximately twenty seconds of earthbound liberty before they would be whisked into the evening sky and secured in the eco-house's ultrasecret safe room, blueprints of which did not appear on any set of plans.

A lot can happen in twenty seconds. And a lot did happen.

Firstly, let us discuss the marksman. When I say Lord Teddy shot the troll, this is possibly misleading, even though it is accurate. He did shoot the troll, but not with the usual explosive variety of bullet, which would have penetrated the troll's hide and quite possibly killed the beast through sheer shock trauma. That was the absolute last thing Lord Teddy wanted, as it would void his entire plan. This particular bullet was a gas-powered cellophane virus slug that was being developed by the Japanese munitions company Myishi and was not yet officially on the market. Known as "shrink wrappers" by the development team, the CV bullet released its virus on impact and then wrapped the target in a coating of cellophane that was porous enough to allow shallow breathing but had been known to crack a rib or two—and did, in fact, crack four of the troll's ribs and both his femurs.

And then there was the physicality of the troll itself. There are many breeds of troll. From the ten-foot-tall behemoth Antarctic Blue, to the silent jungle killer the Amazon Heel Claw. The troll on Dalkey Island Beach was a one-in-a-million anomaly. In form and proportion he was the perfect Ridgeback, with the distinctive thick comb of spiked hair that ran from brow to tailbone, and the blue-veined gray fur on his chest and arms all present and correct. But this creature was no massive predator. In fact, he was a rather tiny one. Standing barely eight inches tall, the troll was one of a relatively new variety that had begun to pop up in recent millennia since fairies were forced deep into the earth's mantle. Much in the same way as schnauzer dogs had miniature counterparts known as toy schnauzers, some troll breeds also had their shrunken varieties, and this troll was one of perhaps half a dozen toy Ridgebacks in existence and the first to ever reach the surface.

Not at all what Lord Teddy had been expecting. Having seen Brother Colman's scars, the duke had imagined his quarry would be somewhat larger.

When the little troll's heat signature had popped up in his eyepiece like an oversize Jelly Baby, the duke had exclaimed, "Good heavens! Could that little fellow be my troll?"

It certainly matched Brother Colman's description, except for the dimensions. In truth, the duke couldn't help feeling a little let down. He had been expecting something more substantial. That diminutive creature didn't look like it could manufacture enough venom to keep a hamster alive.

"Nevertheless," muttered the duke, "since I've come all this way . . ."

And he squeezed the trigger on his sniper rifle.

The supersonic cellophane slug made a distinctive warbling noise as it sped through the air, sounding like a juvenile Swiss yodeler, and impacted the toy Ridgeback square in the solar plexus, releasing its payload in a sparkling globule that quickly sprawled over the tiny creature, wrapping it in a restrictive layer of cellophane before it could do much more than squeak in indignation.

Beckett Fowl spotted the cartwheeling toy troll, and his first impressions were of fur and teeth, and so, consequently, his first thought was *Angry Hamster!*

But the boy chided himself, remembering that *Angry Hamster* was a sculpture he himself had constructed from chewed paper and bodily fluids and therefore not a living thing, and so he would have to revise his guess as to what this tumbling figure might be.

But by this time the troll had come to rest at his feet, and Beckett was able to snatch it up and scrutinize it closely, so there was no need for guessing.

Not alive, he observed then. *Doll, maybe.*

Beckett thought the figure had moved of its own accord, perhaps even made a squealing noise of some kind, but now he could see it was a fantasy action figure with a protective plastic coating.

"I shall call you Whistle Blower, little chap," he whispered into the troll's pointed ear. The boy had chosen this name after barely a second's consideration, because he had seen on Myles's preferred news channel that people who squealed were sometimes called whistle-blowers. Also, Beckett was not the kind of fellow who wasted time on decisions.

Beckett turned to show Myles his beach salvage, though his brother had always been a little snooty when it came to toys, claiming they were for children even though he was patently himself a child and would be for a few more years.

"See, brother?" he called, waggling the action figure. "I found a new friend."

Myles sneered as expected, and opened his mouth to

pass a derogatory remark along the lines of "Honestly, Beck. We are eleven years old now. Time to leave childish things behind."

But his scorn was interrupted by a deafening series of honks.

The emergency Klaxon.

It is true to say that there is hardly a more alarming sound than a Klaxon, heralding as it does the arrival of some form of disaster. Most people do not react positively to this sound. Some scream, some faint. There are those who run in circles wringing their hands, which is also pointless. And of course there are people who have involuntary purges, which shall not be elaborated upon here.

The reactions of the Fowl twins could seem strange to a casual observer, for Myles discarded his seaweed bucket and uttered a single word: "Finally."

While Beckett spoke to his sparkling necktie. "Do you hear that, Gloop?" he asked. "We're going flying!"

To explain: Myles had worked with Artemis to design the security system, so he had a cool scientific interest in putting the extraction drobots through their paces as thus far they had only been tested with crash dummies. Beckett, on the other hand, was just dying to be yanked backward into the air at a high speed and dumped into a security chute, and he fervently hoped the ride would last much longer than the projected half a minute.

Myles forgot all about getting to bed on time. He was in

action mode now as the countermeasure flares fanned out behind his head like fireworks painting the undersides of passing cumuli. NANNI broadcast a message to his earpiece, which Myles repeated aloud to Beckett in melodramatic tones that he knew his brother would respond to, as it made him feel like he was on an adventure.

"'Red alert!'" Myles called. "'Extraction position.'"

The twins had been drilled on this particular position so often that Beckett reacted to the command with prompt obedience—two words that he would never find written on any of his school report cards.

Extraction position was as follows: chin tucked low, arms stretched overhead, and jaw relaxed to avoid cracked teeth.

"Ten seconds," said Myles, slipping his spectacles into a jacket pocket. "'Nine, eight . . .'"

Beckett also slipped something into his pocket before assuming the position.

"'Three,'" said Myles. "'Two . . .'"

Then the boy allowed his jaw to relax and spoke no more.

The two drobots shot out from under the villa's eaves and sped unerringly toward the twins. They maintained an altitude of six feet from the ground by dipping their rotors and adjusting their course as they flew, communicating with each other through coded clicks and beeps. With their gear retracted, the drobots resembled nothing more than the old propeller hats that children used to wear in simpler times as they rode their bicycles.

The drobots barely slowed as they approached the twins, lowering micro–servo cable arms that lassoed the boys' waists, then inflated impact bags to avoid injuring their cargo.

"Cable loop in place," said Myles, lowering his arms. "Bags inflated. Most efficient."

In theory, the ride should be so smooth his suit would not get wrinkled.

"No more science talk!" shouted Beckett impatiently. "Let's go!"

And go they did.

The servo cables retracted smoothly to winch the twins into the air. Myles noted that there had been no discernible impact on his spine, and while acceleration was rapid— zero to sixty miles an hour in four seconds according to his smart watch—the ride was not excessively jarring.

"So far so good," he said into the wind. He glanced sideways to see Beckett ignoring the flight instructions, waving his arms around as though he were on a roller coaster.

"Arms folded, Beck!" he called sternly to his brother. "Feet crossed at the ankles. You are increasing your own drag."

It was possible that Beckett could not hear the instructions, but it was probable that he simply ignored them and continued to treat their emergency extraction like a theme park ride.

The journey was over almost as soon as it began, and the twins found themselves deposited in two small chimneylike padded tubes toward the rear of the house. The drobots lowered them to the safe room, then sealed the tubes with their own shells.

NANNI's face appeared in a free-floating-liquid speaker ball, which was held in shape by an electric charge. "Shall I activate the EMP?"

Myles considered this as he unclipped the servo cable. Villa Éco was outfitted with a localized electromagnetic-pulse generator that would knock out any electronic systems entering the island's airspace. The Fowls' own electronics would not be affected, as they had backups that ran on optical cable. A little old-school, but it could keep systems ticking until the danger was past.

"Hmm," said Myles. "That seems a little drastic. What is the nature of the emergency?"

"Sonic boom detected," said the comforting female voice. "Origin uncertain. Possibly a high-powered rifle."

A sonic boom could be many things, and the majority of those things were harmless. Still, Myles now had a valid excuse to employ the EMP, something he had been forbidden to do unless absolutely necessary.

It was, in fact, a judgment call.

Beckett, who had somehow become inverted in the delivery chute, tumbled onto the floor and cried, "Activate the EMP!"

And for once, Myles found himself in agreement with his brother.

"I concur," he said. "Activate the EMP, NANNI. Tight radius, low intensity. No need to knock out the mainland."

"Activating EMP," said NANNI, and promptly collapsed in a puddle on the floor as her own electronics had not yet been converted to optical cable.

"See, Beck?" said Myles, lifting one black loafer from a glistening wet patch. "That is what we scientists call a design flaw."

Lord Bleedham-Drye was doubly miffed and thrice surprised by the developments on Dalkey Island.

Surprise number one: Brother Colman spoke the truth, and trolls did indeed walk the earth.

Surprise the second: The troll was tiny. Whoever heard of a tiny troll?

Surprise the last (for the moment): Flying boys had sequestered his prey.

"What on earth's going on?" he asked no one in particular.

The duke expertly broke down his rifle and cleaned the component parts with a chamois cloth, still muttering to himself. "These Fowl people seem prepared for a full-scale invasion. They have flare countermeasures. Drones flying off with children. Who knows what else? Antitank guns and trained bears, I shouldn't wonder. Even Churchill couldn't take that beach."

It occurred to Lord Teddy that he could blow up the entire island for spite. He was partial to a spot of spite, after all. But after a moment's consideration, he dismissed the idea. It was a cheery notion, but the person he would ultimately be spiting was none other than the Duke of Scilly, i.e., his noble self. He would hold his fire for now, but when those boys reemerged from their fortified house, he would be ready with his trusty rifle. After all, he was quite excellent with a gun, as his last shot had proven. Off the battlefield, it was unseemly to shoot anything except pheasant, unless one were engaged in a duel. Pistols at dawn, that sort of thing. But he would make an exception for a troll, and those blooming Fowl boys.

Lord Teddy reassembled the rifle and set it on the balcony floor, muzzle pointed toward the island.

You can't stay in that blasted house forever, my boys, he thought. *And the moment you poke your noses out from cover, Lord Teddy Bleedham-Drye shall be prepared.*

He could wait.

He was prepared to put in the hours. As the duke often said to himself: *One must spend time to make time.*

Teddy lay on the yoga mat, which had been his bed for almost a month now, and ran a sweep of the island through his night-vision monocular. The whole place was lit up like a fairground with roaming spotlights and massive halogen lamps. There was not a square inch of space for an intruder to hide.

Clever chappies, these Fowls, thought the duke. *The father must have a lot of enemies.*

Teddy fished a boar-bristle brush from his duffel bag and began his evening ritual of one hundred brushes on his beard. The beard rippled and glistened as he brushed, like the pelt of an otter, and Teddy could not help but congratulate himself. A beard required a lot of maintenance, but, by heaven, it was worth it.

On stroke fifty-seven, Lord Teddy's hunter senses registered that something had changed. It was suddenly darker. He looked up, expecting to find that the lights had been shut off on Dalkey Island, but the truth was more drastic.

The island itself had disappeared.

Lord Teddy checked all the way to the horizon with his trusty monocular. In the blink of an eye the entirety of Dalkey Island had vanished with only an abandoned stretch of wooden jetty to hint that the Fowl residence might ever have existed at the end of it.

Lord Bleedham-Drye was surprised to the point of stupefaction, but his manners and breeding would not allow him to show it.

"I say," he said mildly. "That's hardly cricket, is it? What has the world come to when a chap can't bag himself a troll without entire land masses disappearing?"

Lord Teddy Bleedham-Drye's bottom lip drooped. Quite the sulky expression for a 150-year-old. But the duke did not allow himself to wallow for long. Instead, he set his mind to the puzzle of the disappearing island.

"One can't help but wonder, Teddy Old Boy," mused the duke to the mirror on the flat side of his brush, "if all this troll malarkey is indeed true, then is the rest also true? What Brother Colman said vis-à-vis elves, pixies, and gnomes all hanging around for centuries? Is there, in fact, magic in the world?"

He would, Lord Teddy decided, proceed under the assumption that magic did exist, and therefore by logical extension, magical creatures.

"And so it is only reasonable to assume," Teddy said, "that these fairy chaps will wish to protect their own, and perhaps send their version of the cavalry to rescue the little troll. Perhaps the cavalry has already arrived, and this disappearing-island trick is actually some class of a magical spell cast by a wizard."

The duke was right about the cavalry. The fairy cavalry had already arrived.

One fairy, at least.

But he was dead wrong about a *wizard* casting a spell. The fairy who had cast the spell was a far cry indeed from being a wizard of even the most basic level. She had made a split-second decision and was now pretty certain that it was absolutely the wrong one.